SUPER AMERICA

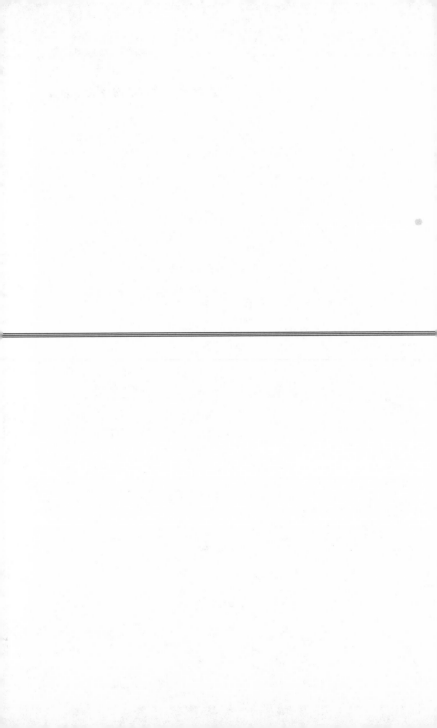

Winner of the

Flannery O'Connor

Award for

Short Fiction

Super America

STORIES BY ANNE PANNING

The University of

Georgia Press

[Athens and London]

Published by The University of Georgia Press

Athens, Georgia 30602

© 2007 by Anne Panning

All rights reserved

Designed by Mindy Basinger Hill

Set in 10.5/15 pt Minion Pro

Printed and bound by Maple-Vail

The paper in this book meets the guidelines for
permanence and durability of the Committee on
Production Guidelines for Book Longevity of the
Council on Library Resources.

Printed in the United States of America

11   10   09   08   07   C   5   4   3   2   1

Library of Congress Cataloging-in-Publication Data

Panning, Anne, 1966–

Super America : stories / by Anne Panning.

        p.   cm.

"Winner of the Flannery O'Connor Award for Short Fiction."

Includes bibliographical references and index.

ISBN-13: 978-0-8203-2996-3 (alk. paper)

ISBN-10: 0-8203-2996-7 (alk. paper)

I. Title.

PS3566.A577S87 2007

813'.54—dc22   2007006700

British Library Cataloging-in-Publication Data available

For Mark,
with love and gratitude

and

In memory of John Mitchell,
professor, poet, friend

CONTENTS

SUPER AMERICA

SUPER AMERICA

My father picked me up from college after my Acting II midterm. He passed me a smoke. It was spring break, which in Minneapolis meant old glacial dung clung to the curbs and sides of houses. Coarse, used snow lay scattered like margarita salt on the street. I was nineteen.

My father's current car was a rusted-out Gran Torino station wagon. It was so big and dark inside it felt like driving around in someone's little cabin. Fifth gear didn't work, so he ground it in fourth the whole way home. Home was New Prague, pronounced like *bag*, which I'd quickly learned was one of many incorrect pronunciations I'd been using all my life. It was my roommate, Van, a Vietnamese American kid from Edina, who told me: "Prague—you say it like *hog*—is the capital of Czechoslovakia. Just so you know."

We stopped for Chuckwagon sandwiches at Super America on Highway 5. I popped mine in the microwave for too long, and the cheese bled out the plastic wrap onto my hands. It quickly hardened like glue. I scraped it off with my top teeth. A couple of airplanes flew overhead, and I remembered Van was heading for South Padre Island right about now. He'd ordered new swim trunks from J. Crew and had been walking around in them the night before.

My father told me he had to make a call. He had an ill-defined job he called "sales rep," though I knew he wasn't a company man. I waited in the car, gray poppy seeds tumbling from my sandwich onto my old wool coat. People looked pissed that we were monopolizing a gas-pumping lane even though we weren't getting gas. Nice cars slid carefully around us, the drivers' noses hawked over the steering wheels like bird beaks. One guy gave me the finger. I made major eye contact, gave him the peace sign, and wolfed down the rest of my sandwich.

My father seemed to be taking a long time. He often made frequent visits to the bathroom, then more phone calls, then asked that they brew a fresh pot of coffee for him while he read the Hollywood gossip magazines. "You'll be in these someday, Theo," he'd told me once. "You got a whole lot more going on than what's this kid—Matt Damon? Dime a dozen." My father knew a little something about just about everything. My mother, a bitter divorcée who loved animals more than people, called him a font of misinformation. She owned exotic, or what I called nuisance, pets like ferrets, chinchillas, and most recently, sugar gliders, these tiny flying marsupials from Australia with huge black eyes and gray fur. One lunged at me when I'd visited last time. It went right for my face, and my mother said, "Poor thing. These little guys are used to a heavily treed environment." Its sharp claws sunk through my thin T-shirt. Then it pissed on me. I nearly slammed it to the ground, but I knew my mother would cry. In Acting II class, we'd had to impersonate a family member for our midterm, and I did her, after one of her sugar gliders had died. For a prop, I used some girl's Beanie Baby sloth stuffed in my shirt pocket as the dead sugar glider. My acting professor, Babe Powers, wiped tears of laughter from her eyes, clapped her hands, and said, "An Oscar contender, Theo. Bravo."

My father was taking way longer than usual. I decided to swing the car back by the dumpster and go look for him. The keys still hung in the ignition, a tiny Rubik's Cube dangling off the chain. It took three tries to get the car started. My father claimed there was a trick to it that involved pumping the gas pedal three times, turning off all the heat and control knobs, and pushing on the brakes at the very last minute. Somehow, I managed.

Inside, I checked the men's bathroom, but it was empty. I peed and took my time. I cruised up and down the aisles in the store—Fig Newtons, travel packs of Kleenex, frozen breakfast burritos—but my father didn't appear. I smoked a cigarette outside and tried not to look like a loiterer. Back inside, I asked the clerk, a woman with gray teeth who could've been my mother's age, if she'd seen a guy in a Carhartt coat and blue jeans, six feet two, big moustache, bushy hair. She thought for a minute, then said, "Problem is I see so many of them types." I nodded. She had a point. When I walked out of the store, she said, "You paying for gas?" and I shook my head.

I sat in the car for a few minutes, flipping back and forth between anger and worry. For all I knew, he'd been abducted. Or maybe he'd met some sleazy woman and gone off with her. Or he'd run into a bad drug deal and had to haul ass out of there with no time to let me know. Who knew? For now, there was really nothing else to do but get in the car and drive around the block looking for him.

As soon as I turned onto the road, it started to sleet. Big cloudy gobs like someone was hacking lugies on the windshield. I turned off the radio and started practicing the monologue I'd have to do for Acting II after break. It was from Eugene O'Neill's *Desire Under the Elms*. I hit a red light, waited, then completely panicked when a hitchhiker practically ran into the car. I pulled over, squinting through the sleet. The Gran Torino wobbled to a stop on the gravel strip. It was my father. He had his hood up and looked wired. He flagged me down and jumped into the front seat. He smelled like fried food and bong water. He laughed and rubbed his jeans.

"Theo," he said. "Pretend you're an actor in a movie and FOLLOW THAT CAR!" He pointed straight ahead at an old Subaru wagon. Its bumper sticker said: "Mean People Suck." Garfield was suction-cupped to the window by all fours. I gunned it.

"So, how's school?" my father asked, as if he hadn't just ditched me, as if nothing were out of the ordinary. The Subaru signaled a left turn, and I shadowed.

"I'm As and Bs," I said.

"Shit. That's good."

"So what's with the car?" I asked. "Why are we following?"

My father told me it was top secret, but if we played our cards right, we'd be sitting on easy street in a flash. My father spoke clichés like a second language. My English professor had done an exercise in class the first week where we had to list as many clichés as possible. Whoever had the longest list won. I did so easily but was embarrassed when the guy then turned on me and told the class clichés were the mark of a lazy writer. He'd said to me, "Smart as a whip. Cute as a button. Sharp as a tack. What fresh life can you breathe into these tired clichés, Theo?" He wore cords and vests. His beard was tight and pubic. He'd fingered his Tweety Bird tie and looked up at the ceiling.

I switched my major to theater the very next week, after my acting professor told me I made a convincing Russian immigrant.

The sky grew dark, and the sleet starting freezing to slush against the windshield. We were now on gravel roads, and I was riding the Subaru's ass. My father told me to keep following as it turned into a long, gravel driveway. A shelterbelt of poplars shook in the wind. We were in the middle of Buttfuck, Nowhere, as far as I could tell. My father ground his teeth in a way that made me want to shake him. An old windmill creaked above us. Finally, both cars rumbled to a stop. A woman ran out of the Subaru, held up a finger to us to wait, then ran in the house.

"Okay, Boss," my father said. "It's show time."

I had no idea what the fuck he was talking about but followed him up to the house. It was white and cruddy looking with plastic stapled over the windows. A big metal tub sat outside full of hay and frozen shit. Some kid's bike with training wheels leaned against the house in a way that made me feel depressed. Empty cages were tossed on top of one another like a small circus had busted loose.

"So, is this a house of ill repute?" I asked my father, who stood, finishing his grit, by the back door.

He narrowed his eyes at me and exhaled. "Don't talk college," he said. "That was my one rule about you going off to the Cities like that. Don't be an ass. You got to talk normal. You gotta stay who you are." He grabbed me by the shoulder and shook it real slow.

"I was kidding," I said.

"Right," he said. "Come on." He stamped out his cigarette on the sole of his boot and tossed it in the bushes.

Inside, the house smelled like hot lightbulbs, wet wool, and an odd citrus air freshener that seemed to be covering something up. We walked through a messy kitchen with clothes tumbling hot and steamy in the dryer, then passed through a dining room full of empty boxes. The woman, to whom my father didn't introduce me, shushed us as we approached the living room.

"Shh," she said. "They're just getting up from their naps." She stepped over what appeared to be a baby gate jammed across the doorway but made us stay out. The living room was divided by a series of little gates down the center. On one side, a miniature horse lay sleeping on the couch. It was no bigger than a golden retriever, but it was gray with white spots on its nose and back. The television flashed brightly, but the sound was muted.

The woman sat down beside it. She rubbed her hand up and down its rump as if it were her lover. "This is Pacman," she whispered. "Little stallion. Parents are War Paint and Bonnie Buster. Good bloodline. He's already been broken to drive."

I sneezed from the rich, ripe scents in the room, and the horse startled. It tried standing up on the couch, but its little hooves caved into the soft cushions. The woman picked it up and set it on the carpet.

"Good-looking horse," my father said. As far as I knew, he knew nothing about horses, but he was sizing it up and down as if he were considering taking it for a spin. "How tall's this one?" It came up to his knees.

"Twenty-seven," the woman said. "That's regulation for the miniature horse breed. Good proportions, too." Then, as if she'd only just noticed me, she reached out a hand and offered it to me. "You must be the son. Nice to meet you," she said. "I'm Tulip." Her name didn't exactly suit her. Her yellow-gray hair fell out of a twisted bun. The Bud Light T-shirt she wore was full of ragged holes, and when we shook hands, we were eye to eye. She was easily six feet tall.

"Theo," I said. "Pleasure."

"Theo's going to be a movie star," my father said. He slapped me on the back, and the horse whinnied. "Whoa, whoa, whoa," he said, and stepped back. "Don't want the little guy getting pissed off." Pacman started minigalloping in circles around his side of the living room. He was like a little toy come to life.

"Tulip and I go way back," my father continued. "We're what you'd call bosom buddies."

My father winked. Tulip blushed. I stuffed my hands in my coat pockets and jumped when the animal on the other side of the room began screaming like a hyena. Luckily, it was all caged up and hidden by tree branches. I couldn't make out *what* it was, though.

Tulip laughed and stepped over the gate. "That's Isadora, my lemur. She's still a little wild but I'm working on her. Your dad says he's good with primates."

"You are?" I looked at my father, who nodded. I was beginning to think the whole thing stunk of something funny. I was anxious to go. It was spring break, and so far I'd spent my time in a Super America parking lot and some crazy woman's house of pets. Was my father drawn exclusively to women who owned exotic pets? Was he a fetishist in this way? This was what I began to wonder.

Tulip lured Isadora out of the cage, then slung her around her hip like a toddler. She had bright, orange-colored eyes and a tail longer than a baseball bat but skinnier. It stood straight up in the air like an antenna. But Isadora didn't seem to like me. She hissed. She bared her teeth at me. She tried pinching me. My father laughed and said I was monkey meat. Tulip looked irritated, as if we had upset her little animal kingdom, and motioned for us to go into the kitchen, which we did. I saw Pacman watch us walk away while an NBA game played behind him on the screen.

"Have some coffee," Tulip said. She gestured to the coffee maker, stained and splattered with brown drops. "It might be cold but you can nuke it. I've got to pee." Thankfully, she took Isadora with her into the can, just off the kitchen. Right after she closed the door, the dryer stopped and made a ticking sound. My father poured himself a cup of coffee and did, indeed, nuke it.

"So," I said. "What the hell."

"Yeah, it's something, huh?" My father lit up a smoke, which seemed pretty ballsy inside someone's house.

"What do you mean?" I asked. My father always talked in circles, and it pissed me off.

He leaned against the kitchen sink with his coffee and cigarette. He looked like a trucker come in from a long haul. "I mean Tulip's gonna set me up with the two of them. Like a rig. I mean, it's a sort of trade deal. Long story, but what's gonna happen is I'm gonna train Isadora to ride Pacman. You know? Like ride on her back like a little jockey?" My father nodded and looked extremely pleased by the whole idea. "Later on I'm also going to get Pacman a little cart to pull and Isadora's going to ride in it."

"And?" I said. Ever since I'd started college in Minneapolis, I'd managed to avoid spending much time with my father. He and my mother still lived in the same town, New Prague, but they'd been divorced ever since I was twelve. He still loved my mother—all three of us knew it—and kept hoping I'd somehow help get them back together. He'd call me up to run ideas by me. Usually they were stupid and poorly timed, like the Christmas my mother had tonsillitis and he'd strung flashing colored lights around himself and stood outside her apartment building, singing "It's Now or Never." The local newspaper had caught it on camera and it was in there the week of New Year's. On my fifteenth birthday, my father strapped a pillow around his stomach, wore a maternity dress, and knocked on our apartment door. "Thank you for giving birth to Theo," he said. This was right after my mother had had an emergency hysterectomy. She'd slammed the door in his face. I had lost count of his pathetic attempts at reconciliation with her and was glad I'd been—until now—removed from them for a while.

"I'm going to bring them to your mother as a peace offering." My father sucked the end of his cigarette down to the filter like a joint. I'd actually been smoking quite a few joints at school. After rehearsals, me and all the gay guys would get high and then go to the bars on Cedar Avenue: Blondie's, Five Corner's Saloon, the Triangle Bar, the 400 Club. I'd never known any gay guys before college, and it turned out to be true that theater was full of them. One of the guys, Benton Riley, from Redwood Falls, told me he'd known he was gay ever since he was about six but never got to *be* gay until he'd come to college.

"You know Mom's seeing someone else," I said. It was true, but not serious, as most of her boyfriends had been. The guy, Bill Lewis, was way younger than her, one of the groomers at the pet shop, kind of a motorhead actually. I knew it would kill my father to hear this, but I didn't care.

"Oh yeah?" he said. "They serious?"

I shrugged my shoulders. "I haven't really been around. But she's told me."

Just then Tulip came out of the bathroom with wet hands, which she wiped on her jeans. Isadora looked agitated and kept crawling up and down her back. She had a face more like a rat's than a monkey's and looked like a miniature Albert Einstein with fluffy white tufts around her face.

"Well," Tulip said. "I suppose I need to start my good-byes." She sighed and took Isadora's tiny face in both her hands. She kissed her on the lips. "Sweetheart," she said, "Mommy's gonna miss you." I swore I saw tears in her eyes.

I looked at my father to make sure I was understanding this right, that we were actually taking the lemur along with us. He raised his eyebrows at me in a way that said, "Cool, huh?"

"Just give me a moment alone with Pacman," Tulip said, and went, with Isadora in her arms, back into the living room.

"I need to tell you," I said to my father when she was out of range. "I am not getting into the car with a miniature horse and a lemur or whatever the fuck."

My father pointed a finger at me. "What did I tell you about swearing?"

"I'm nineteen," I said. "I'm not really yours to discipline anymore."

"Okay, Mr. College," he said. "I don't know what you've got against animals."

"Nothing," I said, "but this is ridiculous. Mom's not going to want them, and then what will you do? Join the circus? You can barely take care of yourself much less a little horse and a monkey." From my vantage point, I could see Tulip nuzzling Pacman and petting her minimane. Tulip knelt down on her knees, and Pacman came just up to her breast. Isadora screeched and leapt from couch to chair to television to Tulip's shoulder nimbly and with height.

"You and your mother always gang up on me," my father said. I realized, as he spoke, that he actually looked dirty, as if he hadn't bathed in a while. He had a grainy face and looked beat. He'd been hustling a buck in the hardest possible way ever since I could remember. I wished he'd give it up, get a real job, and take it easy. But that wasn't in his nature.

"Okay," Tulip called from the living room. "It's now or never. Let's get these guys caged."

My father went to help her, but I held back. I was not about to handle either animal, especially Isadora, who clearly hated me. I leaned against the dryer, still warm from its cycle, and decided to be helpful. I reached in and pulled out the load, intending to fold it while I waited. But among threadbare towels, faded washcloths, and checkered dishtowels were several of Tulip's white briefs turned gray. Some of them had yellowish stains in the crotch panels, and embarrassed, I quickly shoved the whole load back in the machine. Instead, I wiped down the kitchen counters, which were coated with short gray hair.

Back on the road, my father was pumped. He drove faster down gravel roads than the Gran Torino had a right to. The wheels flew over potholes and washboard bumps. Pacman rode in the very back in a molded plastic box with a little door and lots of air holes. Isadora rode in the back seat in a metal cage that allowed her to reach out her leathery humanlike hands and scratch at the upholstery. Each of them made high-pitched yelps whenever the car riled them.

"Hang in there, guys," my father said. "It won't be long now."

I watched drooping electrical wires fly past outside the window. Fields were pocked with old snow, gray on black. I could see the New Prague water tower, pink and domed like a giant pencil top eraser. My acting professor was making me see everything in a new light. She told us we'd never be the same after her class. When one student was doing a scene as Macbeth, she'd stopped him midway through and asked him if he'd ever killed anything, anything at all, in his life. He said yeah, maybe a spider or something. "Then I want you," she had said, "to come to class next time having killed something. A squirrel will do. A mouse. But I want you to kill it with your own two hands. Then we'll talk about Macbeth's sense of guilt." We were all positively shocked, horrified, and thrilled at her daring. Also, we were all—at least the guys—pretty much in love with Babe Powers. She always, always wore skirts with little ballerina shoes and cardigans with matching shells. She was short, muscular, and quick. When we had to say what animal we were, she went last and said soberly, "I am an arctic fox." We believed her.

"So, you making a lot of friends there at school?" my father asked. He was driving with his knee while he fished out a cigarette from the pack and lit it. The Gran Torino still had an actual cigarette lighter that popped up and glowed orange.

"A couple," I said.

"I suppose they all have their parents paying their way, huh?"

"Some," I said. I had a full ride thanks to my parents' piss-paying jobs. I had loads of grants, low-interest loans, scholarships, the works. But to pay for room and board, I still had to work in the admissions office giving tours to prospective students. I also worked at a restaurant, Moose's, as a bus boy. The bartenders there had introduced me to cocaine, so I'd been trying that off and on.

"Any girlfriends yet?"

"Not really," I said.

"That'll come," my father said. "Of course I see Julie around town a lot. She seems good. She always says to say hi."

"Julie's all right," I said. "She'll find someone else soon enough." She'd been my girlfriend from sophomore to senior year back home. Her dad was a dentist and her mom used to be a hand model. We had sex junior year, and after that, almost every weekend. But Julie wanted big things out of me. She said a good job for me would be either dentist, doctor, lawyer, or if I really had to slack, pharmacist. We broke off right around graduation, and really, with both of us going to different colleges, what did it matter? But I sometimes missed her big spooky eyes and her flat little boobs. She was supposedly going into speech therapy, and I had no idea why.

One of the animals seemed to have taken a dump then because the car smelled foul. In fact, it was strong enough to gag me. I had to roll down the window. My father laughed and tooted the horn. "Your mother is gonna die!" he said. "She is absolutely going to flip over these two. Don't you think, Theo?"

"Ah, yeah," I said. "I think that's the problem."

"Let me ask you something," my father said. He put his right arm up over the bench seat, his fingers dangling dangerously close to Isadora's reach. He still wore his gold wedding band, but on his right hand.

"Okay," I said. We were pulling into town, and I didn't know if my father was planning to go to my mother's apartment or the house.

"Are you a homosexual?" he asked. He kept his eyes on the road. Isadora started to screech when a police car sped past us, its siren blaring.

"Why?" I said. "Shut up," I said to Isadora.

"Just answer the question," my father said. He reached his fingers back and let Isadora sniff them out.

"No," I said.

"All right," my father said. He turned right at Sugar Creek Road, named exclusively for the apartment complex where my mother lived. I felt my heart sink to my stomach.

"Why do you ask?" I said.

"What?"

"If I'm gay." I wanted to avoid another mother-father reunion fiasco, but it seemed I was destined to be in the middle of it this time. My father parked near my mother's building, number 30, even though there were only three of them.

"So you prefer the word *gay* over *homosexual*?" my father asked. He cut the engine, leaned back, and didn't seem to mind that Isadora was chomping on his fingernails. I could hear them crunch in her little teeth.

"I'm not gay *or* homosexual!" I said. The shit smell was really cloying, so I opened the car door and got out. "Christ."

My father got out of the car, too. The apartment complex was new and unimaginative. All the buildings were painted gray with white trim. Each had a little balcony, and now, in late winter, gas grills, bikes, lawn chairs, and strollers were all crusted with ice or covered with tarps.

"What if *I* was?" my father said, sucking on probably his fifth cigarette since we'd left Tulip's. "What if I said I was gay?"

I squinted at him. "Are you?"

"Nah," he said.

"Really?"

"Yeah," he said. "I was just seeing what you'd say." He opened up the back hatch, where Pacman's cage had slid up against the window. I felt sorry for the thing and for its shaky future with my father. "So these two guys could actually be a big break for you, Theo. Maybe we could get you on David Letterman or Leno with these guys. Do one of those crazy pet tricks or something. That could be your break." He pulled Pacman's cage onto his knees, then slid it to the ground. "You think you'll change your name when you get famous?" he said. "Or keep it? Theo's pretty good, I think. But I'm not sure about the last name. Rickers. Sounds a little weak. Hey, I could be your agent!"

"Yeah," I said. "That'd be great." Isadora was clearly pissed off that she was being ignored. She leapt back and forth in her cage, hissing.

"How about Theo Prague? You know, put the town on the map."

He said it the wrong way and I corrected him. I thought of Van, how cool he was without even trying. He'd managed to rent a condo in South Padre on the Internet, which is something I'd have never thought of. Van said next year, if I could swing it, I could join him.

"Hey," my father said. "Remember what I said. Don't get college on me now."

"Sorry," I said. For the first time ever, I felt truly superior to my father. To my mother, too. In fact, to the whole damn town. It wasn't an altogether pleasant feeling.

"Hey," my father said. "Why don't you go prepare your mother for what I'm about to do?" He tried to push his hair back, but it didn't look any better. I saw him run his tongue over his teeth. He clapped his hands at me and said something like giddy up.

"Not this time," I said. "It's up to you." I felt like I was playing a role but that I was almost overacting. I was the son who'd had enough.

I did help my father schlep the cages into the complex and up the elevator, but I refused to be standing there when my mother opened the door. Instead, I listened from down the hallway, gathering material for a someday future scene.

D enise and Larry Butters were only two weeks into their new house in the Cherokee Bluff subdivision when the Hillbillies moved in next door. That's what Denise had started calling the three brothers who'd moved in a few days ago—"the Hillbillies." No sooner had they unpacked their U-Haul and pickup trucks then they were shooting off firecrackers at night, blasting up and down Splendorwood Court in their mud-caked ATVs, and letting their three big dogs poop in everyone's yards without cleaning up.

On Friday evening, their third week in the subdivision, Denise had an idea. She went out to tell Larry, who was grilling turkey burgers in the back yard. Ever since she'd been pregnant with Jen-Jen, Denise couldn't stand the sight or smell of red meat, so Larry obliged her with poultry.

"I think we should invite them over," Denise said, "the Hillbillies." She stood next to Larry in their huge, treeless, fenceless backyard. Their builders had promised them two two-inch trees in the contract but so far hadn't delivered. Nor had they finished drywalling the basement. Nor had they cemented the driveway. Nor had they put up any trim in the bedrooms. "That way, once they get to know us and meet the kids, they'll be less likely to disturb us. They'll care about us."

Larry flipped the pale turkey burgers, which looked like crumbly oatmeal patties. He had absolutely vetoed veggie burgers in his household; that's where he drew the line. "You think so, huh?" He reached for his beer in the grill's built-in drink holder and took a swig. He'd taken to drinking dark, heavy stouts, which tasted, to Denise, like rancid root beer.

Denise checked on Jen-Jen and Cole playing in what might be called a sandbox. So far, it was a pile of sand the builders had dumped behind the garage with no box. Cole scooped sand into a coffee can, then poured it out at Jen-Jen's feet, who screamed as if she were being burned.

"I think it would help," Denise said. "It's good to be neighborly, especially in a place like Cherokee Bluff. You've got to show you have class in a place like this."

Larry chuckled. "Well, they obviously don't have any class." Larry, a schmoozer, had done well for himself, despite being from a family of down-and-outers, two of whom were currently in jail. He'd barely managed a community college degree, then hustled his way into the hardware store business; he was now full owner of New Sweden's Hardware Hank and was wheeling and dealing to open another in Waterfield. Denise was very proud of him, even if it did mean she had to live in a town with no real grocery store and only one restaurant, Kick's, which served about ten variations of red meat.

"Still," Denise said. "I'll walk over and see if they're doing anything tomorrow night. Okay? Can you live with that?"

Larry shrugged, nodded, and reached for his beer.

* * *

Denise trekked across the freshly sod lawn to the Hillbillies' house. The smell of grilled hot dogs hung in the air, and everyone in the neighborhood had their two-car garage doors open for the weekend. The Hillbillies' house was sided in beige vinyl with white trim. Denise remembered how there'd been five choices of siding: buff, beige, mocha, vanilla, and frost. As for trim: white, brown, or gray. Denise considered it a coup on her part to have gotten her builder to special order a dark evergreen for the siding with a tasteful sage green trim, even if it had cost them almost $5,000 more, and even if it had pushed the completion date back a couple of months. Every time she pulled her minivan into the driveway, she felt a surge of pride at her rich, green house among the neutrals.

At first she thought the Hillbillies weren't home. She heard the doorbell chime inside but saw no sign of life. She rang it once again, then knocked hard on the steel front door. She peered in through the window. It was roughly the same floor plan as theirs, only the kitchen had cherry cabinets instead of oak, and the sunken living room veered off to the right instead of the left. Still, it had the same pop-out kitchen design (a feature Denise loved) and the same tiled foyer with a step-up entry. She was surprised to see that their furniture was decent (a taupe tweed sectional) and their kitchen looked as if someone actually cooked in it. A blender and toaster were parked in the appliance garage (another feature Denise adored), and canisters of staples lined the counter by the stove. She pressed her face up to the glass to get a better look.

She pulled back when she saw someone come bounding up the stairs from the first level (all Cherokee Bluff homes were four-level homes). It was the tallest and skinniest of the three brothers, and he swung the door open with absolutely no reservations. "Hey neighbor," he said. "Come on in." His face was pointy and pink, and Denise found herself feeling shy. She hung back in the doorway, though introduced herself and explained where she lived. He said his name was Ty. He didn't wear shorts, despite the heat, but wore blue jeans with a red T-shirt, tucked in, belted. She wished she had brought flowers or a bottle of wine.

"So, I was wondering if you and your brothers were busy tomorrow evening, say around six thirty, for a little grill out at our place." She noticed a slightly acrid smell in the house, like burned toast. Ty held the front door open with his cowboy boot.

He looked up at the ceiling (a soaring white cathedral, just like Denise's), scratched his head, then looked at the floor. "Geez, I don't *think* we're busy. Maybe just gonna take the ATVs out for a while tomorrow. But I should ask Mort and Bigs. Sometimes you never know what exactly the two of them got planned."

Denise forced a smile. She would have preferred a simple yes or no. She wanted to get back to her own familiar house, to Jen-Jen and Cole, to the waiting turkey burgers she would serve on poppy seed buns with purple coleslaw (she could get the kids to eat it that way) and garlic potatoes. She noticed from the Hillbillies' kitchen window they had a clear view of the kids in the sandbox, of Larry at the grill, and of Denise and Larry's bedroom windows. She would have to be careful with the blinds. "So, do you want to think about it and get back to me . . . ?" Denise felt a mosquito drill into her ankle for blood and slapped it.

Ty adjusted his ball cap, and Denise couldn't believe how dirty it was, as if he'd literally smeared it around in the mud. His tawny blonde moustache twitched, and Denise shivered. "I'm just gonna say yes. Yes for the three of us. And I'll tell Mort and Bigs that that's what we're doing tomorrow night. I won't even ask but tell."

"Well, all right," Denise said. "Just let me know if anything comes up, though. We can be flexible."

Ty squeezed his hands together, nodded, squinted his eyes, and for a second, Denise feared she was in the presence of a murderer, or at least an ex-convict. But Larry would say she was overreacting, as usual. She had insisted they install a high-tech home security system way out of their price range. She had taught Cole how to phone 911 when he was barely toddling. She was suspicious of strangers and kept an unlisted telephone number. But really, there was nothing out of the ordinary about Ty or his house. Ty was polite enough, even if he did use poor grammar, and their house was clean and beige and just like all the others on the block.

"Again, welcome to the neighborhood," Denise said as she waved good-bye. "See you tomorrow." She vowed next time to bring flowers in a cut-glass vase for them to keep. And perhaps a freshly baked loaf of honey wheat from her new bread machine.

That night, Denise woke up to the sound of firecrackers exploding in the Hillbillies' back yard. Later, when she got up to pee, she lifted the bathroom shade and could've sworn she saw a small bonfire over at the Hillbillies' and the three of them dancing around it. Denise wondered if they were aware of Cherokee Bluff rules and regulations: no loud noise after 10:00 p.m., no inoperable vehicles parked on the street or in the driveway, no lawn ornaments without Cherokee Bluff Residents' Council approval, and absolutely no garbage burning or fires of any kind on the properties.

Denise sank back down into bed beside Larry. Their new pillow-top mattress and Egyptian cotton sheets seemed to allow Larry to sleep even more deeply than before. She reached over and touched his chest: strong, solid, hairy. She remembered in high school he'd had virtually no body hair. He'd been just a boy—tall, gangly, and smooth. He wore loose Levis and sunglasses and drove a rusty Subaru station wagon. He was plagued with acne and shy and always offered her cinnamon gum before heading off to parties with her.

Now, unable to sleep, Denise could smell the garlic on his breath and could faintly hear the deep grumble of male voices next door. She wouldn't put up with it, she decided. She hadn't moved to a place like Cherokee Bluff for this nonsense. She was here because she and Larry had "arrived" here, and as for the Hillbillies, they seemed to have landed here by mistake.

On Saturday morning, Denise heard Jen-Jen crying in her crib. "I poop!" Jen-Jen called out. Denise saw that Larry was already out of bed but was obviously waiting for Denise to change Jen-Jen's diaper. "I poop! Mommy!" Denise could hear Jen-Jen pounding on the wall opposite her.

"I'm coming," Denise said, belting her new seersucker robe. She wanted the mornings to be fresh, unharried, and peaceful, but Jen-Jen continually wore her out immediately.

The diaper was a big, heavy, wet one, and Denise gagged despite herself. It landed with a heavy thud in the garbage can, and Jen-Jen laughed. "I go, boom!" Denise dusted her with baby powder, put on a fresh diaper, and dressed her in little jean shorts and a pink T-shirt. Her bare feet went pattering into the kitchen before Denise had a chance to wash her hands.

Cole and Larry sat in the sunken living room on the second level, bowls of cereal held idly in their laps. Violent, masculine cartoons played on the television at low volume. "Larry," Denise said, "I thought we agreed to no eating in the living room. Remember the furniture?" She and Larry had recently charged a white leather sectional, along with a teak entertainment console and matching teak end tables.

"I thought breakfast was okay," Larry said, and his eyes slid back to the television. Cole dripped milk on his belly and nearly tipped his whole bowl over.

"And Jen-Jen's diaper?" Denise asked. She saw there was not yet any coffee made, and her head ached for some.

"She was calling for you," Larry said. He was already dressed in sweatpants, a football jersey, and big white high-tops. "She wanted Mom."

"Please," Denise said, and ferociously ground up coffee beans to release her anger. "I have a dinner menu to plan for tonight. I've got shopping to do. We do have guests coming, in case you forgot."

"Who's coming?" Cole asked. His dark eyes flashed at Denise, suddenly interested.

"The next-door neighbors," Larry said. "The new people."

Cole ate spoonfuls of milk from his cereal bowl. "You mean the bad guys?"

"Don't say that," Denise said. "I'm sure they're fine people." She looked over at Larry, who smirked. "Well, they are," she said. "We just need to get to know them better, that's all."

Denise waited for her coffee, but before it was ready, Jen-Jen pinched her finger in the VCR and wailed as if she'd been badly beaten. Denise rushed over to her, trying to soothe her.

"Get out of my way!" Cole said, glowering. He wore loose red shorts and nothing else. His chest was concave, his skin almost translucent. "I can't see the TV."

"Cole, zip it!" Denise said, and ran Jen-Jen's hand underneath the cold water. "Larry, I think Cole needs a time-out. Larry!"

"I know," he said. "Come on, Cole." And with that, Denise watched them go outside and get in the minivan and knew Larry was driving him to the store for a box of white-sugar doughnuts. Larry hadn't yet grasped the idea of a true time-out, but Denise was too tired to intervene.

Next door, she heard the ATVs start up in the driveway and watched out the window as the Hillbillies went gunning down the street, their engines sputtering, their big wheels as wide and fat as tractor tires. One of them, not Ty, let his big dog ride along with him as if it were a girlfriend. It sat in front of him, paws crossed over the handlebars, its head turned sideways, tongue hanging out regally. "Oh, please," Denise muttered, and gave Jen-Jen's red finger a little kiss.

Denise had to drive thirty-five miles to Big Top Foods in Waterfield, the only place she could find organic, boneless, skinless chicken breasts, fresh herbs, and hormone-free milk. She'd conned Larry into taking the two kids to the park while she shopped, even though part of her didn't trust Larry's eye for the quickest of missteps, the near-miss injuries, the bold way Cole swung from the monkey bars by his knees. But Larry argued with her. "I'm not 'babysitting' my own kids," he said, buckling Jen-Jen into the car seat. "It's called parenting, Denise. You just have to let me do it my way."

Denise moved swiftly through the big warehouse grocery, which smelled of overripe apples and moist cardboard. She'd composed her shopping list aisle by aisle, so she never had to double back. She stopped briefly in the freezer aisle to sample little chicken nuggets dipped in cheddar sauce but didn't buy any. She was not an impulse buyer and had a specific menu planned for the night's dinner: spinach-and-feta poultry sausages, cucumber and tomato salad with fresh basil, corn bread muffins, and key lime pie for dessert.

She bought an assortment of bottled juices, beer, wine coolers, and sparkling water. She could imagine Ty being confused by all the beverage and food options she would offer. He'd likely never even heard of feta cheese or tasted fresh basil, and the idea of opening up his world made Denise's posture improve. She wheeled her heavy cart to the least busy checkout aisle and, while she waited, tried to calculate in her head how much her total would be.

Her guess: $71.00.

The actual bill: $72.05, including $4.50 off in coupons.

Denise drove through the tall brick subdivision gates with glowing vapor lights: "Cherokee Bluff ⌣ A Unique Countryside Community." Her lot, 28A, was just two streets in on the right, on Splendorwood Court. New homes were going up all around them, and bulldozers, cement mixers, and dump trucks made up the majority of traffic. Prospective homeowners stood in the empty dirt lots, pointing and squinting, trying to imagine their four-level houses with a flagstone patio, or a deck, or a two-car attached garage with a sloping driveway. Would they choose triangular palatial windows, or arched? Side entryway or front? Recessed front porch or open galley?

Denise hefted most of the groceries in herself and found Larry inside, napping with Jen-Jen on the couch. It was a moving sight, and she tried to be quiet, so rare was it for Jen-Jen to nap these days. She looked in Cole's room for him, then down in the den, then scanned the yard outside. She couldn't see him anywhere. "Cole!" she yelled, trying to be calm. "Cole, Mom's home!"

She knelt beside Larry and shook his shoulder gently. Larry came awake slowly, squinting and stretching. Jen-Jen nestled back into the couch and breathed heavily. "Where's Cole?" Denise asked.

Larry sat up, his face creased with deep red wrinkles from the couch.

"Hang on," Larry said. "Just give me a second." He rubbed his eyes and got up to look out the window. "He told me he was just playing outside, in the back."

"He's five years old!" Denise shouted. "You do not let him roam around all by himself while you sleep! God, Larry. Where is he?" Denise's limbs felt loose and watery as she ran around the circumference of their house, then looked in the garage, then looked again in the back yard. Larry followed her, but slowly. Finally, Denise spotted Cole next door, playing with the Hillbillies' dogs. Two of the big things were tied up and staked into the lawn. Cole laughed when the German shorthair pointer jumped up and licked his face, even though it nearly knocked him off his feet.

"Cole Lewis Butters, get your butt over here right now!" Denise said. Cole looked over at her with glowering eyes, then continued to pet the big dogs defiantly. The Hillbillies were obviously still out with their ATVs but had left their garage doors wide open. Denise stormed over to Cole and, without even thinking about who might be watching, swatted him hard on the butt, and then again, over and over. "Do you know how much you scared Mommy?" she said, the tears choking her voice. "Do you know what Mommy would do if something ever happened to you? Huh? Mommy loves you so much. So much!" She held him close to her and soaked in the smell of him. Cole cried and tried to appeal to Larry, who stood, hands in his pockets, as if he were a mere passerby.

Finally, Cole bolted for home, and she let Larry follow him. Denise stood, relieved and trembling and ashamed, in the Hillbillies' front yard. Glancing inside their garage, she thought she saw a gun, or several of them, racked one on top of another against raw drywall. She looked down the street, saw no one in sight, then entered the garage quietly. Hunting guns, rifles, and shotguns hung in plain view along the wall.

"The idiots!" Denise said aloud. She reached up for the garage-door opener, pressed it, then quickly slipped back out before it rolled closed. She didn't care if it wasn't her property; she was quite sure Cherokee Bluff had rules against firearms, and she would see to it that they abided by them.

By six o'clock, the cucumber-tomato salad was made, the pie was cooling on a rack, and the corn muffins were in the oven. The only thing left was to grill the sausages, which wouldn't take long on the gas grill. Larry had wanted to keep their old Weber grill, had argued for the irreplaceable taste and smell of a real fire with some hickory chips thrown in for extra flavor, but Denise had said, "A grill is about convenience, Larry. Who has time to stand around and wait for the coals to get just right? And the smoke in your eyes. And the charcoal, and the lighter fluid. It's so messy! And unhealthy!" So they had charged an expensive gas grill with a warming compartment on one side, built-in drink holders on the other, and a special remov-able basket for steaming vegetables. "We might as well move our real stove out here," Larry had said the first time they'd used it. "It's bigger than our real stove is." But Denise had taken charge, slapped the chicken onto the shiny silver grill, closed the lid, and proved to him how quickly and expertly it worked, even if the chicken did taste about as bland as if it were boiled.

At 6:35, their guests had still not arrived, nor had Denise seen any sign of their ATVs. Strangely now, she longed for the grinding blast of their engines, for their hoots and shouts as they spoke to one another en route. At 6:45, still no sign of them, and Denise was starting to feel embarrassed and angry all at once. At 6:55, Denise said to Larry, "I will not be made a fool of," and took Jen-Jen outside to wait with her on the front lawn. She would show them her indignation and fearlessness by making them look her in the eye and apologize immediately.

At 7:00, she went back in the house, despite Jen-Jen's protests. "Ride a wagon!" Jen-Jen had screamed, clinging to the red wagon in the garage. Jen-Jen tried to climb in and fell, banging her lip. More tears, more injuries, more hassle. And Denise was hungry, so hungry!

"We're eating right now," Denise said to Larry, who was trying to read the morning newspaper in the living room. "Let's go start the grill. Those bastards. Obviously no one ever taught them any manners. I have no idea where they came from anyway. The woods, I think. Maybe the farm. But the Twin Cities? We're supposed to believe these guys actually managed to live in a city? I mean, they're stockpiling weapons, for Christ's sake."

"Watch the language," Larry said. "Cole's got big ears." Cole, who dove from couch cushion to couch cushion on the floor, stuck out his tongue when he heard his name mentioned. He then pretended to have big elephant ears but knocked Jen-Jen down in the process. More tears, and Denise had had enough.

"Dammit!" she said. "Knock it off! Everybody!" But then she heard the ATVs coming down the street. Loud grinding motors, revving and accelerating, loud voices, shouting and yelling. She looked out the living room window (arched instead of the standard triangular) and saw them swerve into their driveway. They didn't seem the slightest bit surprised that their garage door was now closed. Denise watched Ty release the two dogs from their chains, and they disappeared down the street, barking and yelping.

"Let's go fire up the grill," Denise said. "We'll just show them we're bigger people than they are. We'll show them what it means to have a little class."

Denise washed up Cole and Jen-Jen with a wet washcloth, then tied her own hair up in a ponytail. She changed into white jeans and a pink top with brown sandals. Outside, she covered the picnic table with a new floral tablecloth and set out their plastic picnic ware. She waited on a lawn chair, nervously chewing her fingernails, until finally she saw the Hillbillies come filing out their front door. They looked washed and tended, with wet, combed hair and fresh clothes. They all held something in their hands, and Denise jumped up enthusiastically. "Well, hi!" she said, all trace of her anger and indignation absent. "We were starting to think something happened to you!"

"Sorry we're late," Ty said, and introduced his two brothers, Mort and Bigs. Bigs was oddly the smaller of the two with tan, wiry arms, and Mort appeared to have a lazy eye that Denise couldn't seem to follow. They both shook hands with Larry and nodded at Denise. The kids they more or less ignored. "Anyway, we're like the three wise men," Ty joked. "We come bearing gifts."

He handed Denise a bouquet of yellow daisies with some red snapdragons in the mix. Mort set a pink scented candle tied with ribbon on the table. Bigs brought a three-pack of nuts—smoked almonds, cashews, honey roasted peanuts—as if it were Christmas. "Well, you didn't have to do that," Denise said. "You certainly didn't have to bring gifts. Goodness."

Ty shrugged and watched Cole and Jen-Jen play in the sand pile.

Cole kicked his legs in the sand, then pretended he was wiping out on a motorcycle.

"Beer?" Larry offered, and all three said yes. Denise fetched them out of the garage refrigerator and slipped them into can coolers before handing them over. They sat down at the picnic table at her instruction. The poultry sausages were ready, and Larry slid them onto the plastic platter. Nobody spoke, except for the occasional noise of the kids.

"So, dig in!" Denise said. She could feel her smile starting to crack and was wondering why she had invited them over in the first place. They had nothing to say to one another, nothing in common, no anecdotes to exchange. And the guns—she kept remembering how many guns they had openly exposed in their garage. But if she brought it up now, it would surely ruin their dinner, wouldn't it? All she'd wanted was to be neighborly, to show the Hillbillies how nice she and her family were, so maybe they'd quit spoiling her every evening with their noise and unsavory habits. But now, with them quietly eating the food she had prepared, it was harder than she'd thought to bring up any complaints.

"So, what brought you to Cherokee Bluff?" Denise asked. "You came from the Twin Cities, right?" Denise cut her tomato wheels into small bites and fed them to Jen-Jen.

"Mom died," Ty said. He was obviously the spokesman for the trio.

"I'm sorry to hear that," Denise said, her head bowed. And? she wanted to ask. So?

"Got a deal on the house here," Ty said. "Our Uncle Bang knows the builder, and they said they couldn't sell these too much longer, you know, because of the sinking. Figured we could manage a year or so here anyway. Got it on the cheap when Mom's house sold."

Denise nearly choked on her sparkling water. "Sinking?" she said. She tried to catch Larry's eye, but he was nodding politely at Ty's tale. "What sinking?" She managed to fill Jen-Jen's sippy cup with juice and also chop Cole's sausage into little bites like he liked them but was frantic in her movements.

"Larry?" she said. "Did you hear anything about any sinking?" She cleared her throat and tried to calm herself. Bigs ripped right into one of the cans of nuts—the cashews—and shook some onto his plate. She watched Mort stuff the tomato salad right between his sausage and bun as if it were a relish.

"No," Larry said.

Ty seemed unfazed that he'd spilled the beans. He nodded his head up and down and reached for the cashews. "Long story I guess, but Uncle Bang said the land for Cherokee Bluff wasn't inspected right and they got lots of ground water built up under the houses now 'cause it's so close to the river." He brushed a few curls from his face with his finger. "Anyway, Anco Builders is gonna be screwed, so they already left the area. You didn't notice any cracks in your house or anything, did you?"

Denise nearly cried. She *had*, but had been convinced over and over by friends and family that all houses settled right after they were built. Even her own mother had said, "Look at our old Victorian. It's got cracks everywhere, from the settling and shifting over time. Your house is just doing the same. It's part of the process." Denise had seen a large crack right where the kitchen and dining room walls met, even though her house was only *days* old. Larry hadn't seemed to think it was a problem, either.

Ty apparently didn't sense her growing despair and kept on going. "You see those two new lots over there?" he said. He pointed to a couple of faded orange ties fluttering on stakes. "Those are the worst ones. They've stopped construction altogether there. The contractors said they just can't build on a swamp."

"A swamp?" Denise said. She stopped eating midbite. She could feel Jen-Jen, who sat between her legs, grunting and bearing down in her diaper. The smell soon followed, and she didn't know if her guests could smell it. She didn't know if she cared. Cole lined up his sausage bites and stabbed each one with a fork. He hated tomatoes, had eaten the top off his corn muffin, and chewed on the soggy white bun meant for his sausage.

Denise blinked back tears in her eyes. She and Larry had thrown everything they had into this house. They'd paid more than they'd wanted to, simply because they'd been so sold on the Cherokee Bluff aesthetic and sensibility. Their neighbors were teachers and businessmen. The new doctor from India had just bought the lot one street over. One young couple (Volvo drivers) had just moved in with their three small children.

"Hey," Ty said, "don't worry. Maybe something'll happen. Maybe they'll go after them."

"*They* who?" Denise said. Jen-Jen's diaper was reeking in a vaporous cloud all around her. She could see Mort and Bigs pretend not to notice at first but soon saw their hands go up over their noses. Finally, Cole said, "Someone stinks!" He got up and ran over to throw his sausage pieces to the dogs over in the Hillbillies' yard.

"Cole! Stop it! Now!" Denise stood up and shouted.

"Cole, no," Larry said.

"Ha, ha, ha." The Hillbillies laughed.

Denise wanted them to go home. She needed to verify if the Hillbillies knew what the hell they were talking about. Although they seemed a bit dim, what they'd told her seemed too complicated to be anything but the truth.

"Here, I'd like to give you this pie as a housewarming present," Denise said. She handed the foil pan to Bigs. "It's key lime pie. I got the recipe when I was in Florida a few years ago." Bigs nodded and thanked her.

Still they didn't move to go.

"Well, it's been fun," Denise said. "I should go change Jen-Jen, I suppose."

Ty came over and shook her hand. "You're good neighbors," he said. "We haven't heard a thing from anyone else. Haven't even met 'em. Seems like no one else is too friendly."

"Well, we know how it is to move to a strange, new place," Denise said. "It's a challenge. We've got to stick together."

"Amen." Ty saluted her and turned to leave with his brothers. "Thanks again," he said.

Denise watched them walk slowly, side by side, across the big yard and breathed a sigh of relief when they were out of sight.

Later that night, as the dishwasher churned and splashed and groaned, Denise could hear the Hillbillies outside in their yard. Firecrackers exploded; laughter erupted. She thought of the guns hanging on the garage walls. She thought of Cole, who could've reached up and grabbed one. She wouldn't put it past him. Larry was downstairs doing his Saturday evening ritual: ironing his pants, his shirt, and his socks for the following work week. He actually ironed his socks, even though Denise told him only OCD people ironed their socks. She heard another loud explosion and felt her heart rate escalate.

"I'll be right back!" she yelled down to Larry. In her bare feet, Denise went outside and started walking across the yard to the Hillbillies' house. Her feet sunk into the moist grass and got stuck in the muddy soil. One of her ankles was sucked down to the bottom of what felt like a sinking, wet hole. "Help me!" she called out. "I'm sinking!" But the Hillbillies kept on lighting their firecrackers and singing their songs. Finally, Denise pulled herself out and ran, light-footed, over to their garage.

"Excuse me," she said, out of breath, "but this is a family style community. Can you please be quiet?" Ty pulled up a chair and offered it to her, but she crossed her arms.

"I mean it," she said, and stomped her feet. She saw that Mort held a long rifle in his lap, buffing it with a pair of old underwear. "Guns, I'm afraid, aren't allowed in Cherokee Bluff."

"The right to bear arms," Ty said, "comes before Cherokee Bluff rules. We checked that one out before we got here."

Denise glared at him.

"Besides," Bigs said, "this place is going down anyway. You might as well just ride it out like we are. You know, let your hair down. Have some fun."

"It's not going down," Denise said, "but you're bringing it down. Why can't you just behave like everyone else? Can't you do that? What's the matter with you, lighting firecrackers all the time? I've got kids trying to sleep."

"We all make our choices," Ty said, not unkindly. "You do your thing, we do ours." He adjusted his cap and whistled through his teeth.

"Well, next time you disturb my peace, I'm calling the cops," Denise said, and could think of nothing to do but walk away. She ran quickly over the wet, mushy grass, trying to stay on top of it, trying to stay afloat. In the back of her mind, she thought they might shoot.

Inside, the whiteness of her house soothed her. She heard the dishwasher ticking dry. The kids were asleep, and she found Larry in the bathroom, trying to seal a crack above the toilet.

"It's not sinking, is it, Larry?" she asked. She sat on the edge of the tub and rinsed her dirty feet.

"I don't think so," he said. He smoothed spackling over the cracks. It stretched between the space like toothpaste. "Not if I can help it."

"Good," Denise said. "That's good." She thought she heard firecrackers again and sat up, ears pricked. A dozen or so went off in succession. She froze, but the noise quickly stopped. She looked up at Larry, her husband, the father of her children. "There," he said. "That ought to do it." He stood back, tub of spackle in his hand, backwards ball cap on his head. Denise placed a hand on his shoulder; they both stared at the wall in silence.

For a moment, you couldn't even tell where the crack had been. It looked brand new, pristine, perfect.

ALL-U-CAN-EAT

I t all started when my sister Stella tried to convince me that frog legs would be the next big American food craze. "Trust me," she said—she, an animal enthusiast to such an extreme that her freezer had become a pet morgue. "I predict that frog legs," she said, hands on her hips, "will be to 2000 what sun-dried tomatoes were to the eighties! They'll be to western New York what coffee shops were to Seattle! Like sushi in shopping malls. Think about it." She paused to scratch her elbow; she was forever itching with rashes, bug bites, pet hair. "Heck, I wouldn't be surprised if Mickey D's ends up carrying them on their menu. McFrog Legs Happy Meals. What kid wouldn't go crazy for that?"

"Umm, this kid wouldn't," I said, pointing to myself, though I was no kid. Stella—in addition to being thrice divorced, an alcoholic, a liar, and extremely persuasive—was broke. She worked as the cafeteria manager at our town's elementary school but blew most of her wages on lotto tickets, pet food, and bad luck business enterprises, in that order. She often got so excited about her current money-making scheme (most recently: Native American beaded jewelry made in your own home!) that she'd come driving over in her cafeteria whites, plastic food service gloves still covering her sweaty hands. She was as predictable as most con artists, though: no matter what she said, she wanted money, money, money. Unfortunately for me, her "enthusiasms" often rubbed off on my husband, Kenner, and it was all I could do to keep them both under control.

I was—in addition to being hardworking, frugal, a little high-strung, and extremely wary of Stella—flush with cash. When I tell them why, most people are surprised I got such a nice settlement from my lawsuit. The short version is this: about a year and a half ago, I was going about my business as a dutiful letter carrier in a pretty crummy neighborhood when a pit bull attacked me. The thing had been after me for days. I'd warned the owners in one of our special dog-warning letters slipped into their box. It threatened "the cessation of U.S. postal delivery" if they did not take care to "confine" their dog. But I, being how I am—did I forget to mention "pushover" as one of my traits?—gave them one last chance. It was Christmas time, after all. And I had a nice package to deliver for them.

Part of my right foot is now missing. I still walk with a limp and rely on a cane. When the weather gets cold, I'm often in serious pain. Need I say more? But Stella—though she expressed sympathy and concern, brought me magazines and doughnuts, loaned me her VCR and a bunch of stupid movies—has been burning to get her hands on my money ever since. She's a money grubber with grubby little paws, she is! She's a conniving little animal herself (a squirrel? perhaps a rat?), which is what makes her predilection for animal enterprises—in this case, frog legs—so funny. Or should I say ironic?

Despite my refusal, she kept at me for weeks. "We'll have Kenner farm the frogs, then you and I'll serve them up at the restaurant." We were hanging out in my driveway on a humid night in early July. I leaned against her truck, and she sat in my small, scrappy yard.

"What restaurant?" I asked. I had to wear a special shoe on my right foot that made me look like a disabled toddler. It was white with Velcro straps that got grass-stained and crusty all summer long.

"The one we're gonna open!" she said. She ripped clumps of my lawn out by the fistful, then threw them over her shoulder. "God, Faye, how many times do I have to go over this with you?"

Sometimes she could actually manage to make me think I'd forgotten something important. She tried to claim I'd become forgetful after the pit bull incident, but the fact was we had *never* discussed opening any restaurant, and I told her that.

"Bingo!" she said, and pointed at me like I'd said exactly the right thing. Her hair was cut short and boxy just like my husband, Kenner's, and she looked like a man in a white button-up and jeans.

"Bingo what?"

"Bingo to the restaurant we're going to open." She took a swig of her beer after toasting me, although I had no drink in hand. "We'll call it Chez Menagerie, get it? Because we'll serve all kinds of exotic animals. Frog legs'll be just the beginning."

I snorted. "Yeah, right."

"We'll serve ostrich, of course," she said. "Buffalo burgers. Octopus. Stuff like that." She hoisted herself up on all fours to get to a standing position.

"Stella, I am not giving you one *cent* of my money," I said. A mosquito drilled into my leg and I smashed it, felt blood sticky against my skin. "You know I'm saving it for—"

"For what?" she interrupted, rude, loud, and smug. She stretched her hands above her head and looked bored.

"For Kenner's and my retirement," I said. "I've told you a million times! We're going out with a bang! Cruises, winters in Florida, Winnebago." I tried to get her to look me in the eye to see that I was serious, but she was twisting around, trying to crack her back. "Anyway, I think I've earned it." Kenner and I had no kids. We both worked for the United States Postal Service, though I had been assigned to "light duty" after the accident. I now spent most of my days looking up addresses for expired forwards and answering the phone for zip code requests. I missed my route, though, and especially the people. One little old lady had me change her light bulbs and fetch food from her freezer in the basement. A blind man who lived in a collapsing pink house asked me how to run his VCR. You ran into all kinds of odd requests as a letter carrier, and I missed the surprises. I also missed driving my little white truck all over town and waving to everyone.

Stella hung her thumbs in her belt loops like a guy. Her face was dark purple from the stretching. I could see her eyes squinch up in a way that scared me. Then she laid into me. "You think just because a pit bull attacked you, you're better than everyone else!" She was so worked up she was out of breath.

"Oh, yeah, that's exactly what I think." I gripped the bed of the pickup instead of her neck.

"That *is* what you think," Stella said. "People who have accidents are always acting like victims." She hobbled around the truck with an imaginary cane. "'Oh, poor me! My poor leg! I have it so rough! Waaa!'"

When Stella got like this, I had to make a fast exit or things could get ugly. We'd been known to fistfight or wrestle when we were younger, if driven to it. I was almost driven to it now. Bigger than me, Stella usually won and would sit on top of me, her big butt bouncing up and down on my stomach, making me want to puke.

Just then Kenner drove up on his motorcycle. He'd removed the mufflers, and the noise his bike made ripped down the street like machine-gun fire. Dogs tested their chains. Neighbors came running out their front doors, pissed off. Someone yelled, "Not in this neighborhood!" though we were not exactly a high-end block of real estate. He parked it at a jaunty angle right beside us. The engine ticked as it cooled. Its chrome shined bright in the dying day-end light.

"How we doing, ladies?" Kenner got off the bike and popped the helmet off his head like an astronaut. He held it cupped against his side as if he were toting a toddler. "Babe," he said, and kissed me. I saw him raise his eyebrows at Stella in a way that made me feel left out.

"Did you tell her?" he asked. He put the helmet down and crouched on his haunches. I could see his crack and the striped band of his underwear. "Ribbit, ribbit." He stuck his tongue out but looked like a snake, not a frog. I kicked him in the butt with my gimp foot, which probably hurt me more than him.

"You guys are crazy," I said. "Nobody's gonna eat frog legs in this town." I wanted to get inside. I was hungry, thirsty, and cranky. It was a good TV night, and I longed to stretch out in front of its glow. "Are you guys under the illusion that this is Paris or something?" I headed for the back door, which, for me, took considerable effort. "I'm sorry, but the last time I ate out in Rathburg, I was seeing a lot of burgers and fries. Am I right or am I right?"

"You're wrong," they both said in unison.

"Jinx!" Kenner said, and clipped her on the arm. Then they giggled, or at least Stella did in her high-pitched, teeth-grinding way. I went inside, stewing. They could both be so stupid, I thought. Frog legs and buffalo burgers and octopus, in our little town? As if.

In bed that night, Kenner revealed to me that he'd already spent $6,000 of my $50,000 settlement: $5,000 to Stella, to help with a down payment on Chez Menagerie (formerly the old VFW club next to the bowling alley); and $1,000 to Bud "Jupiter" McCombs from Willacoochee, Georgia, the cost of his "Frog Legs: An Informational Video & Starter Kit for the Adventurous Entrepreneur." You'd think the check to Stella would have burned me worse than the frog leg kit, but it was oddly the latter that got my goat. The fact that Kenner had blown a thousand dollars of my money on something so incredibly stupid was more than I could bear. I had my limits. The money, after all, was mine, and since I was the one who'd suffered the injury, I wasn't about to let him squander my stash on another one of Stella's half-assed, get-rich-quick schemes that always, and I mean always, ended badly. How many examples I could pull out of a hat in case he'd forgotten! Tie-dyed T-shirts to sell at our town's Noodle Days celebration had put her in the red. Buffalo Bill aprons, hats, teddy bears, potholders, and bibs had never quite found their market (I still had a couple of stained potholders in the kitchen). Probably her biggest flub was trying to sell deveined filet mignons (from Omaha!) door to door. Her freezer (and mine) had overflowed with them faster than she could move them, and they'd rotted, stinky and brown, on her back porch: another couple grand, which she didn't even have, down the toilet.

"Kenner," I said. We usually slept naked, but tonight I punished him by wearing my stiff cotton pajamas with pigs on them. "I thought you'd be smarter than this! You should know by now that Stella's got about as much business sense as a plate of mashed potatoes." I scrunched up the covers, punched back my pillows. Our two cats, Harley and Davis, got scared by my sudden movements and leapt off the bed in tandem, like synchronized swimmers.

"This time I think she might be onto something," he said. He was propped up on one elbow, and I could see the puff of his dark armpit hair. I could also smell the raw onions from dinner on his breath. "Is it so wrong to want to reach for your dreams? If you don't take a chance, you'll never know what might have been."

Was he reciting from an inspirational greeting card? It sounded like it. "Why do I feel as if I have absolutely no say in this when it's *my* money that's at stake here?" I watched Kenner reach for a cigarette, steady it between his lips, and light it. I hated when he smoked in bed.

"It's about trust," he said through a scrim of smoke. He folded one arm behind his head, gesticulated with the other. "I mean, I can understand your lack of trust after the pit bull thing, but this is me here!" he said. He thumped on his chest with his thumb. "And your sister. I mean, come on. We're all kin."

"Nobody says 'kin' anymore," I said. "Plus, you're not kin."

"You know what I mean," he said. "Don't overanalyze." He tapped my hand. "Just think of it as an investment. We could double, triple, even quadruple our money, then retire early once the thing takes off. Think about it!"

I turned out the light, though he was still smoking. "I hereby banish you from the checkbook," I said. "You don't touch it until I say so." I waited for him to say something, but he didn't. I turned away from him and watched headlights arc across the wall, the ceiling, and the comforter, then hit me in the eyes.

Finally, he settled in behind me, gathering himself against my butt, cupping his knees behind mine. "Tomorrow night me and Stella are going to the Bergen Swamp to scope out some bullfrogs," he whispered. His voice was smoky and soft. "You should come." He grabbed me around the waist, let his hand rest on my curved flank. "*Come*," he said. "It'll be fun."

"We'll see," I said.

The next night, the three of us headed out after dark, a friend's borrowed boat roped to the top of Stella's car. As we turned off onto Old Orchard Road, families of bats swooped away from our headlights. Fallen branches snapped under our tires. I didn't get out when we parked but sat listening to Kenner and Stella grunting and huffing as they untied the boat from the roof. Kenner was educating Stella about amphibian reproduction. In July, Kenner claimed, the frogs were screwing like crazy and making tadpoles left and right. "They'll be lazy and sluggish and tired after all that sex," Kenner claimed. "Should be easy targets."

"And since when are you such an expert on frog behavior?" I said from inside the car.

"Three words." He leaned into my window. "Bud 'Jupiter' McCombs. Best money I ever spent."

I did get out of the car after that, ready to strangle him, but I couldn't see my own hand in front of me and got scared. Plus, I hadn't brought my cane and didn't feel entirely steady on my feet. "What goes around, comes around," I said, unsure of what I meant.

"Exactly," Kenner said.

"Touché," Stella said. As a sister, she could be such a traitor.

Stella carried two spears, a filet knife, a bunch of plastic bags, and a bottle of red wine. I carried two yellow flashlights, big as bricks and just as heavy. Kenner, somehow, bumped the boat along behind us.

We put in at the soupy eastern end of the swamp; the spongy ground pooled up around my ankles. I was sure snakes were weaving their way between my legs; in fact, I cried out when I felt a slick wetness against my calf, but it was only a string of algae slime. Kenner took control of the flashlights while he let us "ladies" get situated in the rickety boat. I kept feeling invisible things brushing against my face and hair, but when I swatted, I grabbed only air.

The boat, painted camouflage, was small and shallow and smelled like cat pee. "I call front!" Stella said, and clambered her way to the bow, almost toppling us both into the water. I sat in the middle seat, Kenner in the stern. It was just after dusk, and the tight thicket of trees and mossy overhang completely obliterated the weak glow of a half-moon. I was put in charge of the flashlights and held one in either hand, training the beams right at water level as we headed out into the unknown. Instantly, dozens, hundreds, thousands of eyes skimmed the surface. It was a pond full of eyes! Round blinking bubbles of eyes. "Lookit there!" I said. "And there!" My flashlight beams grew erratic as my heart rate rose.

"Shh!" Stella said. "You'll scare them. Stay focused." She was leaning way over the boat, spear poised in the air above the water. Kenner was in charge of operating the oars, which groaned on rusty stirrups. We slid through the water, nocturnal hunters and explorers, traveling through thick bands of gnats. I could feel them on my tongue and told Kenner we could get poisoned. I had read that certain gnats in upstate New York were poisonous. I couldn't remember where I'd read it.

"Just keep your mouth closed," Kenner said.

"Then they go in my nose!" I was swatting and trying to breath without inhaling gnats when I dropped one of the flashlights in the water. It sunk.

"Way to go," Stella said. "I was just zeroing in on one!" She sat back in the boat and made waves with her angry movements. I held on, rocking.

"This is crazy," I said. I turned to Kenner. "Didn't they show you any better tricks of the trade on your frog video?" An owl hooted above us and sounded like it was booing. "I mean, I would think a thousand bucks would get you a whole *case* of frog legs, not to mention some how-to."

"Well, here's a little known fact," Kenner said. He sat back, placed the oars inside the boat, and unscrewed the bottle of red. "If you don't feed frogs right, I mean if they're really hungry?" He took a sip, passed it to me. I drank and passed it to Stella, but she was busy taking aim at one of the frogs. "So I was saying," Kenner kept monologuing, "if they're really hungry, they resort to cannibalism. That's one thing McCombs says can be a real problem. Cannibalism. It reduces the harvestable population." Kenner said it as if he were reading out of a brochure.

"Hey, I got one!" Stella said. She rocked the boat a bit getting it inside, but indeed, there was a big grey-bellied bullfrog impaled through the throat. It lay there, gasping, its eyes roving, a desperate little man. "Amazing how easy it is," Stella said. "You can almost reach right in and grab them." She pulled the spear out of it and started going for another.

"You have to put it out of its misery!" I said. "You can't just let it suffer like that." I petted its slimy head, and its eyes met mine, pleading for help. "This is torture."

"You do it," Stella said. "Use your flashlight. Give it a clunk." Again, she dangled over the side of the boat, spear in hand. "Just make sure to smash it over the head without ruining the legs. Remember, this is about frog legs."

I stared at the little guy caught like a common criminal in my flashlight beam.

"Hey, Faye," Kenner said. "It's okay. I'll do it." When it came right down to it, Kenner knew me. He knew I could not kill a frog. I turned away but heard the ugly sound of plastic on cartilage. The rest of the frogs in the swamp seemed to croak loudly and mournfully at the loss of one of their own. "It's okay," Kenner said. "It's all right." He rubbed my sweaty arm and for a second I felt comforted. "Just try to think of it like cows. We kill cows and eat them without a thought. This is the same thing."

"Got another one!" Stella said, and slid it off the spear like a cooked kebab. "I think I'm getting the hang of this." Kenner took the flashlight from me and put this one out of its misery, too. I turned away.

We slid quietly through the dark, spearing, whacking, killing, frog after frog. I sat in the middle seat, sorry I'd come. I missed the Kenner I'd married twenty years ago, who used to wash up on Friday nights and take me to the movies. Back then, we wanted the same things: a little money saved for a rainy day, a decent car, a small house, and a few trips here and there to America's landmarks. We still hadn't made it to the Badlands, not to mention Yellowstone, Disneyworld, or the Jersey shore. Somewhere along the way, Kenner seemed to have drifted into the Harley set, leaving me, I guess you could say, in the dust. All I wanted was what we used to want: to be together, doing nothing much at all, but always seeing the future as a bright place, full of possibility. I didn't even need to go on the trips as much as I wanted to feel aligned with Kenner again, like uniformed soldiers, fighting for the same cause.

After work the next day, we kicked back whiskey-Cokes and fired up the grill at Stella's house. Kenner's theory was that more people would go for frog legs if they were barbecued like any other meat, whereas Stella argued that a breaded, fried version with lemon and garlic would so mask the shape and taste of frog that people would gobble them up with abandon, then be able to say, "Hey, I ate frog legs." They both wanted to test their versions on each other before deciding which one the restaurant should serve. I thought people in our town would rather eat a whole plate of ketchup before they'd eat frog legs but decided that if I wanted to be on the same side as Kenner again, I should at least play along with the whole venture—even if I did think it was ridiculous.

Stella poured about an inch of oil into a deep cast-iron skillet. She stood back, watching it warm up. "My thinking is that if you fry the hell out of it, people will eat almost anything, right? I mean, chicken wings? Give me a break." She finished her drink fast, the ice cubes knocking against her teeth. "Fix me another?" she asked. Granted, I was just sitting there at her very 1970s breakfast bar leafing through a Ladies Plus catalogue, but still. I scowled at her and stomped to the fridge.

Growing up, she had always resented me for being tiny and trim, whereas she was tall and husky. Not only that, but she was a tomboy gone to seed. She played basketball and got thrown out of every single game for fouling. She was a regular pot smoker by age twelve. At sixteen she totaled my parents' Honda and walked away without a scratch. Still, she somehow managed to win their favor. "Stella's spunk," my father, a high school shop teacher, would say, "will take her far. You just watch her go." As for me—their sweet, reliable, goody-goody daughter—my good grades were hastily magneted to the refrigerator, then soon fell down and were replaced by supermarket fliers, court summons for Stella, and photos of our dog, Derek, a blind spaniel Stella had found at the dump and adopted as our family pet.

I could hear Kenner outside hacking the legs off the frogs. He'd wanted to do it at the sink, but I'd insisted it was not an indoor enterprise. I also told him to skin them out there and only bring in the little legs and drummies when they looked like any other meat. It was all I could stomach. But I was glad for the time alone with Stella, who drank her whiskey-Cokes as if they were water. She'd taken to drinking hard liquor the past few years, and I could see it taking its toll. Spider veins covered her cheeks, and her face had grown swollen and splotchy in a way that read alcoholism. Kenner disagreed with me, though, and told me I was always looking for problems when it came to Stella.

She persuaded me to mix up a little beer batter with chive since I was obviously idle. She pointed me over to the flour canister with her elbow and told me where everything was.

"You know, Stella," I said, and shook some salt into my palm. I threw it into the batter. "I kind of wish you'd leave Kenner out of these things. You know he's got a heart of gold. He'd do anything for you. For anyone, for that matter." I snipped up the chive with a scissor. "But he's a lotto-ticket junkie, just like you! We're talking about a dreamer here. All he wants is to quit his job and ride his Harley all over hell."

Her back was to me. She shrugged.

"He's only doing this because he thinks it'll make us all filthy rich," I said. I waited. Nothing. "He wants to blow all my money on this, and then it'll all go to pot, and then what? Huh? You know as well as I do that this thing is never going to catch on."

She still wouldn't look at me. I could see the back of her neck muscles flex. I stirred the batter hard, then let it rest.

"Just because you think you're going to strike it rich," I said, "doesn't mean . . . well, can you just leave Kenner alone for once?" There. I'd said it, and was glad I had.

"He came after me first," she mumbled, her back to me. "It wasn't like I was thinking: Hey, Kenner! Let's do this!" She spun around then, fast, and caught me off guard. I was starting to get confused.

"That's not what he told me." I tried to remember how the whole frog leg fiasco had come up in the first place but couldn't recall Kenner's exact words. "All I know is that Kenner didn't know the first thing about frog legs until you started talking about them. And now—"

The screen door squeaked open, and Kenner came in with a cookie sheet full of frog legs. Their little calf muscles curled tightly around the bones like sea shells. Long black veins ran down the tendons like embroidery floss. You could see the gray hip joints hacked at the ball. But worst of all, he hadn't removed the webbed feet. Each little toe stuck together and looked ready to leap.

"Kenner," I said, "the feet!"

"I'm sorry," he said. "Try not to look."

"The feet!"

He spread them open between thumb and forefinger.

"You're barbarian," I said. "Both of you."

"No," Stella said. She dipped a couple of legs into my batter, and we all stood there, watching them sizzle. "It's more or less we're on the same page, me and Kenner, entrepreneurially."

"That's not a word," I said. The frog legs smelled like garlic, nothing else. They popped and sputtered grease. I took a step back.

"Look it up," she said. "Is too."

I was tempted to say, "Is not!" but crossed my arms and stewed. She could be such a bully. Besides, I comforted myself, I was the smart one. Back in high school, I was on the honor roll and salutatorian and voted Most Likely to Succeed, but whenever Stella caught me reminiscing, she'd say, "Faye, let it go. That was over twenty years ago, girlfriend." I *hated* when she called me girlfriend. I was not her girlfriend.

When the frog legs were done, we sat down at the table, the platter steaming in front of us. I still didn't think I'd quite gotten through to Stella, but I trusted Kenner, if not her. For a while, I wondered if they could possibly be having an affair, but I knew Kenner didn't have it in him to cheat, simply because he was too lazy. Cheating would require him to spend his free time on something other than his bike. Cheating would mean he'd have to make phone calls (he hated talking on the phone) and prior arrangements (he was a "wing it" kind of guy). Plus, there was very little Stella had to offer someone like Kenner except a bossy, know-it-all kind of idiocy. Kenner wouldn't stand for it. I decided they were simply in business collaboration both with and against me, all in the name of getting my money behind their frog leg business. But they were not getting another cent.

"Ladies?" Kenner said. He got three forks from the drawer and set them on the table. "Shall we?"

"Ken, they're really a finger food," Stella said. She pushed aside the forks.

I wasn't going to have any, but the two of them were exclaiming and moaning in such delight that I decided to close my eyes and just do it. What disturbed me about them was how lightweight the bones were, as if they weren't bones at all but airy, birdlike imitations. The fully intact webbed feet didn't help matters, either.

I chewed, but the meat seemed to bounce against my molars.

"Do you think they taste like chicken?" Kenner said. He rubbed some grease off my chin with his thumb.

"I think they kick ass!" Stella said. She was onto her third one, and I could see the grease had already stained her T-shirt. The T-shirt was tie-dyed and so tight around her bust you could see every seam and lacy bulge of her bra through it.

"Umm, I think he was asking me, not you," I said. I kicked her under the table, but she kicked back, harder.

"So?" Kenner said. "Pretty righteous, huh?" He wiped his mouth with the back of his hand. "Tastes like goddamn chicken fingers."

"It's sort of like fat-free chicken," I said, chewing. I nibbled around the knee joint and shivered. "Or somehow it's like fish. And it tastes kind of bitter. A little like algae."

I needed a big swallow of beer to wash down each bite. What really repulsed me, beyond the milky texture and the webbed feet and thick black veins, was seeing the long, gray discarded bones on the pan. The shape and bend of each leg too clearly suggested frog to me. You could almost imagine them hopping away.

"So, are you okay with this?" Stella said. "Are you in?" She sat back and balled up her napkin, then sucked at her teeth and eventually scraped between them with her fingernail.

Kenner looked at me expectantly.

"Meaning what?" I asked.

They exchanged glances, and I felt my heart rate rise. "Meaning we need just a little more money," Stella said. "Please, please, please! If you've ever done anything good in your life, do this! You won't be sorry! I promise."

Kenner moved in before I could even say anything. He was obviously on damage control and tried to placate me and at the same time con me into it. "Babe," he said in his soft I'm-really-sweet-and-understanding voice. "We just need a couple thousand more for the grand opening." He lifted my hand off the table and held it like a fair maiden's. "Just some odds and ends. Tables and chairs. A steam table for the buffet. Advertising and promo stuff. You know."

I pushed the frog legs away from under my nose. "First of all, you've sunk $6,000 of *my* money into this whole thing already." I tapped a finger on the table to make my point. "Without asking me." I glared at Kenner, who nodded, again, in his I-hear-you way. "Second of all, no one is going to want to come and eat freaking frog legs around here! How many times do I have to tell you two that?"

"Why do you always have to be such a downer?" Stella said. She hoisted herself up to get her cigarettes and stood by the back door, half in, half out, exhaling outside as a courtesy, I knew, to me.

"Let me have one of those," Kenner said. The two of them stood with the door cracked open, looking in at me, the lonely nonsmoker, at the table.

"Ever since we were kids, you always had to bring up the practical side of shit and poo-poo on everything." Stella blew smoke inside the house now, as if in revenge. "Whenever Mom or Dad would suggest some kind of vacation to Niagara Falls or Cooperstown, you'd always have to go get the atlas and point out all the problems with it. Or whenever Dad suggested we live a little and splurge on something like a new car or a swimming pool, you'd always band together with Mom and worry about the money. You were worrying about money when you were five years old!" She picked a piece of tobacco off her tongue with her finger.

"It's easy not to care about money when it's not yours," I said. I scraped my chair back and told them I had to go. "And don't think I'm going to change my mind like I always do. Because I won't." I stormed past the two of them—or stormed as best I could with my "disability," a term I loathed. Outside, I sat in the car a minute, rolled my window down, and tried to calm myself. I had read somewhere that you should never drive or operate machinery when you were upset.

"Just think about it," Stella called from the back stairs. "We have to have chairs! Is that asking for so much?"

I pulled out of the driveway, then pulled back in. I hung my arm out the window and pointed at Kenner, who'd just cracked open a beer. "Kenner, get in," I said. "You're coming with me."

He shrugged his shoulders, stubbed out his cigarette, and brought his beer along with him, which I didn't like, not in the car. I drove us away fast without waving at Stella.

"This is getting out of control," I said. I liked driving Kenner around our town and took the long way home. We cruised past the kiddy park, which was clogged with strollers, then down Main Street, past the post office (luckily, we worked the six-to-two shift, great for summer), the movie theater, the comic book shop, and the travel agency with faded cardboard signs in the windows advertising Florida and Hawaii. The signs were ancient, yellowed, and crumbly around the edges. They'd been there as long as I could remember.

"The thing you need to do," Kenner said, and tucked his beer between his legs, "is see the big picture." He mimed a picture frame in front of him and held it up for me to view. "Money down now is an investment for later." He rested his hands on his scuzzy jeans. "You have to spend money to make money."

I rolled my eyes. "I've heard that somewhere before."

"Yeah, it's a saying," Kenner said, "but it's true."

I drove him past the duck pond, a little green pool foul with duck shit and fetid water. Stay-at-home moms sat with their kids, chucking old bread to the ducks, who gorged themselves like gluttons. I used to take walks near the pond, but now those days were over due to my gimp foot. I sometimes wondered if Kenner missed the me I used to be before the accident, the me who could run and jump and dance and wear high heels and really *kick* it; I knew I did. Now

I was a person with "special needs," which I'm sure didn't do much for my sex appeal.

"Check this out," Kenner said. He pointed excitedly to the pond. "There's probably hundreds of frogs in there, right? In fact, when you walk past at night, you can hear them doing their thing." He tapped his lip, which he did when he was really scheming. "Another source of legs for us that's even closer to home! McCombs says on the video that the more free sources you can identify, the better profit you can make. We might not have to farm them at all."

"Don't you think people would look at us a little funny," I said, "if we showed up with our spears, right here in town?" I was trying not to be a downer about it, but the idea seemed pretty unrealistic.

"I've got to tell Stella," he said. "She'll be psyched."

I tried this time to be more positive. If I didn't, I might be spending a lot of nights alone while the two of them hunted dark waters together. "I mean," I started over, "I'm sure there *are* lots of frogs in there. God, yeah." I smiled at him as genuinely as I could, then went out a little further on a limb. "In fact, I could imagine this spot being our little secret. Just you and me. We could walk down here and, you know, make a date out of it. A little adventure."

"That'd be cool." He seemed distracted, though, as if he were already hatching a plan to run by Stella. I had to admit I was jealous of not only their like-minded business sense but of their very mobility, which I was sure they both took completely for granted. Sometimes I felt more like a liability than a helpmate to Kenner, and Stella seemed to fill certain needs of his that I couldn't.

I drove him by the new dollar store that had opened up on the edge of town. Lots of crappy cars and a few rickety ten-speed bikes were parked out front. The building next door to it had been demolished, and little kids jumped around on the crumbly cement blocks.

"So are you and Stella an item now or what?" The idea—however stupid—had been nagging at me for weeks. I signaled left and sort of chuckled. "Should I be worried my big sister is zeroing in on you?"

"God, no!" He exhibited the proper amount of shock and derision so that I believed him.

"Well, Stella seemed to be hinting at—"

"She wants to piss you off," Kenner said. He adjusted his train conductor cap, then wiped off the dust build-up on the dash. He definitely preferred to drive, not ride. "She lives to get your goat. You know that." He seemed genuinely upset by my question. "And come on. Me and Stella? I don't mean to dis your sister or anything, but she's not exactly a looker. You know what I'm saying."

I nodded. "I know what you're saying."

I swung us home, down Briar Street. I could see our little blue Cape in the distance. As we got closer, I saw Harley and Davis on the stoop, whining to get in.

"And the money?" Kenner asked sheepishly. "I don't think you ever said one way or the other." Our car doors slammed, syncopated. I went for the house.

"Let's not fight right now," I said, reaching for the cats. "Okay? I'm too tired to fight."

"Okay." Kenner spanked me on the rear and followed me into the house, whooping.

* * *

On the last Friday night of August, almost two months after we began hunting frogs, Chez Menagerie was ready to open its doors for its grand opening. Kenner and I had harvested more frogs than we knew what to do with. I'd financed the new chairs, tables, steam table, and menus. The grand opening had been advertised in our town's newspaper for two weeks, plus we'd put an ad in the city newspaper the week prior. We were all set to open, and Kenner and I sat waiting for Stella to show up.

I had to admit that even I, the "downer," the "naysayer," was a little bit excited. I had learned things about frogs from Kenner that I'd never known before. Who knew they preferred their food moving, and that the Japanese had actually invented a motorized vibrating food tray that mimicked live bait? The bullfrog, I'd found out, was the largest North American species and grew up to a foot long. How any of this mattered was unclear, but Kenner had relayed it all to me with such relish that his enthusiasm and interest had somehow rubbed off on me. Our nighttime frog escapades were doing wonders for our love life. Plus, the more interested in frogs I became, the better Kenner and I got along and the less time we had to spend with Stella. In fact, we'd barely seen her at all the past couple of weeks.

We'd taken to going on long rides after work on his Harley, me clutching his waist from behind, my hair blowing in strings out the bottom of my helmet. I liked it that way since my bad foot was irrelevant and we could both fly down the highway like the old days. We'd search out new frog sites and evaluate their potential for a harvestable population. We'd picnic by little secluded ponds and listen for the familiar croaks. Our lives had started to center around frogs, but instead of them disturbing me, I had grown to love the little guys, as well as their legs, fried in butter and smothered with garlic and lemon.

"I'm going to give Stella a call," Kenner said now. He turned to the black wall phone, but just as he picked up the receiver, she came rushing through the door. It had started to rain outside, hard, and her red hooded sweatshirt was draped over her head like a cape. She had a bottle stuffed under her arm and shoved it at us like we'd won a prize. "Here you go," she said. "Chinese restaurants usually put a good luck ceramic kitty in the window for prosperity, but I figured some cheap champagne would do us just fine."

She scooted past us, investigating the place. All the tables were covered in dark green tablecloths, and the silverware was rolled up in white paper napkins. To the left of the door, the steam table kept the frog legs hot and covered with sneeze guards. Next to the frog legs were vats of roasted potatoes, buttered carrots, green salad with purple cabbage, and rolls with butter. A sign we'd had commissioned at the local printing press said: "All-U-Can-Eat Frog Legs, $15.95!"

"Isn't that a little steep?" Stella said. She'd dressed up a little for the grand opening, which for her meant a white stretch halter top and black shorts. Her legs looked veiny and weak, like an old person's, and somehow I felt sorry for her. "I thought we were gonna go for $9.95, just to get people in the door."

"Well," I said, "we have to at least break even." I saw her smirk at me, then roll her eyes at Kenner when she clearly thought I wasn't looking.

"It's still a pretty good deal," I insisted.

She shrugged her bare shoulders, which were freckled and leathery. We'd all agreed to help out after our day jobs, just until we were up and running and had some money to pay for help. We decided we'd open at five and serve dinner from Thursday through Sunday nights only. Stella and I had agreed to wait tables while Kenner tended bar, even though we were still waiting on our liquor license. That part made me nervous, but I was doing my best to go with the spirit of things and not present obstacles.

We all huddled back by the bar and waited. There was one window framed by a pink curtain that faced Main Street, and through it, we could see the rain gushing down the gutters and splashing into the street. Cars drove by, spraying through puddles that looked like lakes. We watched the few brave souls who did venture out rush into the bar across the street. We all knew about the two-for-ones from five to seven at the Pig's Eye.

"It sometimes takes a while for things to catch on," Stella said, and tidied the straws and napkins on the bar. She looked away quickly, but I could have sworn she seemed on the verge of tears—or a nervous breakdown.

Kenner's response was to get pissed off. He paced back and forth between tables, then kept going up to the window and rapping on it with his knuckle. "This town sucks!" he said. "I mean, there's what—two restaurants total in this town?" He sat down at one of the tables and drank the water that had ice melting in it. "You'd think people would be thrilled to have another choice! I mean, it's the diner, with their soggy gravy all over everything, or the pizza place, whose sauce tastes like piss, and now us. I mean, we got frog legs! What more could people want?"

I motioned for him to get up when I saw a family of four come rushing at the door. The man held a toddler in his arms, and the woman dragged a small boy by the hand. No sooner did we get them seated then another couple came in. "We're meeting another couple," they said, wiping their eyeglasses off with their napkins and shaking their umbrellas. Within the hour, six tables were filled, but the strange thing was that I didn't recognize anyone, not a single person, and our town was very small. As a letter carrier, I could safely say I knew almost everyone. I asked Stella and Kenner if they recognized anyone. They both shook their heads.

It turned out every single customer was from out of town. Most had driven in from the neighboring city. Apparently, our advertising had paid off. In fact, one of the customers admitted to us, as he paid the tab, that he was writing a review and had decided to give us four stars for the food but only one for the atmosphere. He had a moustache and wore soft green corduroy pants and a blazer, even though it was late August and very humid. "If you want my advice," he said, pen in his hand, "you pretty it up in here and you'll do splendidly. Those frog legs are among the best I've ever had. Where do you import from? Thailand?"

We all nodded our heads vaguely. He left us his card, and a very healthy tip, and disappeared with his companion, a silent but very attractive young man he did not introduce us to.

"He's gay as the day is long," Stella said, and picked up his card. "Rumsford Sage," she read. "Totally made-up name."

"But he liked our food!" I said. I wanted to dance, as if I'd somehow personally made all this happen. "Do you know what this could mean for us?"

Kenner nodded a sly smile and made like he was punching out a time clock. I could already imagine us out on the open road in our Winnebago, my withering stash of money buoyed up by our huge restaurant success. We could open more branches, hire people to run them, and disappear into the great world of leisure.

The table with children spilled milk all over the floor, asked for more ketchup, and complained that the fries were cold. "Well, that's because you're taking a kazillion years to eat them," Stella said. "I brought them out like an hour ago."

Kenner and I gave her hard looks, but when she handed the kid a quarter, everything seemed okay.

Not everyone who came in ordered the frog legs. Some wrinkled up their noses. Some asked for things we didn't have. (A dinosaur burger? What was that?) A couple people even looked at the menu and left. But as the night wound down, I'd occasionally grab Kenner around his skinny waist, snuggle up to him, and say, "I knew you could do it, baby. I just knew." The look on his face told me we were back, and better than ever, and I could hardly wait to run my hands over his familiar, naked body.

Stella watched us coldly; I could feel it, just as I could feel her loneliness every time Kenner and I really got along, really meshed. But I didn't let her ruin things for me this time. I simply stood back and watched her bring out another fresh vat of frog legs. When she pulled off the lid, the steam rose like swirly smoke and, for a second, clouded my view of her. But then I saw her wipe her face and look off longingly, out the window, down the street.

PINNED

hen I was nineteen, I fell in love with a big wrestler from Africa. He wasn't *Africa* African, but a Midwestern white guy who grew up in Kenya, son of missionary parents. What impressed me about Matthew Knudson was not just his big barrel chest and trim little hips but his occasional spouting off in Swahili at parties just when things were getting dull. "What's that you just said?" I asked him the first time we'd met. He said it again, in Swahili, and I shook my head. "No, no! In English. English, *por favor!*" I was a sophomore majoring in Spanish and psychology; I'd probably had upwards of six beers, and it wasn't even midnight. I distinctly remember a big red X on my hand, proof that I'd paid my two dollars for a bottomless cup of Hamm's. I also remember the gray fedora I wore with a feather arcing off the side. I was hopelessly theatrical and in need of attention; it was the mideighties; I had recently escaped a corn & soybean hometown and was ready to exchange my old self for a new.

"I said, 'Baby, anybody want to wrestle?'" With that, he grabbed the beer out of my hand, picked me up over his shoulder, and pinned me down on the moist shag carpet. I remember the wetness seeping through my shirt. More than that, though, I remember the feeling of his hard muscled legs straddling me. He was built tight, his pale skin seemingly strained over an enormous bulging body. His hands held mine up over my head, and I remember I could see his teeth—small, jagged, and widely spaced—grinding together, but also grinning. Big tennis shoes danced and stumbled dangerously around my head. My long blonde hair spread in strings around me. The retainer I wore to correct a childhood overbite slipped loose. Even my little John Lennon eyeglasses flew off, and I remember panicking that they'd be crunched underfoot and I'd have to wander home in a near-sighted fog.

The thing was, I was pretty, if a bit unpolished. I could've had any number of boyfriends who'd have treated me kindly, opened doors, telephoned me daily, brought me flowers. But Matthew won fair and square. After a loud count of ten, he raised his hands in the air and proudly pronounced himself the winner.

* * *

By junior year, Matthew had lost his wrestling scholarship. He was living in his car, a brown Toyota hatchback with a luggage rack, on top of which he kept suitcases of clothes secured with bungee cords. Books filled the bulk of his car, mostly poetry and philosophy, but some gardening and horticulture texts; his most recent scheme was to become a ginseng farmer. Among other atrocities, the U.S. had just invaded Grenada, and Matthew had dyed an American flag black, hung it flapping out his back window to make a statement. "This country is fucked," he said. He kept a can of beer in his cup holder and sipped at it in fast, jerky sips. I watched his Adam's apple, transfixed. "I seriously think we need to get out of here before it's too late. You in?"

I remember the rain wiggling down my window as we drove all

over the city looking for an open diner. The light was pearly gray and sad and put me in a mood I couldn't name. Matthew had terrible, sporadic acne, and his normally pink face looked purple with pain. Everything seemed ready to erupt.

I'd just won a big scholarship to keep me going, tuition-wise, for another year and asked Matthew to attend the ceremony at school as my guest. "But you have to dress up," I told him. "It's steak and champagne." Somehow I hadn't yet learned to anticipate his flare-ups. They always blindsided me when I should have seen them coming. I remember the silence he issued after my invitation.

"You don't get it, do you?" He ran a red light, because as he always said, no cop, no stop. A neon Open sign glowed up ahead, and Matthew gunned it into the parking lot. "This isn't about books!" He ground the stick into first, cranked on the parking brake with a flexed arm. "This is about values and beliefs! Who does this country think it is? My parents had the right idea. Fucking Kenya." He placed a big warm hand on the back of my neck and squeezed. He was always offering me massages, but the presses felt like pinches and hurt more than helped.

Finally, he got out, slammed his door, but I still sat there. The rain sprayed in gauzy sheets across the pavement, and I could see it drenching Matthew, who wore no coat, carried no umbrella. He knocked on my window and jumped up and down. "Come on!" he said. "I'll go to the damn thing if it's so important!" He pointed to a big sign in the window that said Breakfast 24/7, then patted his stomach. I remember the way he laughed then, raised his hands up to the rain, and shouted, "I love you! I fucking love you!" He sunk his knee down into a puddle and opened his arms to me. I couldn't resist, but I remember worrying about how I'd ever get through school when he seemed perpetually perched between failing out and dropping out, not to mention driving me crazy.

At the ceremony, I felt proud and important, as I should've. I'd won a prestigious full tuition waiver plus living expenses for a year and had a chance to repeat the scholarship the following year if I kept my grades up. I listened hard to the speeches; I wore hose and borrowed pumps; I remember holding my knife and fork European style as I ate, something new I'd learned from a foreign student. Matthew drank heavily. He ate too quickly and complained of a sore stomach before they'd even brought dessert. There were carnations on the tables; I remember they were pink, edged faintly with white, and just when I dared to give Matthew a glare to behave, he reached right out and ate the carnations in the vase, one right after the other. He patted his lips with a napkin when he was through, then gave me a look I knew I'd never forget. It was both sorry and contemptuous.

* * *

I'd been seeing Matthew over a year before I had my first orgasm. It was the end of junior year; I was studying for my art history midterm, trying to sear images of Tintoretto and Daret and Greuze into my memory. Matthew, long since dropped out of school, was giving me a foot massage, only his hands kept creeping further and further up my leg. My roommates at the time were at a football game. The apartment we lived in was cramped, and Matthew's nearly constant presence had been the source of numerous "house meetings." Their ultimatum, "He goes or you both go," hadn't seemed to register with Matthew, but instead of confronting me, my roommates had taken to vacating the apartment whenever he was around. To his credit, Matthew tried to make himself indispensable to them. He'd change the oil in their cars, make them pancakes and bacon for breakfast, shovel the walk, and write their Shakespeare papers for them when they'd waited until the last minute and were bereft of ideas.

I remember on that cold, slushy Sunday, I didn't care. I let the heavy art history textbook slide to the floor and let Matthew's hands wander. Sex with Matthew was, if not always satisfying, at least a sensual feast. He was forever rubbing almond oil onto my shoulder blades, burning cinnamon-scented candles, playing Bolero or Billie Holiday in the background, draping us with silken sheets the color of sherry, then drawing us a bath laced with cream and nutmeg. That afternoon, we kissed, undressed, caressed. On my tiny single bed, we rolled on top of each other. I remember looking out the window at a squirrel running furiously up a bare maple tree. We were doing it, and then it happened. I remember my body locked tightly into position and wouldn't move, so Matthew kept moving. In fact, I remember him cheering when he realized what was happening. When it was his turn, he shouted, "Let's wrestle!" then rolled me over. I remember gazing out the window as the sleet turned to snow, and it all seemed so beautiful, every blink felt positively luscious, until I heard my roommates come home.

I shared a room with Janet, who stood in the open doorway and said, "Oh, okay," and walked out. I stiffened. Matthew whispered that in the big scheme of things, it shouldn't matter. "I mean, when you get old and ready to die, what will be more important? Your first big orgasm or your bitchy roommate Janet?" His armpit hair gave off a slightly ripe odor. He did not believe in deodorant.

"I heard that!" Janet shouted from the tiny galley kitchen. I remember the sound of them all discussing what to do about us, but Matthew was focused, tender, tracing my jaw line with his calloused finger.

"*You*," he said, hot skin radiating, "are amazing."

That night I made him sleep in his car, even though it was cold. He said he liked to park down by the Mississippi River and listen to the radio. I guessed he would drink himself to sleep. Still, I was desperate to fit in with the girls and spent that night eating popcorn and watching "The Lawrence Welk Show," which they, for some reason, enjoyed mocking for entertainment.

My mother called just as I was dozing off next to Janet on the couch. "Nor, it's Ma," she said. "Your dad's leaving me. In fact, he's already gone." My parents owned a bakery, Rolling in Dough, and as my mother had long been predicting, the early morning hours and lack of sleep would eventually kill them. "Can you come home?" she said. I remember her voice sounded as if she'd been smoking, though she'd never touched a cigarette. "Please?" I was her only child. I told her to wait, that Matthew had the car but would be coming around soon.

"That Matthew," she said. "He's a keeper."

"Yeah." We agreed to arrange details later, then hung up.

My body still pulsed with a deep mystery inside. I knew Matthew would be back after my roommates had gone to sleep, and sure enough, around midnight, I heard a snowball smack my window. At the door, his eyes were bright, his thinning hair matted to one side, the pattern of the vinyl car seat woven firmly to his cheek.

"Do you want to try it again?" he asked, meaning sex. "We should see if it works again." He pulled me close to him; his heartbeat pounded under my ear.

"Shh," I said. "They're all asleep." I ran my fingers over his soft corduroy coat.

"We could do it in the kitchen," he said. "Right here." I let him lift me up and carry me to the counter. It was covered with empty cereal bowls and coffee mugs. I remember the streetlights seeped in through the blinds and made our bodies looked striped. He kissed my neck just below the ear.

"But my mother," I said. "My father—"

I remember it did work again, and this time, it was difficult to be quiet. A cookie sheet crashed to the floor, and both of us froze, waiting for my roommates to come running.

Later, we slipped out the door quietly and drove to my parents' small house an hour away. "We could just keep driving," Matthew said. He braked for the single stoplight in the center of town; it flashed red at the late hour. "We could run away and never come back." The blinker glowed green onto his face.

I shook my head no, but the way Matthew smiled at me in the dark, I could tell he was already gone.

* * *

After my parents divorced, I proceeded cautiously with Matthew, scared of disaster. On weekends I went home and helped my mother bake early morning muffins: orange and peach and blueberry. Matthew drove me there, though he had traded his Toyota for a used motorcycle. I remember my hair flying out the back of the helmet like tentacles in the wind. Matthew laid it on thick with my mother. When she came home exhausted from a long day's work, Matthew massaged her shoulders, asked her probing questions about her life, made her tea in mugs he'd hand-thrown himself.

Little by little, he started going too far, though. He asked if he could borrow her car, then didn't return it until early the next morning. He brought over sacks of clothing and began doing laundry there regularly. When my mother discovered money missing from her wallet after we'd visited, even she began to suspect the worst. What she didn't know but what I did was the crystal methadone habit Matthew was falling prey to. During the week, when I was studying for my classes, Matthew would come over harried and frantic, running his hands through his hair. I had been talked into a premed major by my advisor and had no time for his antics. I was serious and driven, hopped up on coffee but committed to the study of cell division and anatomy. At that point, I preferred the human body from the distance of books over the actual up-close version.

I remember Matthew wore the same dirty black jeans for days; he did not believe in underwear. Unlike most junkies, he'd gained weight instead of lost it and started letting his hair go "native." I remember the thin blond strands looked more like fuzzy snarls than dread locks. He wore sunglasses indoors because the light hurt his eyes. One night he stood in front of me, dropped his pants, and threatened to urinate all over my room if I didn't just this once drop what I was doing and go take a motorcycle ride with him.

"You're insane," I told him. It was raining and after midnight.

"You've lost your spirit," he said. "They've taught it right out of you! Man, what a waste."

"What a waste *you*!" I barbed him right back. "At least I have a life! At least I'm not like you, Mr. I-Can't-Deal-with-the-Mundane-Ordinary-Life-So-I-Think-I'll-Just-Mooch-Off-of-Others-and-Snort-Meth-and-Get-Fat!" There was silence then, followed by a quick movement I couldn't at first identify. I remember seeing his worn leather book bag fly across the room, but I had no idea it was heading right for me. It hit me in the face. It knocked me to the floor.

I scrambled up to my feet. "I am a smart woman!" I said. "One hit. That's all it takes. Just one hit." I remember my cheek throbbing where the buckles had broken the skin. I could feel my own warm pulse rise to the surface, and then I saw the blood. "Some women would take this but I won't," I said. I stormed around the room, pumped on adrenaline. "I can't believe this. Just go! I never want to see you again! Isn't that what I'm supposed to say?"

"I didn't hit you." His penis hung between his pale legs like a dead bird. It reminded me of the ducks my father used to shoot and carry by their necks as if they were made of rubber.

"Excuse me?" I remember, despite the physical pain, a deep sensation of loss. He'd made it impossible for me to be with him now and forever. "Did the bag hit me on its own?"

He shook his head. His eyes were all pupil and artificially bright.

"Semantics," I remember saying. "You know what you did."

He reached for the door. My roommates were around; I remember hearing the whir of the blender making margaritas over the sound of televised sports. They laughed and puréed and clinked glasses. Suddenly, I had become older, more jaded, less innocent than them.

When Matthew turned to leave, I could tell he was going to say something else, so I said, "Go. Now." But he talked over me.

"You know you'll never stop," he said. "Either of us—we can't. I mean, it's not possible, right?" His eyes, so deep set and blue, looked pinched. The attraction was like a magnet, pulling me against my will.

"What did I just say?" We stood mere inches from each other so that I could smell his worn, woolly sweater the color of yams; he always wore clothing in warm, tropical colors, thrifted from the Goodwill. I remember all I had was a tissue to hold against my bloody cheek. He reached out to touch it, but I recoiled. "What did I say? Don't touch me. Just go."

"No one will ever love you as much as me," he said. "That I can promise you." I scoffed at the cliché.

"Well," I said, "just look what that much love does." My heart beat hot and tight when he finally left. I could hardly swallow. "Bye, Matt!" I heard my roommates say in chorus; they had no idea.

I sunk to the carpet, thinking: "Smart, you're smart. You have to be smart." I picked up my anatomy textbook and looked up the cheekbone, the *zygomatic bone*, which was starting to swell.

The next day a hastily written note was shoved into our apartment mailbox. It was loose leaf notebook paper, folded in sixes. I read it right in the vestibule before anyone could see.

Norah,

This will sound crazy, but I want you to marry me. It's the only way. The world will tear us apart otherwise. What we have only comes along once. You know it. I know it. Everyone knows it. That's why it's so hard. I don't even need to think about it. Do you? You're the single best thing in an otherwise piss-ass world. When I look in your eyes, I see madness. And light.

Love,
M.

I didn't respond. I didn't see how.

* * *

The day I graduated from college, I cut off all my hair. I remember how free and skinny my neck felt without the weight. My mother and father both came to the ceremony with their respective new spouses. Within a year, each had managed a romantic turnaround and slap-dash wedding. Neither new spouse seemed sure how to act around me other than smile hard and grip my hand tight like an aunt or uncle. I was, amazingly enough, selected to be valedictorian because of my seamless 4.0 GPA, and with that honor came an obligatory speech in the gymnasium. I had been accepted to medical school in Lincoln, Nebraska; I had secured funding for the first year. My new boyfriend, Walt, had also been accepted there, and we'd found an apartment near campus that we'd leased in both our names.

My speech was perfunctorily optimistic, though peppered with pithy quotes from artists and poets. An old Chinese proverb: "Live each day as if your hair is on fire." St. Augustine: "We are restless hearts, for earth is not our true home." There were others. My general thesis was that we are all given only one life; you get one chance, so make it count. I remember Walt, who'd read the rough draft, thought I was being fatalistic. He believed that we were given many chances and that life was nothing if not a learning curve. I argued no; you get one chance.

As I was concluding my speech, I saw Matthew slip in and lean against the back wall. I literally lost my breath, then I lost my place. I remember seeing the big leather book bag, *the* book bag, slung crosswise over his chest. I was too far away to see his facial expression, but I noted he wore a faded jean jacket I'd never seen before and looked taller, less manic, from a distance. I cut the speech short. I could just hear him cringing at all my gung-ho platitudes imploring my classmates to be better citizens, make safer communities, seek bigger challenges. My ankles felt watery and without bone as I stepped down to my seat. Polite applause masked my coughing fit. I could barely control it.

My parents and their new spouses took Walt and me out for hamburgers and malts at a 1950s-themed restaurant with too much chrome and neon. It felt more like a triple date than a celebratory, life-marking dinner. Walt asked and answered all the right questions. You could already see the doctor in him. He was hoping to specialize in pediatric medicine; the way he nodded at my father, ate French fries with his fork, and pushed up his eyeglasses with two fingers made his calm bedside manner apparent. My mother got up twice to use the ladies' room. I could tell by the way she raised her eyebrows that she wanted me to come gossip with her about my father's new wife. I stayed put.

As I drained my strawberry malt, I saw Matthew again. He was paying for a meal at the counter and buying gum, so it was impossible to know if he'd been there first or if he'd followed us. My straw sucked loud emptiness and the whole room stared. He nodded at me. I made sure my parents didn't see him. I nodded back, just a little. Every fiber of my being wanted to rush up and throw myself against him. At our table, Walt tried paying for the meal like a gentleman, even though he was broke. My father threw down three twenties. My mother asked if I was all right. I said I was.

By the time my parents paid and left a tip, Matthew was gone. I was despondent. I excused myself to the restroom and found a note wedged between the door frame. It was folded up like a little diamond.

Norah,

You're the smartest, after all. Didn't I always tell you? I'm going to work the strawberry fields in upstate New York this summer. I'll be living in a tent, sleeping under the stars by Lake Ontario. I know you're all set to become a doc and all, but you're only given one life, right? Want to come?

Love,

me

ps I still stand behind my claim that no one will ever love you as much . . . esp. this bozo. Nor, are you for real with him?

pps No, I'm not stalking you. If you're around tonight, so am I.

ppps Your hair!

I found him that night standing outside the library. It's where we used to meet to walk along the river when I was done studying. I remember how sweet the air felt. It was mid-May; little trees were just struggling back to life after a long winter. I could feel the soft air against my bare legs under the skirt I wore. Matthew had a car again, this time a huge late-sixties Oldsmobile. It was truly large enough to serve as a small apartment.

A great distance sat between us in the big front seat. When he turned a corner heavy, I slid closer to him by force of gravity and smooth vinyl. His right arm wrapped around my shoulder. Down by the river, our headlights cut through the darkness. The moon spilled silky light on the water. I looked at Matthew to gauge his thinking. He'd snipped the dread locks off and had hair now as short as mine. His hairline had receded. I remember his skin, usually so pink and full of fury, looked milk white in the light. "You and me," I remember him saying. I didn't know what he meant, but I nodded.

We sat on the big warm hood of his car, our backs flat against the windshield. We took off our shoes. "You know," I said, "I'm a person who not only talks the talk, but I walk the walk."

"Meaning?" He uncorked a bottle of wine between his legs. There were no glasses, so we sipped and shared.

"Meaning we're only given one life," I said. I was quoting my own valedictorian speech. The wine was sweeter than I liked, and cold red.

"So . . ."

"So don't you get it? I'm coming with you this summer," I said. "Strawberries."

Matthew stood on the car and bellered like a madman.

"But only for the summer," I was quick to add. "I'm not giving up med school. Don't even think it."

"Who, me?" Some birds lighted on the water and made it look like ink. They settled in, adjusting, then went silent. Above us, traffic streamed along the Washington Avenue bridge, and from below, I remember the lights—red, white, green—looked festive, like Christmas. I'd utterly abandoned Walt with lies, and felt a momentary rush of guilt.

"So, you wanna wrestle?" Matthew placed a hand over my heart. That he was still using our euphemism after all this time unnerved me.

"I don't know," I said.

I remember the oddest feeling then, as if I were cheating on myself. I was breaking my own rules, the rules of smart women.

I did let him hold my hand. "Tell me about Kenya," I said. "You can say it in Swahili if you want." I felt him nod in the dark.

I remember the sound of his words in the quiet May night. Each sentence sounded like little music. Each little story I already knew in English. "Say the one about your mom baking cakes in leaves," I said. My head lay back against the cool glass. "Or the one where your dad made a swimming pool for everyone in your back yard. Wasn't it out of tires?"

He talked and talked. He was happy to tell. I, on the other hand, needed to listen to take back some of what I'd lost.

That night we slept in the car like vagrants—me in the front, him in the back. In the morning, a family of ducks waddled around the car, waking us. Somehow I knew, rubbing my eyes against the bright sun, that Walt was no longer a contender.

* * *

My mother tried to talk me out of what she called some "dangerous choices." I was temporarily living with her and my new stepfather, Victor, a landscape architect. They hadn't even been married a year, and he'd ripped out all her shaggy forsythia and holly and replaced them with tiny geometric hedges that looked like blocks. I remember I spent a lot of time in my old bedroom reading magazines, waiting for Matthew to give word we were ready to go. I'd never been to New York before, and although I knew we were heading upstate, I couldn't quell the excitement of heading to the Big Apple.

"Norah," my mother began one rainy Saturday in late June. I remember she leaned against my doorway and tilted her head in a way that suggested tenderness. "You really don't have to go through with this," she said. I remember how elegantly her toenails were polished. Her bare feet grazed the carpet. "I mean, I don't want to interfere here, but I think you need to remember this is the boyfriend who hit you once. And you know what they say. . . ."

I had regrettably told her about the book bag incident way back when, and now it was coming back to haunt me. I almost said, "He didn't actually *hit* me," but managed to stop myself. I remember the odd mix of sun and rain outside the window; the sky glowed pink-yellow like an old bruise and seemed to radiate heat through the raindrops. "I know what I'm doing," I told her. "It's just a summer adventure." I smoothed the white eyelet comforter I'd had since sixth grade. "Life's going to get serious soon enough. I've got to explore while I've got the groove."

My mother picked up a piece of lint from my floor. "That's not you talking," she said, prim. "That's him." She put the lint piece in her pocket. The phone rang, thankfully, and since Victor didn't believe in answering, we heard the machine pick up. It was Matthew. "Be ready tonight," he said, not indicating any specific time. "I'll swing by."

My mother sighed. I punched my pillow down and lay back. I remember thinking: we create ourselves by our choices. It was something I'd read somewhere that had stayed with me.

"I don't like this one bit," my mother said. "But you're a grown woman. You have to know."

I looked down at myself in blue jean cutoffs and a red T-shirt. For an instant, I felt like I was twelve again and we were having the menstruation talk; I was that antsy and uncomfortable. It seemed my mother had me wrong, though: I was not yet a grown woman.

"Just trust me," I said.

"Oh, okay," she said, closing up tight. My father had always complained she was no risk taker. She'd always needed the safety net of compliance.

* * *

We ate strawberries with every meal: in sandwiches, on pancakes, sprinkled in salads, studded in ice cream, chopped in stir-fry. "Oh, look! Strawberries!" we joked, as if they were the greatest treat. My fingers were stained red but felt softened by all the juice. Later, every time I smelled strawberries, I would be catapulted instantly back to that summer in Alton, New York. Our little khaki tent, our sex inside it, our pink skin, and the very taste of berries on our tongues at all times.

If Matthew had failed miserably at college, he quickly rose in rank in the strawberry business. Our boss, Leo Benning, made Matthew crew captain after the first week. Matthew had a way of making people feel at ease but of getting them to do what he wanted, as well. Half of the workers were poor college and high school students like us; the other half were Mexican migrant workers with little English and even less money. Luckily, some of my Spanish became very useful. I was the only one who could understand what they were saying, which made Matthew paranoid. He was convinced they were talking about his leadership as captain. I laughed. "They're talking about what they need to get at the grocery store later, you fool." But Matthew wasn't sure he believed me.

After our first week there, we were all run ragged. The novelty of working with my hands quickly wore off. My back ached deeply. The hot sun had burned my fair skin and then reburned it before it had time to heal. My joints creaked and popped from the constant crouching. After the first big rainstorm, life in the tent was no longer such an adventure. When it began to thunder and lightning one night, Matthew suggested we try to "wrestle" and "pin" each other in synch with each boom in the sky. I remember I went along, but my heart wasn't in it, and it never really worked.

Leo Benning turned out to be a tyrant. Though he did not actually wield a whip, he may as well have. We were paid by the bushel, not the hour, as we'd been told, so everyone began speeding along to make a decent wage. Matthew decided the working conditions were inhumane. After dark one night, we sat around the fire and drank beer. Matthew had prearranged a secret meeting with both the migrants and the students. I remember sitting there exhausted, worrying about whether or not my student loans had come through for medical school and how I was probably missing some very important pieces of mail. After all, we had no television, no radio, and no mail service, save for when we could get into town, which was seldom. I remember worrying that so much sun was doing damage to my brain and that I'd never be able to compete with the other students, who were likely lazing around their rich parents' air-conditioned homes, brushing up on their biology and anatomy. I remember also daydreaming about hot showers, movie rentals, and a much-needed professional haircut.

Matthew stalked circles around the fire, hands clasped behind his back. I could tell he liked the power. Of course he needed me to translate for the migrants, which slowed the whole process down, but the long and short of it was that he was spearheading a labor movement, initiating a strike, and was trying to get everyone to go along with him. The migrants sat on one side of the fire; the students sat on the other. Neither group ever mixed. The all-white students nodded eagerly in agreement, their herd mentality and susceptibility to peer pressure much apparent. I tried to soften Matthew's rhetoric in my translation to the migrants, but even then they immediately shook their heads and stubbed out their cigarettes; they had heard it all before.

"What's wrong with you people?" Matthew shouted. "Unless we rise up and *do* something, we're nothing but slave labor. Come on! Fuckin' spiks." His voice echoed across the dark fields. I remember the air was gauzy with leggy, moist mosquitoes. Clouds of gnats floated in waves above our heads. The migrants, of course, understood some English and knew they were being insulted. Beer flowed, and consequently, if not inevitably, one of the migrants made a dash for Matthew, swung at him, and floored him. A quasi fight ensued, and I remember feeling two blurred parts of myself split and divide: the desire to walk away for good, and the need to go for blood myself. I had never hit anyone and could almost taste how good it would feel.

But I didn't. I didn't know whom to hit.

The next day Matthew was licking his wounds, wanting me all over him as if I were a sort of bandage. "Sex," he said through clenched teeth, "is the great healer." I remember my inability to speak after he said that. I had sacrificed a great deal to be with him, and my body now seemed too much to ask.

I remember sitting inside the tent sipping instant coffee. We had no days off and had to rush each meal before getting to work. I missed my mother; during one of our rare phone calls, she told me she'd sent fresh muffins from Rolling in Dough by overnight express, but of course, having no mail service, I never saw them.

"You don't love me enough," Matthew said.

"What's enough?" I asked. Among other things, my mother had accused Matthew and me of overanalyzing everything.

"I'll tell you what's *not* enough." Matthew chugged more coffee straight from the thermos. "What's not enough is that you're just here slumming this summer before you go off to med school and play with the rich kids. You think you can just slip in and out of this tent on a whim."

I remember the sun rose higher and higher and hit the top of the tent hard. It was very hot inside, and we were both sweating heavily. Across the camp, the migrants' cassette player blasted Mexican polka. The same tape played day after day. The scent of their breakfast—beans, rice, eggs, and salsa—blew towards our tent and made my stomach hurt from hunger. We were having nothing but the coffee. I'd dropped several pounds already and could feel myself disappearing.

"What do you want from me?" I asked. I remember my pajamas—Matthew's T-shirt and briefs—stuck to me, and stunk.

"Marry me," Matthew said. It was now the second time he'd proposed.

"Marry you?"

"We'll move to Kenya," he said. He wore only briefs, and his chest, slightly pigeon breasted, protruded and swelled. You could count his chest hairs on one hand. "My parents said they'd fly us over. They love you! You know that."

I had never met his parents.

"Aren't you forgetting something important?" I said. "When I agreed to come here with you this summer, what did I say?" I sounded like a parent or teacher, I knew, but couldn't help it.

"Depends," he said. He reached out and stroked my cheek with a pink finger. I had had it with the strawberries and couldn't eat a single berry more. "Depends on how much you love me."

I knew somehow I had to end it right there or I'd look up years, maybe decades later, and find myself still without a medical diploma. I told him all of this, and more.

We were going to be late and have our pay docked, but neither of us cared. Matthew lit a joint and pinched it between his fingers as he smoked. "Med school will always be there," he said. "But will Kenya?"

The pot smoke made me dizzy. I got up, ducking low under the canvas. "I don't know," I said. "Don't you have it reversed?"

I stayed three more days, just long enough to collect my pay, say good-bye to the migrants, and ship a bushel of fresh strawberries to my mother's bakery. On the third night, I saw Matthew ducking into a student's tent. I had seen him talking to her earlier, helping her carry the baskets heavy with fruit, leaning in close. He didn't come out until morning.

My mother would be so proud of me, I remember thinking as I walked down the long gravel road to the highway; I could almost hear her cheering me on.

* * *

I remember Nebraska as grassy plains, gigantic truck stops, and competitive, blue-blooded medical students who skied and played tennis, cutthroat to the core. Much of my time was actually spent in study carrel 16 on the third floor of the library. Occasionally I peeked out the window at the tar-topped parking lot and muddy puddles, but only occasionally. The flat gray sky depressed me; the absence of trees served to expose me for the sham I really was. I remember I had to press my fingers to my temples in order to fully grasp the words and images in front of me. I was most fascinated by the vascular system and spent hours tracing tiny blue blood vessels with my fingers.

One professor, short and mustachioed, who wore bow ties, told me the money was in oncology. "Sounds morbid, but it's true." Another, a woman with long gray braids and braces, tried to lure me into obstetrics. "Think of the joy you'll see every shift," she said. "You'll see life pouring out right in front of you." My classmates, when they did manage polite conversation, seemed destined for the newly popular ophthalmology (laser eye surgery) or cosmetic medicine (plastic surgery). I didn't know where I belonged, only that I preferred the human body inside out, so beautifully red and blue and brown, instead of the pale sad colors of the flesh. I did run into Walt occasionally, though I tried to avoid such run-ins. He still seemed bitter about my summer betrayal, but some attraction gave itself away in his trembling voice, his jittery hands, the glint behind his nearly invisible eyeglasses. I rarely dated, save for a few courtesy setups arranged by fledgling friends. I simply studied with the intensity of a true beginner. Maybe the sun on the strawberry fields had burned up some of my brain cells; maybe I wasn't as smart as I'd thought I was; maybe my heart was stronger than my will; maybe I missed Matthew but didn't even realize it.

Matthew. I remember the day I saw him sitting on a bench outside Carney Hall. It was early spring; a pair of squirrels chased each other up a tree behind him. His leather book bag was flopped open like a yawning saddle sack. Books and papers tufted out the top like a strange bouquet. A loose lock of hair swung in front of his eyes, and he pushed it back casually, with two fingers. We create ourselves by our choices, I remember thinking. But who'd said it originally? Nietzsche? Kierkegaard? Nietzsche, I thought, but wasn't certain. I saw him before he saw me and stopped, stunned, my heart nearly throwing itself up my throat. I remember he was eating pistachios and throwing every other one to the squirrels. The empty shells accumulated in his black beret, which he held on his lap. When he saw me, he stood, the blue of his eyes brightly visible even from a distance. Up close, I could see how red they were, as if from tears or too much sun. The pistachio shells tumbled to the grass.

"It's my mother," he said. "I've got to go back. To Kenya." He said something in Swahili, and I nodded. I didn't quite understand. I wanted to know—illness? accident? death?—but I kept the questions quiet. He reached a hand out to me, and his flesh looked so pale, so clearly veined in violet blue, he would have made an excellent cadaver sample. I could imagine myself separating the vessels with a tweezer clean and cool in my hand. We were especially taught to look for vascular bundles, like small gray embroidery knots my mother stitched into dish towels. I could've sworn when he hugged me, I smelled strawberries. I pulled away.

"You'll come?" he said. My next lab was in five minutes and was clear across campus. I could miss it but would instantly lose points as others rose in rank. As if on cue, a balmy, almost tropical breeze came out of nowhere to tempt me.

"I don't know." I didn't want to give him false hope, but compassion prevented me from declining him outright. The books weighed heavily in my bag and cut a deep pain through my shoulder. I could almost hear my watch ticking and knew lab would be starting any second. "I don't know."

"You don't?" Matthew's innocence often surprised me. At times, I thought it was an affect of his he used wisely, even manipulatively, but as he stood in front of me, under the big beech tree, I saw his honest wonder. He really wanted to understand my elusive response.

There were so many ways things could have gone after that. I could have walked away, as a smart woman would've. I could have slapped him; I could have kissed him; I could have told him to kiss my ass. A thunderstorm might have blown in and sent us scurrying for cover; a tornado might have swept us away. I could have sat down next to him and explained all the reasons why he was wrong for me, and I, for him. Instead I stood mutely, the weight of inevitability pinning me to the spot where, for the third time, Matthew asked me to marry him.

As leaves spun above our heads and the sky rumbled impatiently like an empty stomach, I remember thinking how small we must have looked underneath the big tree. I looked up to gain perspective. Dark branches arched and curled, reaching for a sky bigger than either of us.

For the first time, I did not say no.

T his morning at 10:30, Angela Mayer's husband died on his bicycle; he was wearing a helmet, in case any of you are wondering, though it hardly mattered. And Angela is doing all right, too, despite so many things beyond the obvious, despite the fact she lives so far away from both sets of relatives it will take them a day and a half just to get there. What comes next is how it went, what came before and what came after an event so circumstantial yet conclusive. What comes next is an account of how people steer themselves through tragedy and freak accidents, and of who Angela and Michael are, or were, together. What comes next is something similar to—though far more detailed than—an article you might read in the newspaper and find yourself unable to stop thinking about. It is exactly the kind of thing you hope will never happen to you or anyone you love, yet it intrigues you, propels you forward into a strange pursuit to know more. Why, then, do we seek blood, tragedy, horror?

Earlier today, a Monday morning in June: Angela and Michael putter around the apartment, and Michael finishes off the last of a second pot of coffee, despite the heat. In Honolulu, the only apartment they can afford is a small cinderblock walk-up on Date Street that gets very humid and cloistered and dark by afternoon. Angela is off to teach an English as a second language course at the Vietnamese Community Center, and Michael, a marine biologist, must run to the university and do research in the library. They Velcro into sandals, Angela swoops her long blond hair up into a tight knot, Michael fills his water bottle, and they kiss in front of the stove. Angela runs her hands up and down his back, over his stiff, line-dried T-shirt.

"Maybe we can go to the beach later," Michael says, and straps on his bike helmet, which looks, to Angela, like a peculiar, blue, shiny beetle perched atop his head.

"Yeah, maybe," Angela says, "unless I'm too exhausted." She slowly maneuvers her backpack onto her shoulders, trying to keep perspiration to a minimum. She must do everything slowly on days like this—walk slowly, eat slowly, get dressed slowly, think slowly. Outside, on the busy street, the sun pounds down like an assault, and Angela lingers by the door, imagining its rays pounding into her scalp, fermenting her brain, sunburning the side part in her hair. "I hate to go. It's too hot. God, why does it always have to be so damn hot here?"

The question is of course rhetorical, but Michael bristles and jeers. This bone of contention is old: Michael, an East Coaster, spent most of a year begging and pleading and campaigning for Hawaii Pacific as the school where he'd do his postdoc. With so many foreigners there, Angela could teach English as a second language, but as a Montanan, she had shirked. She had coiled up like a snake and spit, "Hawaii? Me going to Hawaii is like putting a polar bear in the desert! It's like putting a herd of cattle in the jungle!" And it's true—her parents were cattle ranchers, and it did get fantastically cold in Montana so much of the time. But still Michael hoped and held on to dreams of the clear ocean blue and all that heady sea life: bright yellow angelfish practically jumping into your hand! Parrotfish, dolphins, whales! About all of this, and more, he had read. For the rest of winter, Angela sat poised on top of a decision which would alter everything, and she knew it, and she roosted there long-term.

But they were married. Within three tiny chaotic years, they had already learned, like soldiers, to advance and retreat, listen and fight, give and take, and finally, to think things over in the kind selflessness of private time, which, when one is much in love, is the giving-in time. At last, Angela gave in, or agreed to try it, because she loved Michael: it was that simple. Yet, although Angela agreed that he should at least *apply*, she had no intention of going there; at her insistence, he had also applied to Oregon, California, and North Carolina. But as everyone knows, life more often than not throws you where it wants to. So when the Hawaii forms came and the funding was so good, even Angela couldn't say no. She, too, had job prospects waiting for her there, too good to refuse.

At the time of their decision, they were both working loathsome temporary jobs in a city they did not so much hate as endure. Angela was a clerk at a life insurance agency, and near the end of her as-signment, an older female coworker with deep, smoky breath and tinted glasses took her aside and gave her a quick little lesson on how to hold a pen better so as to fill out forms more efficiently. Angela, a college graduate, had nearly fainted in exasperation and horror. Michael had fared no better on the temporary job scene; he had ended up in the county's social-services phone pool, with twenty-eight telephone lines ringing in his ears in a basement office, sans windows.

But this morning in June, in Hawaii, it is hot, both are distracted and busy, and from the window, Angela watches Michael unlock his bike. He weaves through traffic and stops, poised, at the light before heading up the hill and out of sight into Manoa. She, too, mounts her bicycle and is off. As she rides, heading toward Diamond Head, something in the air feels entirely too heavy, as if it might rain, though there is not a single cloud in the sky. Still, the air is thick and hard to get through. She plans in her head: she will teach, come home, make a cold fresh-vegetable sandwich, then, yes, go to the beach with Michael. They simply do not go to the beach as often as you might think, living in Hawaii.

Pay careful attention to Angela's return home, for upon arriving at work, she finds her two classes canceled, due to reasons of which she is unaware. There is simply a single white sheet of paper taped to the outside door, which reads, "Classes canceled today. Report tomorrow as usual." This note both angers and relieves Angela. Of course she is happy for the sudden freedom, but irritated at the knowledge that she could have slept in, that she has ridden halfway across town in the blinding heat and is soaked with sweat, that she had spent two hours last night preparing an innovative lesson plan having to do with restaurant menus and job applications. But she steers back toward home, coasting mostly downhill, sensitive blue eyes shielded by sunglasses.

The first indication that something is wrong is their friend Nate standing right outside their door, up on the second-floor landing. He never comes over in the mornings, and he never looks as sickly in the face as he does now. Angela waves to him, locks her bike, then sees in the lot a police car and knows then, knows for certain, there has been an accident. Her first thought is her family in Montana. Perhaps her father has been crushed by a horse; it has happened to people she knows. Or her mother in a car accident. It has to be her family; Michael seems practically indestructible—so careful, so smart, so beautifully alert and on top of things. She wonders if he is still at the library and how she can reach him in the stacks quickly.

Here is how Angela approaches the scene, in a way you may not expect: cheerfully. "Hey, Nate," she says, taking the cement stairs by twos and gasping, out of breath. "What's up?" She looks him bravely in the face.

Nate shuffles his feet and looks, for the first time, actually pale, despite his dark coloring. "Why don't we go in," Nate says, and Angela, for some reason, resists. She notes the policeman advancing up the other staircase.

"No, here," she says, and dumps her backpack, purple and worn, at their feet. "Tell me here. What is it?" She reaches out and touches his arm, which is warm, hairless, and smooth. Nate is their best friend; he is in Michael's department and a Hawaii local. He has shown them everything, driven them around in his Honda, warned them about dangerous beaches and jellyfish.

"It's Michael," he says, and puts a hand on her shoulder. "I really think we should go inside. I don't know how to tell you."

"Tell me here," Angela says again, and feels the sharp prickle of salt crystals form as the sweat dries on her face and back. "What is it? Is he all right?"

The policeman approaches them, introduces himself, and looks down, waiting for Nate to say it. And finally, Nate is able. "Michael was in an accident. It all just happened so fast—on his bike."

Angela feels fear rising in her chest, and her ears ring high and spinning. "Is he all right?" The sun makes her head throb, makes all the blood in her fingers and toes and chest pound and pulse and beat loudly inside her ears.

"Angela, Michael died," Nate says at last, then immediately opens up his arms and pulls her close to him. He begins to sob dryly, despite his aim at control, but Angela stands immobilized by the news.

"He died?" she says, patting Nate on the back, soothing him until he pulls away. "He couldn't have died! I just saw him an hour ago. He was right here."

The policeman takes his lead and intervenes as the force of authority and stability. "We wanted to contact you before we called his parents." He takes a small notebook out of his breast pocket. It has a hard silver cover, which Angela notes curiously. "I'm really very sorry," he says, pink in the face. "It was a fluke accident. There was really nothing anyone could do. Are you sure you don't want to go inside? It's so hot out here." He wipes his forehead with his hand, then wipes his hand on his pant leg.

Angela murmurs back at him incoherently and unlocks her apartment door in a blur. Was she in shock? Yes. Was she about the throw up? Yes, to this question, and to all the rest, but she was merely functioning mechanically, as our bodies are somehow able to do in times of crisis. Later she will throw herself on the couch and sob and scream and grab her gut; later she will become nauseous at the mere thought of eating; later she will gather in her arms their stale pile of dirty laundry in the closet and suck in the smell with a terrifying thirst and stay there, stay in the closet, afraid to come out for hours; but for now, she is sedate with miscomprehension, glazed by the confusion of it all.

Oddly, once inside the apartment, she feels safe and immune, and seeing Michael's navy blue coffee mug sitting on the kitchen counter settles her somehow. She perches uncertainly on the edge of the couch and puts her hands on top of her head, trying to control the thoughts which are swimming like fish in her brain. "So tell me, I guess, what happened. I need to know this, right? I mean, I need to know." A slight breeze passes through the open doorway, and she jerks her head up, expecting Michael's lanky frame to walk in, his familiar, grainy face to lean against the door frame, his deep, kind voice which will laugh and tease and help her get through this.

The policeman sits on their one good chair, a rose-colored recliner, purchased at the Salvation Army; Nate hovers over the sink, cleaning up some unknown mess. The policeman explains the details of the accident in a calm, respectful manner.

This is what happened, what was told to Angela and later to Michael's parents in Boston, and later to everyone who watched the local news: Michael was biking up the tiny road between the library and the medical school, which was also the road to the construction site for the new cafeteria. Large trucks and general campus traffic streamed through periodically. A line of parked cars was on Michael's right, and a large truck was chugging uphill on his left, going slowly, carrying construction supplies to the building site. Michael, probably in a hurry, decided to pass the big, slow-moving truck; he looked left, to see if any cars were coming, but in doing so lost his balance, ran into a parked car, tipped over into the street, and fell directly under the double wheels of the truck. He was crushed to death instantly.

More could be said, more fruitless attempts at "But why?" or "I just don't see how," but there are no answers, and even if there were, it wouldn't matter. Whether it's classified a fluke or a freak accident or bad biking depends on how you, as secondhand listeners, choose to interpret it.

Angela listens, hearing, head down. The policeman says Michael was wearing thongs, and that might've been part of the problem—he lost his footing. Angela snorts at this information; she doesn't know why. Michael loved his Surfah thongs with the bumpy, black massage soles, and to think of these innocuous $3.99 drugstore slippers causing his death is more than Angela can accept. Then suddenly, it hits her with a striking wet clarity: What is she going to do? What will she possibly do in the next ten minutes, or tonight, or tomorrow, or in a week, or for the rest of her life? Will she leave Hawaii? She thinks she will leave Hawaii, and sits with her own private thoughts, trying to plan and figure it out.

Nate must see fear mounting in her eyes and comes to sit beside her, to touch her and make her feel real. But another wave of disbelief comes over her, and she knows she will have to go see. It could've been her; it could've been Nate; it could've been her friend Patrice, who bikes Honolulu fast and furious, like a madwoman—they all bike cramped roads all the time, and so does everyone, but nobody gets killed. What could have gone through Michael's head as he made the short flight off his bike and out of his life? Angela tries to think of it, of what he would feel, but decides there was likely no more than three or four seconds of pure panic to think of anything.

Angela makes a motion now to go see the street, the exact sight, if she is ever to believe it. She agrees to let the police and the university handle the initial phone calls, since she cannot yet imagine talking to Michael's kind and loving parents, who were due to visit them in August. His father, Larry, will cry immediately and have to hand the phone to Michael's mother, Babs, who will stay on the line, pen in hand, notepad to her right, exacting facts and details. But then she, too, will hang up and stand in the kitchen, quaking with shock and grief. She will pray to her lord for strength, and they will slowly begin calling the siblings. Angela will talk to Larry and Babs later, after she has gathered herself, *if* she ever gathers herself.

She will also let Nate call her own parents in Montana, which momentarily seems an acutely remote and foreign place, as if, were she there, this death, this horrifying news would not be true. It could be a story told from the outside that they would all gasp and remark over but not have to endure firsthand. She will talk to them later when she actually understands more of what's happened. Everything, details, will be handled later, as if then it will all be okay, as if then the death will be old hat and yesterday's news, as if then Michael will be back and she'll be able to sit on the couch with her feet in his lap and tell him how awful it all was.

But on she moves through the confusion of the day, the hottest day she can remember since moving to Hawaii: ninety-nine degrees. Grabbing only her purse, though she feels as if she's forgetting something, she takes a ride in the police car. Nate sits in front; she sits in back. She is happy with it that way, so she can watch quietly out the window, try to discover what is happening to her life. All over Angela sees bike riders cruising slick and speedy between cars, helmets or no helmets, all of them sure footed and positive they will stay afloat. Be careful! she wants to shout. She wants to pound on the bulletproof glass window and warn them. Be careful! It could happen to you! But the big, bloated police car motors forward in air-conditioned silence.

They reach the accident site. This part may sound like television to you now, for you are used to seeing tragedy up close and immediately. *Cops. Hard Copy. Rescue 911.* But here, in real life, yellow Do Not Cross the Line tape is wrapped and knotted around trees. Police personnel stand around the sidewalk, taking notes and interviewing people. A fire truck is even on the scene, with one man in street clothes uncoiling lengths of canvas rope. He turns the water on, and—you may not have seen this part on TV—he washes away the pool of blood on the street. It rolls down the curb, watery red on dull concrete, and finds its way into the sewer drainage grate. The huge truck is still in the middle of the street, and a man, apparently the driver, paces the road, explaining, bending down over and over again to look underneath the wheels. He is wearing dirty working clothes—a tan T-shirt, jeans worn out at the thighs, dust-coated boots. You can imagine his guilt, the way that, even though it was no one's fault, it will always seem like his fault. To him it will. TV news reporters gather around him with microphones, and he speaks, though no one inside the police car can hear what he says.

"You okay?" Nate asks Angela. "You don't want to get out, do you?" But as he's asking, Angela does get out. She wanders, knowing no one will recognize her, feeling as if somehow she will forever share a relationship with this man, this truck driver. He is done with his interview, and she approaches him slowly.

"How are you doing?" she asks, and tries to meet his gaze, but he is busily looking again from the truck to the curb to the Honda Civic that has a small white paint scrape on its driver's door. This is the car Michael ran into.

"Not good," he mutters, hands on hips, as if, should he continue his investigation of the accident site, he will figure out why this happened. "Did you see it?" he asks, wiping at his nose. She can't place the gesture as from habit or tears. "I just didn't know what he was doing. He came from out of nowhere. You know, I got kids. I'm never gonna live this one down. I'm just never gonna get over this. Nope. Makes me not even want to get in that truck again. No,

I don't think I can do it. Ah, Jesus. The poor kid. And his parents." He flips off his cap and scratches through his hair.

Angela glances back at the police car, which still houses the officer and Nate, who look back at her warily, as if she might commit murder. "I'm his wife," Angela says with neither conviction nor blame. "That was my husband."

The man reels. "Oh, God. No. I'm so sorry. I'm telling you—I just . . . I don't know what happened! I don't know what to say—he just . . . I saw him, you know, out of my right mirror, but—I guess he just tipped over or something and—and I was going real slow, too. I'm sorry—I'm just—so sorry." The man starts to cry, but Angela doesn't. She reaches out to him, sets a hand on his arm, and just then a newspaper photographer captures the moment on film. A woman comes running over with her clunky camera bag and begins snapping, which sets off a chain reaction of other reporters rushing over to get in on the beat.

"You better go," the man says. "They'll be all over you." He takes her hand away and leads Angela over towards the police car. Nate gets out and tries to shield her from any more people. As she's getting into the back seat again, the truck driver leans down and says to her, "I'm sorry. I just want you to know I'll be sorry for the rest of my life." He grimaces at her as the door is closed.

As they drive away, Angela looks back out the window. It's Michael's Surfah thong lying in the street. Or does she imagine it? The one lost thong—seeing it lying there haphazardly and overlooked finally opens up a well of agony for Angela. It starts in the pit of her stomach, rising, and she can feel it surrounding her heart: a new uncharted pain. Nothing will ever be right again, she thinks, as they deposit her back at the apartment, where friends are waiting. This, so many peoples' love and concern, must mean Michael is truly gone, and Angela sits for a moment with the thought.

"I can't believe it," she says, to no one. But, for lack of choice, she looks out the window, and starts to believe it. She makes an effort that will have to endure. For you, this is where the story ends. You can go back to your own lives—read and dream, eat and sleep—but Angela starts over, alone. She gets out of the car, squints up at the sun, and feels the heat pressing down like a punishment.

TIDAL WAVE WEDDING

Rob had seen it happen so many times since coming to Hawaii, he immediately picked up on the telltale signs: a handsome, sunburned young couple combed the beach hand in hand, the woman in tears, the man determined and morose. A sympathetic group of onlookers helped the two honeymooners search in vain through the damp, sparkling sand: a lost wedding band. Rob, a lean and stylish hairdresser with bleached white hair, waded out of the water with his big blue flippers flapping against the current. His snorkel mask gripped tightly to the top of his head like a small yellow bonnet, and he approached the couple, hoping to help.

"Did you lose something?" Rob asked, and pegged the man instantly as military. The haircut was undeniable: a closely shaved neck, a half-inch buzz up to the ears, and a gentlemanly, little square patch at the top, parted to the side. Rob removed his flippers and tried to remain steady as the strong waves lapped against his calves.

"Oh, God. Yeah, my wedding ring," the man said, and massaged the empty spot on his left finger. He was pale and muscular with small blue eyes and a tank of a chest; every time a new white wave broke against the shore, his eyes searched desperately among the glimmering white sand and nuggets of battered coral. He pressed his hand to his forehead. "God, we just got married, you know, and—shit—it was my dad's wedding ring—he's dead. Is that it?" He reached down into the sand with two fingers but pulled out a deceivingly shiny pebble. "Fuck, we're never gonna find it. Trish is really bummed—you can't blame her—" He turned to search for his new wife, and Rob noticed the smooth ripple of muscles flexing from his back to his ribs. He was well built and reminded Rob, in a way, of his partner, Jeremy, who worked out every day at the Y and was a beautiful, solid, smooth, toned man.

"Well, let me help you look for it," Rob said, and lowered the mask over his eyes. He pulled himself through the soft, silky water, pumping hard with his thighs to propel himself forward to where the water shifted from pastel blue to a hard, rich green. His hands looked pure white and delicate in the water, despite the many nicks and cuts from the small golden scissors he used at work, Society Salon. He didn't like the name—its connotations too sober and aristocratic—but the owners, Claire and Ann-Ellen, had targeted Honolulu's cream of the crop, the idle rich who could afford the luxury of beauty and glamour. The entrance boasted pale granite columns, and each station was built of custom cut slabs of green marble, special ordered from a small island in the Philippines. It was a heavenly place to work, as far as Rob was concerned: air-conditioning, classical music, cappuccino served in tiny blue cups, a thirty-foot ceiling, and three walls of windows. He was well liked there and made more than his weekly salary in tips on any given day.

Suspended by the buoyant salt water, Rob hung over a network of purple coral. He saw no wedding ring but watched a small school of yellow-black angelfish swim past coyly like little kids. The parrot fish were much bigger, glummer, and hung toward the bottom of the reef; as usual, Rob wished he'd brought his spear gun. He could surprise Jeremy, who'd be tired and sweaty from working another dinner cruise, with the beautiful blue fish, grilled, belly split, stuffed with lemon and zucchini and tomato. They would laugh, drink white wine, and massage each other's bare feet, leading them, as always, into the bedroom, painted a soothing mint green—Jeremy's idea—to help alleviate the heat. Only lately, Jeremy hadn't been much fun to be with. He was cool and distant and slunk away whenever Rob tried to talk about their future. In the back of his mind, Rob worried that Jeremy was sleeping around, seeing other people in some kind of effort to stay young, attractive, and single.

Rob turned back toward shore, raising his head briefly like a turtle to get his sense of direction; in doing so, he heard a long, wailing sound, like a fog horn. He looked back toward the ocean to check for boats or helicopters but saw none. Confused, he quickly swam to shore, peeling back layers of ocean to channel his body through smoothly. When he reached the sandbar, he unhooked his fins and yanked off his mask. He shook his head and smacked lightly at his ears with his palms and, indeed, heard the sirens.

The new husband still paced up and down the beach, and Rob noticed his wife, a short, suntanned woman in a geometric-print bikini, lying face down on their beach towel, shoulders shaking. Her hair was poorly dyed a yellow-blonde and revealed dark roots, which Rob would've liked to get his hands on. Rob approached the husband, uneager to give him the bad news. "Hey," he said, calling over to him. "Sorry, I couldn't find anything. No luck here either, huh?"

The man stood, hands on his hips. His nose glowed red from sunburn. "Nah, we looked and looked. Just—nothing." He shook his head and dug his toe in the sand. "I suppose it's impossible. I mean, it's—" and he gestured toward the horizon, purple and pink with streaky clouds. "It's the damn ocean. I mean, what we say in the navy is, it gives and it takes, so you gotta respect it." The man fixed his eyes on Rob for what seemed to be the first time and held out his hand. "I'm Collins, by the way." They shook hands and then stood back awkwardly. "So, you live here or what?" Collins asked, and crossed his arms, looking back periodically to check on his wife lying on the towel. Rob noticed his jagged teeth, with small spaces between each one.

"Yeah," Rob said, "it's my day off. I like to get out and enjoy the water when I can." He swung the snorkel mask as if to illustrate.

Collins stuck his hands underneath his armpits and stood tall. "Yeah, I hear ya. So what do you do?"

"I'm a hair stylist," Rob answered, and anticipated Collins' dismissal.

But Collins surprised him by rubbing his fuzzy head and scratching the back of his neck. "Oh yeah? That's funny because I was thinking I could probably use a trim. Getting a little long." Suddenly, the sirens rang again, long and shrill and disconcerting. Rob wondered if it wasn't the first Wednesday of the month, testing time, but it was definitely Monday, his day off for the past twelve years.

Collins stuck a finger in his ear. "What the hell is that?" he asked.

"I'm not sure." Rob watched people gathering up their beach chairs and coolers, staring out at the water and then toting off frantically to their cars. Then it hit him. On the way over, he had heard about the big earthquake in Japan on the radio but hadn't put two and two together until now: the vibrations rippling secretly underneath the Pacific Ocean, brewing potentially giant waves that could hit the Hawaiian Islands with a fierce slap. A tsunami warning. The two lifeguards began making the rounds, clearing the beach, and soon

Collins' wife came scrambling over with all their stuff in a huge tote bag.

"There's a tidal wave warning!" she said, and grabbed Collins' elbow. Her eyes were puffy and pink from crying, and her diamond ring glittered brightly. She seemed to take note of Rob warily.

"This is Trish," Collins said, and grabbed her around the waist. Her skin looked healthy and rich and dark, and soon she began crying again.

"It's just so symbolic!" she said, talking through sobs, wiping her made-up eyes with upturned palms. "I mean, we just get married, and he loses the ring? It's just too awful! How can we go on after this? I mean, it was his dad's, and it's just not replaceable!" She turned and looked out at the ocean, as if it might respond and spit the ring back out at her feet.

"Hey, I don't mean to be unsympathetic," Rob said, startled now by the evacuation going on behind them. "But I think we should probably clear out of here. You just never know with these tsunami warnings."

Collins looked uneasy and eager to leave, but Trish held tightly to his arm. He grabbed her hand and squeezed it. "Hey, baby, we better go call a cab. We're just not gonna find it, okay? We'll get another one, somewhere, I promise."

"But we can't go until we find it!" she said, and ran a hand through her short yellow hair. "Oh, it's just too awful. It's no way to start a marriage!" She kicked the sand as sadness turned to anger.

Rob, growing a bit tired of them, offered a suggestion. "Well, I don't mean to tell you what to do, but when my grandparents were honeymooning in Hawaii, a long, long time ago, my grandpa lost his ring in the ocean, too, and instead of buying him another, my grandma decided to throw her ring in, too. So they were joined at sea. Kind of romantic, huh?" Rob was chilled now and wanted to get showered and dressed. He felt his hair drying in ridiculous spikes.

"That's a great idea!" Collins said. "Trish, let's do it." He grabbed the bulging red bag from her shoulder, threw it to the ground, and reached for her left hand. But she pulled away.

"No!" she said. "I love this ring! You worked so hard saving up for it, and I'm not going to throw it in the ocean. I'm sure!" She glared at Rob, turned away from Collins, and began combing the beach again, head down, body bent at an almost perfect right angle, hands clasped behind her back like an inspector.

Rob apologized to Collins, said good-bye, and walked up to his little beach spot: striped mat, fold-up yellow chair, small mesh bag for his fins and snorkel, large bottle of mineral water, book. But when he'd gathered his things and was turning toward the parking lot, he saw Collins and Trish standing in the water, arms wrapped around each other, staring out at the stormy surf, the color now of spit and bullets. Her breasts curved into his ribs; his knees nudged her thighs, and the water threatened to take them down, but didn't. It was a snapshot honeymoon moment, but somehow, Rob could not turn away. He felt a deep, hollow ache inside of him, not necessarily for what they had, or didn't have, but for what he knew did not exist: a true union of human spirits, a binding of two souls forever, without fear or pain or loneliness pending.

He breathed in the salt air and was transported, through memory's passage, to his first lover, Cesar, a wealthy, mustachioed Brazilian he had met years ago in San Francisco, when Rob was not so much a prostitute as a companion, a paid accomplice of sorts. Cesar, with his flashy eyes and black felt hats, flew Rob to Brazil, where they had lived in a luxurious tile-floored mansion in the middle of the rain forest. Rain dripped upon the shiny blue roof and slid like oil;

monkeys laughed with abandon, far off. It was the jungle, Cesar had always reminded; he would then twirl his thin brown cigarettes in the air and shout, "Green!" in Portuguese. There was a maid to empty the chamber pots, a boy to cook sausages and onion with rice, an uncle to drive them to town; Rob had lived there for ten long years—a beautiful, tall, blond North American boy with aviator glasses—until something fell apart. Cesar had begun trying to control his every move. There were family riches to hold over Rob, and Cesar would sometimes punish him by withholding money for something as simple as postage stamps. He'd sought to keep Rob isolated and removed from the rest of the world, all to himself, like a bribed best friend. But Rob began slowly dying inside, withdrawing in anger and suffocation, until he finally, secretively, convinced Cesar's wealthy father to buy him a ticket back to the States, promising to stay away from Cesar for the rest of his life.

As the tsunami siren quaked across the island, the few remaining cars drifted onto the narrow highway and sped away. Even the lifeguards, after stabbing "Dangerous Swimming: Tidal Wave" signs into the sand, began to close up their orange towers. Rob stood in the middle of the deserted beach and cupped his hands around his mouth. "Collins! Trish! How about a ride?" He watched them break apart, argue, negotiate, and approach. They stood in front of Rob, beach towels saronging their hips. They were out of breath and seemed to cross their arms stubbornly, as if challenging Rob.

"Yeah, we'll take a ride," Collins said, "if it's not too much trouble. There's no way we're getting a taxi out here now." He reached into the red tote, which was back in Trish's possession, pulled out a crumpled white T-shirt, and put it on. It said: "KOOL, Kool Radio 98.5 Des Moines" in orange letters, and Rob began to make assumptions about his background.

"Thanks," Trish said, "we really appreciate it, you know, your being so nice and everything." She seemed more subdued to Rob now, as if she had given up on the ring. They all toed through the sand, burdened with heavy beach gear and regret.

They brushed off their feet and got into the small gray car. Rob shifted into reverse, hung his sunglasses on the rearview mirror, and made a right. "So, where are you staying? Waikiki, right?"

"Yeah," Collins said, and touched his lip in a way Rob found sexy. "But what's our hotel called again, honey? The Outrigger? Or Surf Rider or something like that? Or no, it's Waikiki something."

Trish leaned up from the backseat, which comforted Rob. She smelled like Coppertone and vanilla and hung her arms between the two men. "No, it's the Waikiki Grand. On Kapa—lua—God, what's that street again? I forget."

"Oh, right," Rob said, relaxing finally and sliding down in his seat. "On Kapahulu. It's not too far." With that reassurance, Trish sat back, staring quietly out the window; Rob glanced at her in the rearview mirror and made no more attempt at small talk. Collins, in the seat beside him, radiated warmth from sunburn.

When Rob reached Waikiki, there was pandemonium everywhere. Cops redirected traffic, banning all cars from the Waikiki strip. Official yellow tape was wound around large white sawhorses, making the entire beach area off limits. Rob's head pulsed with a smashing headache, and he began to wish he had not been so friendly, had not gotten involved in this couple's plight. It was just as Jeremy said: Rob was a pushover, he had to learn to say no, he had to keep to himself more. Still, Jeremy sat at the other end of the spectrum: he was a yes-or-no man, had clear-cut divisions of what was right or wrong, didn't believe in saying hello to strangers on the street, and still clung to harried, frantic East Coast habits in the middle of the Pacific. It frankly worried Rob, Jeremy's life speed: he would run across the street on red lights, finagle his way into the grocery store's express line with more than nine items, and worst of all, would give slow drivers and befuddled rental-car drivers the finger and lay on the horn if they so dared to hold him back a fraction of a second.

"It doesn't look like we're going to be able to get you to your hotel," Rob announced, and was surprised that neither of them took the news with any apparent stress or disappointment. Collins shrugged his shoulders and leaned his elbows on his knees. "Well, wait," Rob said, rolling down his window and turning off the A/C. "Let me ask this guy over here what's up." In the lilting local accent he'd picked up over the years, Rob asked a cop what he should do.

"Tsunami," the man said, and jammed his walkie-talkie into its pouch. "Nobody's going into Waikiki. If these guys are staying down here, they're evacuating to the high school in Manoa. They can get a bus by the zoo. Over there." He pointed to a group of tourists dressed in pastels.

"How long will it be until it opens up down here?" Collins asked, ducking his head low to peer through Rob's window. The cop laughed, tuned into his walkie-talkie, responded in code, turned it down, and took a step away from the car.

"Never know," he said, and started to wave them away. Traffic was building up behind them, mostly shiny new rental cars. "Gotta move along now. Could be thirty-, forty-foot waves. Never know."

"Thanks for the info," Rob said, and rolled up his window. He was starving and hoped the tsunami warning meant Jeremy had not gone out to work the dinner cruise. Perhaps he'd even be at home, cooking something Rob loved, like lemon fettuccine, or broiled salmon with that wonderful tarragon sauce Jeremy had invented.

"So, I don't know what you guys want to do . . ." Rob asked, cocking his head back to address Trish more than Collins.

She seemed startled out of a daydream and ran her hands through her hair before answering. "Well, it seems pretty hopeless at this point. It's just not anything like I'd imagined it would be, you know?" Rob watched the tears well up in her eyes again, but she fought them back this time.

Rob murmured quietly in response. Collins sighed. The traffic moved so slowly, Rob held the steering wheel with two fingertips. He tried to get a station on the radio for an update on the tidal wave, but it was either slow-time hula or classic rock. "You know, I guess you guys could come to my place until this blows over," Rob offered, knowing that bringing two unknown guests into his home would illicit a silent but obvious irritation from Jeremy. "I don't live far, and I'm out of the tsunami zone, so it'd be safe. Sometimes these things blow over really quickly. They just have to take precautions. You could come over until it's all clear. It'll be better than the high school gym, believe me." Traffic lurched forward a block, two, then stopped. Tall, now-empty hotels flanked the street on either side, creating a tunnel-like dimness.

"Oh, we don't want to bother you," Collins said, and placed his big flat hands on top of his knees like a king. His fingernails were square and healthy and pink; his leg hair was golden, curly, and delicate. Rob could clearly imagine him naked, could see the firm buttocks flexing with muscle power, hollowed out on the sides where Rob would sink his hands and press deeply.

"Oh, it's no bother. My roommate, Jeremy, is probably whipping up dinner as we speak." Growing impatient, Rob changed lanes and wove his way to the right, grinding into third, and finally turned off on Hinano. Sometimes Jeremy was his "friend," sometimes "partner," sometimes, rarely, his "lover." In this case, "roommate" seemed appropriate, although anyone could guess the nature of their relationship, considering the blatant kiss Jeremy enjoyed smacking on Rob in public.

"There we are," Rob said, and felt relief to be on the nearly empty, quiet street where he lived. "This is the home stretch. Boy, you guys must be exhausted. It's been quite a day for you." He hadn't meant to remind them of their loss but knew instantly he had. Collins fingered his left hand again and squeezed the emptiness. In the back seat, Trish brushed out her hair frantically; Rob parked downhill, turning the wheels to the right, so as not to roll away.

His apartment was actually more of a double bungalow—the owner, Webster Ming, a small, old, nosy Chinese man, lived in one half, and Jeremy and Rob in the other. A narrow concrete stairway ran up between the dwellings—Rob's door to the left, Mr. Ming's to the right. There were always rows of shoes and slippers lined up like an offering outside Mr. Ming's door. He and his wife, Letta, in addition to being landlords, also worked a souvenir stand just down the street at the weekly Kodak Hula Show. Rob guessed they probably had plenty of money, though, considering the steep rent he and Jeremy paid and the shabby, threadbare frugality evident in the Mings' clothing, car, and furnishings.

As Rob ascended the stairs, Mr. Ming stuck his head out the door, with his usual plucky gray crew cut, and beckoned. "There's a tsunami warning, you know!" he said, and hung back in his dark doorway, barefoot, wearing khaki trousers and a white T-shirt. He glanced warily at the two strangers and thumbed at them. "Who's that? You have visitors during the tsunami? That's too bad for them." Mr. Ming clucked his tongue, and Rob saw Letta Ming peer out from underneath his armpit, to see what was going on. By now, the Mings were used to a steady flow of mainland visitors lugging bags to and from Rob's apartment, though that had tapered off once they'd been in Hawaii several years.

Rob enjoyed the Mings, even though they kept increasing the rent, little by little, every six months. "No, these two are on their honeymoon—" Rob stopped and made brief introductions. "They were over at White Beach when the tsunami warning started, and they didn't have a car, so I brought them here. Their hotel's been evacuated."

Mr. Ming looked disappointed for them. "Oh, that's too bad for you. Don't worry. It will get better. The water will calm down. It always does." Sometimes Mr. Ming spoke like poetry, but other times, he swore viciously, as he did when he was losing at poker. Rob could always tell when he was losing, too, because he could hear Mr. Ming slam his hands down on the table and start shouting, "Dammit! Goddammit already!"

Trish leaned against the railing, looking exhausted and fried, still wearing nothing but her bikini top and a towel. Bits of white sand stuck to her chest, and Rob wanted to wipe her off briskly with a towel. "My husband lost his wedding ring in the ocean today," she said, as if Mr. Ming could help her somehow. "We've got to go buy him a new one when this big storm is over. Although, it sure doesn't look like a storm to me." She glanced up at the sky, which was void of clouds and still bleeding a strong white sun.

"Sure doesn't," Collins said, and looked bored, as if he regretted accepting Rob's invitation to his home. "Looks like maybe they'll open up our hotel soon." He crossed his arms over his huge chest and seemed ready for a long delay, despite his hopeful statement.

"No," Mr. Ming said, "with the tsunami, you never know. You can't tell if it's coming or not. Once, a whole two hundred houses were swept into the ocean, just like that." Mr. Ming raised his arms high, miming the disaster, then brought them crashing down. Mrs. Ming, meanwhile, disappeared, then returned with an old cigar box. Mr. Ming, confused, turned to see what she wanted. "What? What is that?" They spoke briefly in Chinese to each other, and Rob made a motion to leave. Often, as much as he enjoyed the Mings, these exchanges in front of their doorways lasted too long.

"Well, we better get going," Rob said, and couldn't tell if Jeremy was home or not. The screen door and the interior door were both closed. "See you later."

"Just a minute," Mr. Ming called, and nudged his wife over to Trish and Collins. Her gray hair was wound up like braided bread in back and fastened high with a metal clip. Her dark eyes shone, and she wore red lipstick in the middle of the afternoon. She displayed the cigar box with a small, curious grin on her face. "Rings," she said, and opened the box up like a mouth. "I've had these for so many years now."

Inside were rings in various sizes and colors. Most of them were tiny and silver with Chinese characters etched into them; others were thin, pale, jade, or chunky cuts of garnet wedged in cheap gold, but there were three plain gold bands in what looked like small, medium, and large.

Trish stepped forward and started browsing. "My God," she said, trying some on, "where did you get all of these? They're beautiful." She turned to Collins, who stuck one of his big hands in the box, going after the gold bands.

"Over the years," Mrs. Ming said, "I've bought and sold. Maybe you can find your new husband a wedding ring."

Rob stood back, exchanged glances with Mr. Ming, and wondered what was going on. Meanwhile, the tsunami sirens began blaring again, and Rob noticed that the Mings did not wear wedding bands themselves. Nor did he and Jeremy for that matter, although he considered them partners for life. Rob had always dreamed of a big wedding with Jeremy, out on a catamaran, all their family and friends smiling under a bright sun, a tall orange cake with lemon glaze, a case of champagne, and he and Jeremy tossing a brick into the sea for luck and longevity.

Trish watched to see if the largest gold band would fit Collins' ring finger. Mrs. Ming even got a bottle of dish soap and squeezed a drop on his finger for lubrication. Collins winked at Trish, grimaced slightly as he bore down, and managed to jiggle the ring back and forth until it finally grazed over the knuckle.

Everybody cheered. "All right!" Collins said, then picked Trish up in his arms and kissed her on the mouth. Mrs. Ming nodded her head and said, "It is meant to be."

Suddenly, Rob's apartment door opened, and Jeremy emerged. Trish slipped slowly out of Collins' arms, Collins examined his new ring from every angle, and the Mings retreated slightly back into their own doorway. "What's going on out here?" Jeremy said. He spoke from behind the screen door and didn't come out. Rob couldn't tell if he'd been sleeping or was simply in a bad mood. He wore a faded blue T-shirt, tan shorts, and a black cotton vest; his dark hair was pulled back in a short ponytail, and Rob wished, for the thousandth time, that he'd let him cut it.

Rob explained briefly the day's twists and turns. Jeremy listened, leaning one arm on the inside doorway. "Can I talk to you for a minute, alone?" Jeremy said, and drove a long glance at the others. Rob could see his sharp blue eyes flickering.

"Oh, sure," Trish said, perked up now by the new ring, by the miracle of the fit. "We have to talk business with Mrs. Ming anyway." She waved a hand at them. "You guys go ahead."

Rob left Collins and Trish with the Mings and stepped into his apartment, where the fan spun a semicircle of coolness around the room. Jeremy sat at the small kitchen table, a bag of chips and a bowl of salsa in front of him. He uncapped a bottle of Mexican beer. "You want one?" he asked Rob, and although Rob's head was pounding, he said yes, gripping the cold bottle in his hands, then touching it to his cheeks, forehead, wrists.

"So what's going on?" Rob asked wearily. "Obviously something's wrong." He took a sip of beer and let the sting settle in his mouth before swallowing. It seemed to improve the headache instantly.

Jeremy's jaw muscles flexed, his slim nostrils fluted in, then flared out, quickly, like fish gills. "Don't you know?" Jeremy asked. "Think of what's going on right now, and I have to tell you?"

Rob knew that soon he would have to deal with Collins and Trish, if only to finish what he'd started, and he knew there wasn't time for an argument with Jeremy. "Please don't make me guess," he said. "Just tell me what's wrong, and maybe I can explain." His knees cracked under the table, and smoothing his hands over his bare arms, he saw he'd gotten a good tan.

Jeremy scoffed, but acquiesced. "Ah, *hello*? There's a *tsunami* warning and sirens blasting *all* day long, and *I'm* sitting here, knowing *you're* at God only knows *what* beach, and you don't think I might be a little worried? You couldn't have called to say, 'Hey, Jeremy, don't worry. I'm on my way home'? Of course not, because you're too busy hauling around some sleazeball tourists! I mean, what the *hell* are they doing here? For all I knew, you were swallowed up by a fifty-foot wave and on your way to Palmyra Island!"

Rob paused a moment, making sure Jeremy was finished, and noticed the curve of his large biceps through his T-shirt. Rob also noticed that Jeremy did not have a tan but was quite pale from spending all his free hours in the gym. Rob sipped the beer, which was already losing its chill. "All right," Rob said, and placed a hand over Jeremy's, which sat, flat and lifeless, on the table. "You're right. You are absolutely right. I should've called. I guess I just—I got so confused when this couple lost their wedding ring, and I was trying to help them find it, and then—well, the tsunami warning came from out of the blue, and I just—I had to help them out. They didn't have a car or anything." Rob weighed what he'd said and tried to guess if it sounded valid.

"Let me ask you something," Jeremy said, and pulled his hand away. He pushed one loose black lock of hair behind his ear and leaned over the table, face to face with Rob. "Why do you *care*?"

Rob shifted. "What do you mean?"

Jeremy bowed his head in exasperation and tried again. "Why do you *care* about all these total strangers you're always helping out? Can't someone *else* do it? And what about me?" He sat back, arms crossed. "Did you ever think, when you heard the tsunami warning, hey, I hope Jeremy isn't out on the boat? I hope Jeremy's okay? Let me call and see! Don't things like that ever *occur* to you?"

It was true; Jeremy was right and had every reason to be upset. Rob sat there, unthinking, staring at their beautifully decorated apartment, the white gauze curtains, the low gray couch, the wonderful, round glass coffee table held up by brass elephants. The kinds of thoughts that Jeremy had just mentioned did not occur to Rob regularly. When he was at the beach, he was a lone man, soaking up the warmth of the sun, kicking in the froth of the salty ocean, helping people out when they needed it like a contemporary saint. Jeremy was "other" to him, close, but not self. Was this what marriage was, then, Rob wondered, to be joined so that the separation was not so apparent? Suddenly, foolishly, he had an idea.

"Jeremy," Rob said, and slid their bottles of beer aside. He held Jeremy's smooth hand, which smelled perpetually of lemons and limes, which he cut by the dozen for the cruise ship bar. "Will you marry me?" As he asked the question, Rob saw them as old men; they would hobble along the seashore together in cuffed pants and plaid shirts. Gray haired, they would salute the passage of years by drinking Scotch and kayaking the islands. They would travel to Switzerland, Bombay, Belize, and Turkey and always celebrate the Chinese New Year. "Well?" Rob said, eyes misting over with a peculiar twist of emotion. "We can just do it on our own, with all our friends. What do you say?"

"I say—" and there was a knock on the door. "Dammit," Jeremy said, rising for another beer. "I say, dammit."

Rob went for the door. It was, of course, Collins and Trish, all but forgotten already in Rob's mind. Likely, they felt sheepish about disturbing them, and hopefully they had figured out some sort of arrangements for lodging elsewhere. Rob opened the door and forced a smile.

Trish looked much more radiant than he'd remembered, and her hair sparkled golden, not yellow. Her nose was thin and elegant, and her teeth, perfectly white and straight. She still wore her bikini top, revealing the rise of modest breasts. Collins hung back behind her. "Umm, sorry to bother you and everything," Trish said, and seemed breathless. "But we just wanted to ask a big favor of you. If you wouldn't mind." She wrung her hands nervously, and out of the corner of his eye, Rob watched Jeremy turn on the television.

"Sure," Rob said, hoping, whatever it was, would be brief.

Trish leaned against the doorframe, neither in nor out, and presented her proposition. She listed things off on her fingers. "And so, Mr. Ming said with this ring—which we bought, by the way, for 150 bucks—can you believe it? an antique from China!—we should have some kind of ceremony." She paused, glancing at Collins, who was transfixed by the TV. "He's going to do the ceremony, you know, just unofficial, and so we were wondering if you could climb up Diamond Head a ways with us and be witness at our second—well, sort of our second wedding."

Rob's first thought, oddly, after hearing an undeniable snicker from Jeremy, was how the Mings could possibly climb the Diamond Head crater—so old and wrinkled and small they were. He asked Trish this.

"Oh, they do it every morning at 5:00 a.m. It's easy for them, they said. Please come," she said, and grabbed Collins' hand in a fit of passion. "You've been so nice to us and everything."

Collins and Jeremy were both involved in an NCAA basketball game, and Rob knew he should've said no, knew it would put him at even greater odds with Jeremy, but the idea sounded so spontaneous and splendid, in the midst of the tsunami sirens and the hot, humid afternoon. "Yes," he said, hoping, even, that Jeremy would hear. "Yes, I'd be honored."

Jeremy surprisingly agreed to accompany them, and Rob held tightly to his hand, even though that was a risk they didn't always take: no public displays of affection in front of the Mings, in front of strangers, in front of relatives. But up the three couples climbed, first on the lip of the paved road leading into the crater, then up the gravel path that led to the peak. The Mings led the way and did not hold hands but strode diffidently ahead, short arms swinging; Mr. Ming carried a candle in one hand and a bottle of wine in the other. Trish and Collins were next, arm in arm. Rob and Jeremy walked behind them and pressed sweaty palm to sweaty palm, gripping tightly, as if, were they to let go, the connection might slip and dry and fade.

The trail was practically deserted, due to the tsunami warnings, except for a few intrepid joggers. Diamond Head was up high enough to avoid any danger of a tidal wave, and Rob almost missed, for a moment, the threat of danger, of a huge splash that could wipe out cities. When they reached the top, after passing through the claustrophobic, dark tunnels and spiral staircases originally built for a military lookout, Mr. Ming stopped, turned around, and held out his hands, as if to prevent them all from falling down the cliff.

The view was all of Waikiki and part of the eastern shore and immense. Patches of ocean twinkled blue, green, and white, and islands of coral poked out from the surf. "Now," Mr. Ming said, without any warm-up or chitchat. Rob and Jeremy stood on either side of Trish and Collins, and Rob could still hear, despite their great altitude, the faint shrill of sirens.

Trish and Collins held hands, and Collins removed the ring, only to put it back on again when he was coached to do so. "Love long, and always remember the ocean for bringing you together," Mr. Ming said, and uncorked the wine. He splashed a little near Trish and Collins, who giggled and jumped, then he handed his wife the bottle, who drank from it, wiped her mouth, and threw it over the cliff.

"Shit," Jeremy whispered. "They can't just do that!"

"So now you are husband and wife, again," Mr. Ming whispered in a solemn staccato, and Rob could tell he was making it up as he went. "And you'll probably remember this old volcano in years to come."

Jeremy whispered in Rob's ear. "Please. This is ridiculous." But then Jeremy placed his hand on Rob's shoulder and squeezed, and this felt hopeful to Rob. Mr. Ming lit the small candle and set it on a rock.

"Now you can kiss each other," Mr. Ming said, clapped for Trish and Collins, and then turned around to kiss his own wife of forty-five years. They kissed passionately, her head turned into his. "You, too," he said to Jeremy and Rob, and waved them together with his hands. "You're already married, right?"

Jeremy and Rob looked at each other dumbfounded, confused by the question. They stammered and shrugged. "Well, not exactly . . ." Rob said.

"Let's say you are," Mr. Ming said, "and you are. Married. *I thee wed.*"

Rob and Jeremy, too stunned to know what to do, held hands and leaned against each other. Jeremy, despite his earlier anger, seemed less upset. He rubbed his bare shoulder against Rob's.

"Look," said Mr. Ming. "The tsunami's coming in!" Mr. Ming pointed down to the shore, and all three couples gripped the railing, mouths agape. The water stood like high, tight walls of beautiful light blue, then snatched down upon the sand like a cat leaping at a mouse; the hotels, the buildings were splashed with surf that crushed and tore and broke. Then up again, another taut, quivering blue wall lifted, high as a house, and went charging down the streets.

If you were one person standing underneath a tidal wave, Rob thought, you would seem small as a bug, and lonely. You could be wiped out.

The Whites' room was in a hotel in Taxco, Mexico, which, until 1620, had been a monastery. Toby, Alice's husband, had mentioned this several times. Once inside their room, Alice collapsed on the bed. Above her, large black beams supported a red clay ceiling.

"Do you think those tiles could fall on us?" she asked. "Do you think they've been up there since 1620?"

Toby emptied his pockets of loose change, keys, receipts, pesos. "Do you want some water?" he asked.

Alice sat up and marveled at the medieval cast-iron door latches. She imagined small Spanish monks pulling them open, their dark robes brushing the cool floor. "Is it purified?" she asked. "Because I can't get sick right now. I can't. Not now, not when we're so close to—"

Alice had brought along not only a basal body thermometer but a five-day ovulation test kit. She'd urinated onto a small white stick in the Mexico City bus station. At first she'd been confused, not realizing she was supposed to pay two pesos just to use the *sanitarios*. Then, when she realized there was no toilet paper, she'd had to step out of the stall and pay a small girl two more pesos for a small wad of tissue. She'd crouched over the seatless toilet, her sandals wet, the hem of her dress grazing the wet, dirty floor. The felt strip had shown two dark purple lines. She had felt her cheeks flush with nervousness and excitement.

On the bus to Taxco, she'd tried deciding on the best position in which to become impregnated. Not with her on top, which was their customary position and pleasurable for both of them. Perhaps with Toby coming from behind would be the best. But the bus ride had been long and curvy, and she'd grown exhausted. She'd tried to ignore the booming movie on the tiny television screen above her, while the sharp scent of the toilet mint in back made her head ache. Toby had insisted on buying Primero Plus bus tickets, complete with air-conditioning, plush reclining seats, movies, and a bag of snacks, which included chili-dusted peanuts and a can of Squirt. He'd said he didn't want *bandidos* to stop them, rob them, or harass them, as he'd read could happen. Alice did not fear such things, but she'd agreed simply because sometimes it was just easier to let Toby win.

Alice got up to investigate the bathroom and ran her hands over the blue and yellow painted tiles. "Oh," she said, "I love these! I'd like some in our bathroom at home. Aren't they gorgeous?"

"In our Queen Anne Victorian?" Toby said, and stepped out of his khakis. He was nothing if not a culturally sensitive and appropriately dressed traveler. He folded them and hung them carefully over the chair.

"Well, I know," Alice said. "I just meant . . ." Toby took everything literally. Of course she wouldn't *really* want Mexican tiles in their high-ceilinged, period-wallpapered bathroom back in Rochester, New York. The 1880 house now felt too large and ornate, too complicated in comparison to the simple white walls of Hotel Los Arcos. Who needed so much space? she thought. Five bedrooms, two living rooms, and two baths for just the two of them. When college was in session and they were both teaching, often Alice would find herself grading quietly in her study—the moss green north bedroom—and realize she could not hear a sound from Toby in the entire house.

Alice had been the only one in her family to break away from her hometown of River Falls, Wisconsin, and go to college, much less graduate school. Being a psychology professor who researched attachment relationships between parents and children, she knew there was some guilt associated with her transcendence, which she sometimes confused with abandonment. Her parents had still not visited in the five years she'd been married to Toby, and the most they could say about her job as associate professor of psychology was what an awful lot of days off she seemed to have. Alice felt it was better for her to disassociate, though she often dreamed at night of her parents' small pink house as a symbol, she suspected, of her desire to return to the safety of the womb.

In actuality, a simple three-bedroom house would have sufficed for her and Toby—always working, reading, writing, preparing for classes. But Toby, who taught architectural history, had bought the house the year before they'd married, and Alice had simply moved in with him after vacating her small but cozy two-bedroom apartment on East Avenue. There was definitely something of herself she'd left behind as she'd rolled up her tatami mats and taken down her vintage movie posters. Her life, which had previously been a collage and collision of influences, had changed into something serious and dignified, as represented by their beautiful, well-appointed Victorian home.

"So, *vamos mirar el zócalo*," Toby said. He'd changed into khaki shorts of modest length and had already brushed his teeth and splashed cool water on his face. His shirt still looked crisp.

Alice's Spanish was terrible; she admitted it but wasn't proud of it. She spoke some Italian from a year's study abroad back in college, which sometimes helped her Spanish, but most often confused her.

"*Inglés, por favor*," she said. On the airplane down to Mexico, she had joked with Toby that her ugly American gambit was going to be "*Inglés, por favor!*" Toby had laughed, too, and so she'd said it over and over, loving it when he found her funny. "They'll ask me, '*Cómo está usted?*' and I'll say, '*Inglés, por favor!*' They'll say, '*Buenos días*,' and I'll say, '*Inglés, por favor!*'"

"Let's go check out the town square," Toby said, and looked at his watch. Why would he look at his watch? Alice wondered. And why must they immediately storm out into the town and investigate when they had all day, and the next day, and the next day, which would be their five-year wedding anniversary? "Or do you want to wait here? Rest?" Toby smiled at her, but Alice sensed he was forcing himself to be patient and pleasant.

Alice sighed. She walked to the window that boasted a view of twisting cobblestone streets, a hodgepodge of chalky white buildings with clay roofs seemingly built on top of one another. Streams of white vw Bugs, the ubiquitous Taxco taxis, groaned and sped up the tiny winding streets.

Toby came up behind her and held her. She leaned back against his solid chest and enjoyed the sense of being enveloped by something larger than herself. He smelled brightly of the hotel soap and of slightly worn deodorant. She rubbed his arms, dry and hairy and familiar. "Did you know," he said, and she could feel his warm breath on her hair, "that Taxco is a historic district? The entire city. There are actually rules that state residents can't paint their homes—or rather, the exterior of their homes—anything other than white. It's a Spanish colonial city, and you can see how the roof lines reflect . . ."

Alice let him go on, amazed by his inability to turn off his professor-lecturer role, even with her. She could hear his voice change into a smoother pitch; he paused more emphatically and drew out the ends of his sentences.

"Toby, please," she said, and he stopped. Although she was also a professor, she welcomed the opportunity to abandon her role of Dr. White whenever possible. Whenever a student called her Dr. White, she felt as if a surgeon should come rushing around the corner, ready to perform emergency surgery. "Call me Alice," she'd tell them at the beginning of each semester, but they would never dare. A couple kind-hearted but dim students, always female, would routinely call her Mrs. White, which she didn't like either, but she never had the energy to correct them.

"Don't you care about the history of the place?" Toby asked, suddenly sounding angry. "There's a quote by someone about travel—I can't remember now who said it, but it goes something like: 'He that would bring home the wealth of the Indies must carry the wealth of the Indies with him. A man must carry knowledge with him if he would bring home knowledge.' I believe it goes something like that." Toby pulled open the curtains of the other window, which overlooked garbage cans and dust mops.

"What if you're a woman?" Alice asked. She fished out her Ziploc of Tylenol and shook two into her palm.

"What?"

"If you're a woman?" she said, and swallowed the pills dry. "It says a man must carry knowledge, but what if you're a woman?"

Toby sat on the edge of the bed beside her, and the rocklike mattress barely budged. For a moment, he hung his head. "Come on," he said. "Let's not do this. We're tired. Let's go get something to eat."

He reached for her hand and she took it.

The only place they could find to eat with a balcony was called Vicky Cafeteria. To reach the restaurant, Alice followed Toby up a tiny spiral staircase inside a silver shop. Toby hit his head at the landing, and Alice cooed with him to be careful. Their small table overlooked the busy town square, and Alice was so distracted she couldn't focus on the menu. She looked out over the *zócalo*, which was full of people listening to an odd vocal medley from *Cats*, in Spanish. Three people dressed like cats sang into a fuzzy microphone, spun in circles, and clapped their hands. On the corner, a man with upwards of thirty straw hats atop his head yawned and stretched. Another man sold bright pink cotton candy, and Alice could see, even from this distance, how it melted in the humidity.

The waitress came by, and after Toby handled the formalities in Spanish, Alice was pressured to order. "Burritos with *queso*," she said. She always ordered the easy items she could pronounce: tacos, burritos, enchiladas.

The waitress, a plump young woman with large curled bangs, looked at her eagerly. "*Con jamón*?" she asked.

Alice looked at Toby for translation. He asked her did she want ham. Did she want ham in her cheese burrito?

"Well, I suppose," she said. "Okay."

When Toby said *sí*, the girl walked away quickly.

"Sounds kind of breakfasty, though," Alice said. "A little like McDonald's."

"Maybe," Toby said.

The burrito that came for Alice was nothing like the fold-and-wrap variety to which Alice was accustomed. These tortillas were smashed flat and flipped in half like a taco. The cheese was a bright yellow spread; the ham was a single smooth sheet. Toby's meal looked luscious. Two large fried tortillas smothered in a rich brown sauce called *mole*. It came with a dollop of bright green guacamole, a circle of dark refried beans with a single tortilla chip sailing in its center, and a gravy boat full of green salsa. The waitress uncapped two bottles of Corona for them and was about to pour them into glasses with ice.

"Please, no thank you," Toby said. He looked at Alice to instruct her also to refuse the ice, for health reasons, but her hand already covered the glass.

At last, they ate.

"So, I'm about to ovulate," Alice said. "If ever there was a more perfect time." She squeezed lime and sprinkled salt in her Corona. She figured this would be the last of her drinking.

Toby raised his eyebrows, and Alice thought she saw him wink. "So tonight's the night," he said.

"Or this afternoon," Alice said. "The sooner the better, really."

This endeavor was not new; still, Alice felt a manic glee, a certain boisterous anticipation at the sheer *maybe* of it all. So far, nothing was "wrong" with either of them. Their doctor had told them to just keep trying, even though Alice feared it was almost too late for her, at age thirty-six, with so many good, unused eggs gone to waste ever since she was fourteen. The doctor told her that 80 percent of healthy couples took up to a full year to conceive a child. The important thing, she'd said, was to relax and just keep trying. They'd agreed a trip to Mexico might be just what they needed.

A small girl in a yellow dress wandered up to their table, selling tiny packets of Chiclets: purple, pink, red, white, and green squares the size of postage stamps.

"*Señora*," she said, and looked up at Alice with big, pleading eyes. "*Chiclet. Barato. Por favor. Barato.*" She rubbed Alice's arm softly with her hand.

"Toby," Alice said, "ask how much. How much for one pack."

He did, and told Alice in English.

"Ten," Alice said. "I'll take ten little packs." The girl didn't respond to her English but looked as if she knew she was in for a good sale. She leaned her elbows on the table and waited patiently. Alice could see her flip-flops had been many times repaired with tape.

"It would be three pesos," Toby said. "For ten."

"That's thirty cents, right?" Alice said.

"More or less," Toby said.

"Let's give her twenty pesos," Alice said. "That's only two dollars." She fished through her trim black travel pouch, which she kept inconspicuously inside her dress, strung around her neck. "Here," she said.

"Don't flash all your money around," Toby said, and physically shielded her from the street, even though they were up two stories.

"I'm not," she said. She paid the girl, scooped up her ten packs of Chiclets, mostly pink and maroon, and set them by her plate. She didn't even like gum, but the girl was so charming and such a convincing little salesperson. What was two dollars to Alice?

She gave Toby a look that said *what?* but soon a group of children flooded around Alice, hawking their wares: beaded necklaces, silver chains, brightly painted ashtrays shaped like sombreros, Aztec paintings on sheets of bark paper, clay vases banded in cobalt blue, bags of fried pork rind drenched in hot sauce like splattered blood.

"No thanks," Alice said. But the children wouldn't go away. One of them pointed to Alice's plate, where the ham and cheese burrito sat cooling, hardening, and Alice could feel a pained expression cross her own face.

"I'd give it to her," she told Toby, and crossed her legs uncomfortably. "But then the others—"

"It's okay for you to eat your meal, Alice," Toby said. "I'm sure they scam all the tourists. They don't look emaciated or anything."

Eventually, much to Alice's relief, the waitress sent the children back down the curving black staircase, and Alice watched them spill into the street below and zero in on other easy targets.

How she hated to say no to children, to anyone for that matter.

On the way back to their hotel, Alice feared they'd be run down by the white taxis constantly speeding through the narrow streets. She pulled herself up against buildings whenever one passed. She never turned her back on the traffic. She leapt into open doorways when a taxi got too close. As it turned out, it was Toby who got hurt. He did not get run down but lost his footing on the steeply pitched, wet brick street and twisted his ankle. Luckily there'd been a break in the taxi traffic. Alice had never seen him in such a state before. He lay on the ground, grimacing, gripping his leg at midshin, his face a dark shade of red. Fortunately they were just two doors down from Hotel Los Arcos, and the proprietor came rushing out and helped Toby hop down the street and into the hotel courtyard.

"I think it's sprained," Toby said, back in their room. Alice pulled the drapes closed and sat on the opposite bed, unsure what to do.

"Should we try to find a doctor?" she asked.

Toby tried moving his ankle around but winced. "No," he said. "Maybe just an Ace bandage. I think there's a little pharmacy around the corner. Do you think you could do that? It's really swelling. Maybe some ice, too."

Alice panicked at the idea of venturing out on a shopping trip, alone, with her poor Spanish skills. "Sure," she said, then fished the dictionary out of her bag. "I just need to look a few things up. Give me a sec."

Toby lay on the bed with his eyes closed as Alice frantically flipped through pages. Even the simplest request, the simplest sentence, caused her stress. She wanted to be good at it, to blend in, even though it was impossible with her rich, red, bobbed hair, her green eyes, and her milky white, obviously North American skin.

Finally, when she felt ready, Alice grabbed her money pouch and slid into her sandals. It was almost dark outside, and loud salsa music drifted in through the windows. Maybe she would buy an ice-cream treat, or a couple bottles of beer, or some garlic fried peanuts. She felt the Chiclets in her pocket as she reached for the door.

"Babe?" Toby said, startling her. He opened his eyes, sat up, and looked at her with an odd combination of apology and love. His beard, she noticed, had gone more gray than black, and she wondered, if she ran into him on the street, a total stranger, if she'd be attracted to him. It was his eyes, those piercing dark brown eyes, that got to people. He was dashing, you could say. He looked smart. He looked like someone who took good care of his belongings and drove a sensible but not unattractive car.

"Yes?" she said.

"It's probably not going to happen," he said. "I mean, with this ankle and everything. I'm good for nothing at this point."

"Right," she said, and although she tried to sound upbeat, she couldn't help the disappointed flatness that lingered in her voice. "It's just—I mean, of all possible times. You know? This is it," she said. "I mean, the doctor said as soon as the ovulation test is positive . . . I was just so hoping this time."

"I know," Toby said. He held up his hands in surrender. "I'm really sorry."

"Don't be silly," she said. "There's nothing to be sorry about. It was an accident! At least you didn't get run over by those crazy taxis." She strode over and planted a quick kiss on his cheek, which landed more on his ear. "We'll try again next time."

"I love you, you know," Toby said, and blew her a kiss with two fingers.

"You, too," Alice said, but her heart fell.

Out in the street, Alice imagined herself a single, reclusive ex-patriate. She exchanged knowing glances with a couple of young backpackers who had to be in their twenties. At home, they could be her students. They would hate her for giving them poor grades. They would call her Dr. White and complain about her difficult Introduction to Psychology exams. Here, they nodded at her in solidarity as if to say: This travel thing's a trip, isn't it? Around the corner, dogs barked and growled at her. Men glanced at her in her linen sundress as if she were merchandise for sale. Her new sandals creaked and groaned at the straps.

At the pharmacy's glass counter, a woman dressed in nurse's whites looked at her expectantly and asked what Alice assumed to be "May I help you?"

Alice's carefully practiced Spanish melted away. She was without words, utterly incapable of asking for anything, much less an Ace bandage or ice. She couldn't remember the verbs or the nouns. Nothing. Without Toby as her guide, she was rendered mute and ridiculous. Here, all her education couldn't get her a single bag of ice. The woman spoke again, in Spanish, this time more rapidly.

"*Inglés, por favor,*" Alice said, her own worst joke, but the woman wrinkled up her nose and shook her head.

"Okay," Alice said, in English, and slowly. "I need some ice and an Ace bandage. For a foot?" She lifted up her own ankle and pointed to it.

The woman looked at her blankly, then produced a small package of Band-Aids from underneath the counter.

Alice shook her head but felt they were finally getting somewhere. She acted out walking and then twisting her ankle. She made a painful face, then pointed to her wedding ring. "*Mi amor,*" she said. She didn't know if that was the right word, but the woman's eyes lit up.

"*Sí, sí,*" the woman said, and walked purposefully back among shelves of supplies. She returned quickly, placing a bright red condom packet in front of Alice. *Profiláctico*, it read, the absolute last thing Alice needed. Clearly, they'd reached an impasse.

Alice was about to give up but couldn't stand the thought of Toby's disappointment at her returning empty handed. Hands in her pockets, Alice came upon the Chiclets and fished them out, as if they could explain something. She set them on the counter, pink and maroon, like little valentines, sweet nothings. "You can have these," Alice said. "Give them to your kids. You have kids, right? Everyone in this country seems to have plenty." The woman looked at her suspiciously, then said something else that Alice didn't understand.

Alice shrugged her shoulders apologetically. The woman finally produced a small notepad from under the counter; she pushed a pen towards Alice and stood back. Alice took the pen, thought for a second, then wrote, in English, "I'm out of luck. It's not your fault." She lay the pen down and left.

On the short walk back to the hotel, she gave money to every beggar who asked for it. She gave until her pockets were empty, then went back to Toby, who lay waiting in the dark.

I first started eating chalk when I was in kindergarten, and couldn't keep my hands off the box of pastels, which reminded me of miniature colored marshmallows. My teacher, Mrs. Finch, who actually looked like a bird with her clipped little mouth and tight white nose, caught me gnawing on a pink stick behind the kitchen center. I remember trying to hide the mushy, grainy mess in the toy refrigerator, but she reached in and grabbed my arm like I was a criminal. Later, Mrs. Finch told my mother, who thought it was very funny, that she was merely afraid I would choke and die. I'll never forget her famous line, which our family still quotes to this day: "I don't care to be picking up any corpses in my classroom due to chalk!" That was the end of it, although my craving never ceased, and I've since read about women who cannot quench their desire for dirt and eat it, pure black and crumbly like an Oreo, right out of their yard with cupped, savage palms. So I am not alone in this earthy, mineral insatiability.

I'm twenty-one now, in my sixth month of pregnancy, and the craving is back. I'm a thin woman and have barely gained more than the baby's weight so far, but every night when I'm lying in bed, I get such a craving for chalk that I finally walked down to Ben Franklin the other day and bought a stash, which I keep in my nightstand, tucked in the drawer. My sister, Ardeth—a law student and my roommate—thinks I need to eat more and sleep less. She's a constant, sensible woman with short auburn hair, round tortoise-shell glasses, and heavy limbs. Most often you'll see her in long, floral dresses, navy leather flats, and dark blazers, all ordered from the same catalogue she's been steady with since high school. She's older than me by five years, and smarter than me, and more disciplined than me. You couldn't exactly call her matronly or dowdy, but she rides the edge: she wears only white cotton briefs, listens to country, and won't dare zip from the bathroom to her bedroom unless she's got her full-length "Little House on the Prairie" robe wrapped around her tight, even when no one's home. I know because she told me. We live on Main Street above Paesano's Pizza Parlor in Greenwood, Ohio. It's a small college town, but we get a lot of traffic. She's afraid someone might see her dripping wet, half-naked in a towel—that's what she's concerned about. We're very close, actually, which makes what's happened worse, or rather, very complicated.

My due date isn't until December 30, which is nice because I'll be able to finish out fall semester and keep working at Briante's Basement Bistro, which is the best restaurant in town. The professors from the university like to go there with their spouses, cozied against the brick walls, elbows leaning on the red-checkered tablecloths, little candles flickering in jelly jars. Occasionally one of my current professors will come in and sit in my section, which used to be awkward, but if they're men—bearded, balding monologuers—I flirt and wink at them, then sashay off with my empty tray, leaving their wives to wonder. I don't have too many male professors anymore, though, since I'm a junior majoring in women's studies and have most of my core requirements out of the way, except for biology/chemistry, and an annoying, worthless physical education requirement that demands two bogus semesters of exercise. I'm planning to take ballroom dancing and golf, but still.

I also make quite a bit of money at Briante's, and it's because I know how to flirt. Ardeth gets very upset with me about this, too. When she comes in after prowling in the dark, musty stacks of the law library all day, her pupils still dilating, then retracting, I bring her the usual, which she only drinks since I taught her to: Jack & Ginger. She loves it and always asks for it with a maraschino cherry, then sits there mournfully dragging it by the stem around and around in her drink. Meanwhile, by Happy Hour, I have a whole bar full of young and old men who come in here, so they say, just to see me. I'm propositioned constantly and have developed a slow, sweet smile, eyes lowered, as I twist a lime into their drinks, which says: you rascal, you just never know what can happen now, do you? The more I flirt, the more money I get, and I try to explain to Ardeth—who says I'm not the kind of woman who should be a women's studies major—that it's only my way of manipulating a male-dominated, capitalistic society in *favor* of women. She grows gruff at my lame excuses, slides out a slim, white cigarette, lights up, blows smoke straight up like a chimney, then shoos it away with a cupped hand. She has impeccable smoking etiquette.

Frankly, I'm glad Ardeth drinks, and especially glad that she smokes, since these vices give her some much-needed credibility and edge. She was actually married and divorced already by age twenty-five to a guy named Jack Slade, referred to ever after as "The Loser." She met him back home in Michigan between college and law school and, against her better judgment, married him in Ann Arbor's City Park. I was a senior in high school and thought it was risky and frolicsome and spontaneous, but our parents feared it would upset her career in law, which it likely would've if she'd stayed with him. Our father is a theater professor at the University of Michigan, and every other summer he hires a bunch of poor graduate students to scrape and paint their rather large, lemon yellow house with white trim.

Jack Slade was one of the bunch that year, an actor wannabe, and while he stood high on an aluminum ladder, dribbling sunny yellow rain from his paint bucket, he'd recite lines from Shakespeare to me and Ardeth, who sat tanning in our bikinis in the backyard, flipping through magazines. I secretly think he was after me, at least at the beginning, because whenever Ardeth ran in the house to pee and get us some more iced tea, Jack would point his finger at me, and then at himself, and then shrug his shoulders as if to say, why not? That was also the summer I bought my best bikini ever. It was a low-cut, underwire top with tiny straps and small hip-hugging bottoms in pale blue. I have to admit, with my tan and my dark hair and eyes, I looked pretty good in it.

But Ardeth would come out in her red plaid bikini, which smashed her breasts down like pancakes. She has a very fair complexion, with a light sprinkling of freckles over almost every inch of her, including her lips and eyelashes. She would look up at him, then look down at me, and roll her eyes. Somehow—I'm still not sure how it happened, since we spent almost every second together that summer—he asked her out. First, they went to see a Jodie Foster movie, Jack's favorite actress ("She's a fucking *goddess*," Jack always used to say), then the next weekend they went camping on the Upper Peninsula, and then suddenly it was wedding time. I was the flower girl, for effect, and wore a tiny black sundress and carried a huge bouquet of Gerber daisies in bright, primary colors like a Doctor Seuss book.

My mother, a gifted musician, played the dulcimer and sang a poem she had written herself called "Hither and Thither, Love." My father, ever the flaky, flamboyant dramatist, performed a skit in which he reenacted Ardeth's childhood in abstract, elliptical scenes, then went on a mythical journey through love using mime and a black box. No one really got it except for the coalition of actors who were the only guests at the wedding, dressed extra-funky in Salvation Army clothes: sombreros, gold sandals, peasant skirts, batik sarongs, and silk pajamas. They clapped furiously and patted him on the back when he was done, even though he had all but upstaged Ardeth on her one special day.

When it was time for Ardeth to start law school in Ohio, after Jack had finished his degree, everyone began asking him what he was going to do there. "I'm going to be married to a rich lawyer," he said. "Who needs to work?" This didn't sit well with our family, and as we saw them off in their big twenty-foot U-Haul, intonations of doom were probably evident in our voices. Ardeth drove and dragged her blue Subaru wagon behind the huge truck, its front pointed backwards. Jack's bare feet gripped the dashboard, and he waved happily as they pulled away. "It's never going to last," my mother said, and grabbed me around the shoulders. "Now, you, Winifred, can wait a while before you jump into something like that. Right? Isn't that right? There are big things ahead." She then steered me up the sidewalk, and once inside the house, I felt the absence of Ardeth echoing everywhere.

They divorced a year and a half later, and when I called to ask Ardeth why and what and how, she said, "He's a loser. That's all it is. He's a total loser." I didn't question her further, because if Ardeth said it, it had to be true. At the same time, she tried to get me to transfer to the university in Greenwood, and at first I resisted. "No way! It's out in the sticks!" I said, and it was, but then I looked around and realized, living at home, having a free ride at Ann Arbor because my father taught there, going to all the same bars and seeing all the same people, I needed a change. My parents were naturally unhappy because a) I was the only kid left and my leaving made them feel sad and old, and b) the university in Greenwood would not be free. That was the main issue, I soon discovered: money.

"Half," my father said, pacing the kitchen floor in his usual scroungy black turtleneck and gray jeans. "We'll pay half. That's the best I can offer." He spun on his heel, looked at me long, then spun towards my mother, who sat at the breakfast nook, buttering an English muffin.

"We'll miss you," she said, and crunched down on the jagged disc of bread. I worked all that summer as a waitress, gathering valuable experience that would land me my future job at Briante's. With a huge wad of cash, I rolled out of town in August on the Greyhound, my choice: far more romantic than a ride with my parents could've ever been.

When I moved to Greenwood that summer, Ardeth was living in a big apartment complex on the edge of town, despicably plain, all of the buildings painted tan, running parallel and dangerously close to the railroad tracks. It was a one-bedroom with a windowless kitchen, although it did come with free cable and a dishwasher. I'd sleep on the nubby beige couch and yawn and stretch and watch TV in the morning, while Ardeth sat at the tiny kitchen table, head bent over thick green books with yellowed pages. When the trains came past, which seemed to be on the hour, the windows rattled, the TV went mute, and the deep, moist carpet beneath our feet shimmied and vibrated like an earthquake. We had to shout to talk to one another, and Ardeth would sigh, pinch her fingers around her forehead, trying to concentrate. Finally, she would stalk off to the law library, her second home.

Still solvent with my Ann Arbor earnings, I flipped through want ads at my leisure, went for long bike rides in the afternoons, and whipped up interesting, healthy meals for Ardeth. Her favorite that summer was a simple salad of chopped red tomatoes, cubed mozzarella, and fresh mint tossed in olive oil. I would pace the hot, humid apartment, waiting for her to get home, and with great pleasure, sit and watch her eat the bright, wet food. Most often she would fall asleep sitting up in the chair, reading, and I'd nudge her, pat her on the hand, and say, "Ardeth, Ardeth, honey, time to go to bed," then walk her down the short hallway to her tiny white room with a daybed and rocker and five-drawer filing cabinet.

I first suspected Ardeth had a lover when the phone would ring, I'd answer, and someone would hang up. But Ardeth and I sound amazingly alike, and when I'd say hello, there was often a brief pause, thick breathing from the nose, then a dial tone. Sometimes Ardeth was home; sometimes she was not. When she was not, I would catch the phone on the first ring, breathless, and instead of saying hello, I'd say, "Who is this? Just tell me. I'm Ardeth's sister, Winifred. Talk to me." Still, I failed to elicit a response.

In order not to embarrass Ardeth, for she was a very judicious, discreet person, I began watching her more closely, pretending I was asleep in the early morning hours when she was most active. Mostly Ardeth studied and drank coffee, and sometimes did a series of stretches where she reached her arms up to the ceiling, then slowly lowered them, swaying from side to side. It was sad to see all the work she did with her brain and to watch her body becoming ever more lumpy and broad for lack of real exercise. Her hips had bloomed and bloated, and although she was certainly not fat, she was what you might call solid or heavyset, and I knew this bothered her. I also knew it bothered her that I could eat whatever I wanted, drink practically a twelve-pack of heavy beer, and never gain any weight. Not so with Ardeth, who was always merely picking at her food, fasting, campaigning herself into new diet programs, only to drop out after a week or two. I was always supportive and encouraging but knew our physical differences were an unspoken agony for Ardeth.

One morning, however, the phone rang for just a fraction of a second, and Ardeth was on it like fire. I pretended to be asleep when Ardeth turned her back to me and dragged the phone with her into the bathroom, the door ajar. I could hear every word and lay there, breathing slow and shallow. Finally, I picked up on a name. "Well, Tim," Ardeth said, the disappointment thick in her voice. "When do you have to pick him up? Uh-huh. Uh-huh. Well, what about Lori? Can't she pick him up?" There was a long silence, during which Ardeth sighed loudly and peeked around the corner to check on me. Luckily, I'd kept my eyes closed, but she might've known I was awake, given the tense, flexed stiffness of my body, straining so hard to listen. She must not have noticed, though, because she kept on. "Is she really? Oh, God. When did she go in? Yeah. Yeah. Yeah. Well, what does that mean for you? Or for us, I should say?"

Who was Lori? Was he married? Kids? I couldn't bear the suspense any longer and sat up, stretching loudly so Ardeth would know I was awake. She heard me and came quickly out of the bathroom, her voice newly tight and wiry. "All right then," she said, and I tried to read into her code. "Yep. Thanks for calling. Gotta go. Yep. Bye-bye."

She replaced the phone on the wall and ran back into her room to grab her car keys.

"Who was that?" I asked, and right away began folding up the pink bed sheets like Ardeth asked me to every morning.

She came out of the bedroom finagling her earrings, dark topaz drops, into her ears. She wore a long, brown calico dress, which laced up in back like a maiden's, and soft, buttery leather sandals. "Oh, friend from law school," she said, head cocked, nose wrinkled. "Shop talk." She shrugged her shoulders, grabbed her big wine-colored attaché case, and looked at her watch. "Better be going. See you for dinner?"

I nodded, yawned, wiped sleep from my eyes, and poured myself a cup of her leftover coffee, which had a burnt, black look to it by now, like unrefined maple syrup. When I added milk, it turned a bleak slate gray, so I tossed it down the sink. Ardeth never said things like "shop talk," so I knew something was up, but I didn't know why she was keeping it a secret from me, her only sister. The only reason I could think of was her constant fear of me stealing her boyfriends, which she had accused me of countless times, and which was entirely fear based and unfounded. Well, except for twice, but I was young and stupid then and hadn't been able to control myself. Plus, I had to be better at Ardeth at *something*; she had beat me on almost every other count. I decided I would have to confront her head-on, but in the meantime, I would look for a job. Although it boasted a good-sized, well-respected university, the town of Greenwood was so small the shops and restaurants spanned only five blocks on Main Street until they gave way to huge old houses all broken up into apartments.

I wore a sleeveless periwinkle shift and fisherman sandals and carried a small leather bag filled with loose money, ID, and three pens. It was a hot, humid Midwestern afternoon, and since I wore a dress, I couldn't bike but had to walk across town under the driving sun. When I came out of the prefab apartment building, checking in a panic for my keys, I saw a man in a blue car, watching me, watching our apartment door. I didn't like the feel of it and, being much more street-smart than Ardeth, decided to go ask him what the hell he was doing.

As I approached his Ford family sedan, he fiddled with the side mirror and smiled. "You must be Winifred," he said, and squinted in the glaring sun. "Wow. Quite a package."

I crossed my arms and looked adamant. "And you are who? Somebody who likes to lurk outside peoples' apartment buildings because he has nothing else to do?" My father had taught me to psych people out, to be mean and defiant, and to throw all cards on the table when dealing with creeps.

"Hey, sorry," he said, and flipped down his sun visor to beat the glare. "I'm a friend of Ardeth's. Is she home?"

I didn't know what to make of him, and had also known women who were too gullible, had gotten in cars with men just like this, and had been beaten, raped, and robbed, so I wasn't taking any chances. "What's your name?" I asked, thinking this would be a perfect test.

He answered quickly. "Tim. I've talked to you on the phone before." His eyes, a merry, flickering blue, met mine, and there was an awkward silence. His face was nicely sculpted and angular, freshly shaven, and his dark hair rolled back from his forehead in waves.

"How come you never identified yourself on the phone then?" I asked, and could feel cool drops of sweat dribbling down my ribs. I was braless, which I'm able to get away with, but could feel my nipples graze against the rough fabric of my dress.

"Because I'm supposed to be a secret," he said, then adjusted the side view mirror and winked at me. His fingers drummed against the side of the car. "You know how Ardeth is."

I nodded that I did, and then maybe, simply because of the heat, or his soft, blue eyes, or because I had these certain insatiabilities, I said, "Would you like to come in for some iced tea? It's really too damn hot to go anywhere." My forehead was dotted with sweat, and my palm came away wet and shiny when I swiped at it.

He raised his eyebrows in surprise and gripped the steering wheel with both hands, as if ready for takeoff. "Sure," he said, "if it's no trouble." Probably, if we had known then what we were getting into, I'd like to think neither of us would have done it, would have crossed that line. But I had no friends in town, no job, and Ardeth had all but abandoned me for school. I went ahead as he locked up the car and met him in the doorway of the apartment, bolting the lock casually behind us.

There was no iced tea, so I drew us tall, clear glasses of water from the tap and plunked big, frosty ice cubes into them, which sizzled and popped and split. The glasses soon beaded up with the humidity, and water trailed down both our hands and wrists. He sat on the couch, my bed, and I sat in the yellow director's chair, facing him, legs crossed. It was hard to tell if he was on his way to work or had been to work, since he wore Levi's and a purple polo shirt, tucked in; it was about noon. His blue eyes stood out shockingly in the whiteness of the room, and he looked around, jumpy.

"You're married, right?" I asked, and sucked on a sliver of ice, cold and sharp and small. It padded my speech.

He put his glass down on a magazine, spread his arms across the back of the couch, and nodded. "But it's very complicated. I mean, yes, I am technically married, but my wife, well—she's got some problems. She's—"

"Like what?" I asked. "Specifically." My foot jiggled up and down involuntarily, so I grabbed my sandal and held it down.

"Well, she's manic-depressive, right? So she gets in these fits and has to be hospitalized for weeks at a crack. It's really bad for her, and there's nothing I can do. I mean, when she gets like that, she doesn't even want to see me. You know?" He rolled his head around in circles, vertebrae cracking and shifting, as if the conversation were tensing him up. "Anyway, it's a real mess. I don't know." He folded his hands together and set them on his stomach.

I wasn't satisfied, and grilled further. "Kids?"

"One," he said. "Patrick. He's seven, good kid. He knows Ardeth—did you know that? A lot of times the only way I can see her is when I'm picking him up or some shit like that. He really likes Ardeth, you know, something about her good nature." He tapered off, and I imagined then the look on Ardeth's face if she were to come home, carrying a huge stack of law books in one arm, toting an expensive six-pack of beer in the other. Her jaw would not drop. She likely wouldn't scream or yell. She'd sit on the edge of a kitchen chair, trying to understand and infer meaning out of the meaningless.

"It sounds confusing," I said, in a manner I hoped did not connote sympathy.

Tim stood up suddenly, and I realized he might leave, that perhaps he'd had no ignoble intentions after all. "You know Ardeth wants me to leave my wife, right? She said it's no good for me, living like this. But there's Patrick, and you know Ardeth said she'd love to be his stepmother, but I don't know. Kind of tricky business—" He cracked his knuckles and quickly scanned the titles, mostly Ardeth's, on our bookshelf by the door.

"It is tricky," I said, and I've since replayed over and over in my mind what I did next, which was walk up to Tim, put my arms around his neck, and press my lips to his very, very softly. His warm hands came around my waist, then slid down my hips, and pulled them into his. I'd like to think I was saving Ardeth from what sounded like a dead-end affair that would surely culminate in favor of the wife, who was ill, and therefore more vulnerable and pitiable, but I suppose that's a shabby excuse on my part.

To my credit, I'm glad to say we didn't do it in Ardeth's bed, but instead groped our way over to the couch. I quickly poofed a pink sheet over it and pulled Tim down beside me. He had a practically hairless chest, smooth skin, and tiny, narrow hips, and as I lay there on top of him, naked and gasping and flushed, I remember thinking: Please, please, Ardeth, do not come walking through that door. In a matter of minutes, I was gripping the back of the couch, practically hyperventilating. Ardeth, to my utter relief, did not walk in, and we got quickly dressed and arranged.

"So," I said, after washing up in the bathroom a bit. I had scrubbed my hands with Dial and sprayed a plume of air freshener around the living room. From the kitchen, I watched Tim fold the sheet and stick it behind the couch. "That was interesting. Now what happens? You'll have to keep *another* secret, I guess." After over a month of no sex, my body felt loose and languid with release. I sat down on a kitchen chair but couldn't stay upright; I was practically horizontal again, my head leaning back against the chair, my butt sliding off of the seat.

"I don't know what to tell you," Tim said, and stood behind me, stroking my short wavy hair. "But I could fall in love with you. I'm already halfway there. I adore everything about you. God, your hair." He bent down and kissed the top of my head, and I shrieked.

"Please!" I said, turning around to look at him. "Do you say that to all the girls? You do! You do, don't you?"

But we heard a door thunking open downstairs, and although it was thankfully not Ardeth, it reminded us of her, and of our carelessness. I ran outside and did a thorough lookout for Ardeth, then waved Tim down with the all-clear sign. He got in his car, which was dense with closed-up, new-car heat, and rolled down all the windows. I stood a few feet away, just in case, wearing the same original job-hunting outfit, though feeling a bit discombobulated. My hair was now a frizzled mess.

"Now what're you going to do?" Tim asked, and started the car.

"Apply for jobs," I told him. "I'll just be a waitress. It's really the best money."

"Briante's Basement Bistro. It's the best place in town, seriously, and my friends own it. Tell them I sent you. I think they're hiring!" With that, he shifted into first, drove off, and yelled out the window, "I *will* see you again."

But what about Ardeth? I wanted to say, but was too full of self-loathing to even speak her name.

I was hired on immediately by the Briantes, a middle-aged Italian couple from Toledo for whom Tim had done some drywalling when they first opened, just two years ago, to huge success. Mr. Briante was short and compact with a hook nose and thick dark hair that was obviously dyed; he said to call him Big Daddy, as everyone did. His wife, Marie, had dark, slightly graying hair parted dead center and cut blunt to the chin. They said they liked my looks, kind of dark, kind of ethnic, trim. "Are you Italian?" they asked. I smiled, said, "Yes, of course!" though I wasn't. I found out it was the only Italian restaurant in Greenwood, and people were crazy for their bubbling red sauces, laced heavily with garlic, their creamy alfredo twirled over handmade spinach fettuccine, their osso buco with saffron lemon risotto.

I was also happy to look at the menu and discover most dinner entrees began at around ten dollars: good tips, likely, plus they served wine by the bottle, another sure way of jacking up a bill. They gave me a red apron with deep pockets on the front and a pad of green order slips, metered out by the number. I would need black pants, they said, tight—stretch pants were okay—and a white blouse, no T-shirts. Heeled black shoes and only black socks or hose. They gave me a tall, fizzy ginger ale with a twist of lemon, then sat back in the booth, hands crossed, both of them looking pleased as I drank it through a straw.

I must've been working at Briante's for two, three months, with a full load of classes, when Ardeth came home one night and told me everything about Tim. I remember I was sitting on the couch, my stockinged feet up on the end table, highlighter in my mouth, reading my large, pointy-cornered psychology textbook, when she came home teary-eyed and broken down. My face froze in a mask of panic, and I tried to ignore the fact that I'd been having sex with her boyfriend any time we could both arrange it, often in Ardeth's and my apartment. "I have to tell you something I should've told you a long time ago," Ardeth began, and peeled off her heavy, tan trench coat. She poured herself a glass of milk and sat down at the kitchen table. "Come here, will you?" She tapped the seat beside her, and I jumped up like an obedient dog, terrified of the master.

Ardeth ran her hands through her auburn hair, freshly cut, clipped around the ears and shaved at the neck. She removed her glasses and set them like a protective wall around her milk. "I have a lover," Ardeth said, gazing at me levelly, and the way she said it made me think for a moment she was going to tell me it was a woman. "It's been going on for some time now. Maybe, I don't know, five, six months. Before you even got here. Anyway—" She inhaled sharply before continuing and began to scroll for me a similar though slightly skewed version of Tim and his manic-depressive wife, Lori, and his son, Patrick, and how she had never meant to get so involved, but it had just happened. "You know how things just *happen*, and it's as if you have no control?" she said, clicking her glasses against the milk, then rolling up the corners of a glossy supermarket ad. "So, it was getting to be that he and I never spent any time together anymore, although he wouldn't break it off either. See, his wife's in the hospital now, in very bad shape, and they think it's going to be long-term this time. So—"

At this point, I had to get up and get myself a beer. We always had a few strays somewhere in the refrigerator, and I dug around and found a Heineken behind the ketchup. "Go on," I said, sitting. "Sorry." I didn't know how much more I could take without alcohol.

"Anyway, Tim and I had a very long talk tonight, and we finally made some decisions, which actually involve you," Ardeth said, and gestured to me with her hand in a way that I knew would make her a great lawyer someday. "So I told him I'd speak to you first and see what you thought."

My heart pounded in a furious, jumping frenzy. What was this? I thought. What was going on? I gulped my beer and licked my lips, waiting for life, as I knew it, to end.

Ardeth must've sensed my discomfort, because she reached out a parental hand and rubbed my arm. "Don't look so worried, Winifred!" she said, and leaned her elbows hard on the table, getting to business. "Now, what's going to happen is that Tim's son, Patrick, is going to stay with Lori's parents, who know about Tim and me now, and would have it no other way. They're going to let Tim see Patrick on weekends, but they don't want me to, but, really, how can they stop it? Anyway, after a lot of discussion, Tim and I decided to take this beautiful apartment we looked at—I didn't want to tell you until I knew for sure, okay? You understand, right?" She looked at me with her green flecked eyes, and I nodded, still fearful.

"It's a great apartment—it's above Paesano's Pizza, just down from Briante's. Have you seen that sign in the window?"

Again, I nodded silently like a shy child in school. I was gripping my beer so hard I thought I might shatter the bottle.

"Well," Ardeth continued, and began to spin her glass of milk around and around in circles across the tablecloth. "We decided, actually it was Tim's idea, that you simply have to move in with us. I mean, the place is huge! You can have your own bedroom towards the back, even though it's a little small—I hope that's okay. Tim's and my bedroom will be in the front, towards the street, and there's a huge kitchen with a brick wall behind the stove and a stainless steel oven and an overhead rack for all our pots and pans. It's really beautiful. The living room's a little dark, but very cozy with a fireplace! Can you believe that? And the place is cheap, considering we'll all split it three ways. You'll be paying the same as you do for this place and be right on the same block where you work. So what do you think?" Ardeth said, squeezing my arm, more excited than I'd seen her in years. Her eyes glowed with hope and warmth. "He's really leaving her for me, Winnie! I *knew* he would. I mean, I feel kind of guilty, of course, because she's sick and everything, right? But Tim deserves some happiness. I tell him that all the time, too, that he's entitled to a normal life just like anyone else."

I wanted to tell her right then, to absolve myself and flee town, but I was in too deep. I would shatter this newfound happiness she had worked so hard for. But I did vow, that night, on my soul, that I would never, ever sleep with Tim again. I could not dupe my own sister any longer. "So when do we move?" I asked, and felt the beginning of emotional terrorism.

Two weeks later, huddled over the toilet in our new black-and-white tile bathroom, I peed over a white piece of plastic and found out I was pregnant. The faint blue line grew darker when I held it up to the light, and I cursed every expletive I knew. I hadn't been with Tim for two weeks; I moved brusquely past him in the hallway, stoically watched videos with him and Ardeth in the living room, then stole off to bed early during the credits. We had used condoms in the past, since I'd learned about the ramifications of The Pill in a class I took called Women, Sexuality, and the Politics of Reproduction. We had always been careful, Tim and I, and I'd watched him carry the slightly full condom like a beaker, rinse it in the sink, and roll it up in mounds and mounds of toilet paper. Then it was shoved deep down in the wastebasket. That had been the ritual. Apparently the 99.7 percent effective rate did not apply to us.

I also vowed never to tell Ardeth the truth. The truth does not necessarily set you free, I decided, but would separate us for the rest of our lives. I did, however, decide not to inform Tim right away about the pregnancy but to let the fact slowly unfold before his eyes, as my stomach bloomed and swelled like a small pan of dough.

These days, working at Briante's, I wear a loose white poet's blouse that drapes almost to my knees, and customers are none the wiser. My black stretch pants are starting to give at the elastic waist, and soon I'll have to break down and buy real maternity clothes—so ugly, with big off-color nylon panels over the stomach. My breasts are truly starting to ache, and many nights when I get done with a nearly $100 shift at Briante's, I rush right home, peel off my heavy, garlic-scented clothes, and hold my breasts in my hands, alleviating them from the heavy impending weight.

Ardeth knows about the baby; I finally told her when it was just the two of us home one night, drinking cinnamon tea out of big ceramic mugs, reading the newspaper on the living room floor. Ardeth had made a fire, and it warmed the room so completely that I was barefoot. "Well, who's the father?" she asked, peering at me logically out of her tortoise-shell frames. "Is he going to take responsibility?"

"Just someone from school. Drunk at a party. Big mistake," I said, and brushed it off as if she would just forget it. But she wouldn't let up.

"So what are you going to do?" she said. "You're not going to keep it." It was a statement, not a question, another good lawyer tactic Ardeth had already perfected, and hearing her say it made me wonder, how *could* I keep it?

Suddenly, I was awash with hormones gone out of control, and tears filled my eyes. I didn't want to cry in front of Ardeth, because if anyone needed comfort it was more her than me. But she took me in the crook of her arm, and I sunk my face into her fuzzy alpaca cardigan. She smelled like Heaven Scent, which no one wore anymore but Ardeth, true to her brands till the death, and I bawled like a baby out of shame, fear, and regret. I could see the clear, gelatinous strings of snot I'd left on her sweater, and when I pulled away they hung between me and her arm until I swiped them.

"Shh," Ardeth said, cooing me. "It's okay. We'll figure it out. You can give it up for adoption. People will pay big money for babies, you know. It's perfectly legal now to sell a baby, if both the mother and the adoptive parents agree to it. In fact, I had a course last semester dealing with adoption. Just let me—"

We both heard the door open, and knew it was Tim. I listened as he hung up his jacket on the hook in the entryway, then heard his footsteps peep in the kitchen, and then he came to us. He leaned in the doorway, cheeks red with cold and blue eyes sparkling.

"Hey, you two," he said, and shoved his hands in his back pockets. He wore a black sweatshirt speckled with drywall shavings. "Having a pity party or what?"

With me still leaning against her shoulder, Ardeth looked up at him with loving tenderness, like the Virgin Mary. Then she looked down at me. "Can I tell him, Winnie? We have to tell him. He's like part of the family now." Her voice, for the first time, sounded like when we were kids, when Ardeth still knew how to play and let loose as I'd pump her high, high up on the swing set with an underdog and she'd squeal in frenzied joy.

"Tell me what?" Tim asked, and sat down on our new blue couch, which had been his and Lori's and was now covered with an afghan Ardeth had knit—a dark green and tan popcorn stitch.

Before I could speak, Ardeth whispered solemnly, "Winnie's pregnant. Can you believe it?"

Tim knelt beside us on the floor and threw his arms around me. "Oh, baby," he said, kissing my cheek right in front of Ardeth. "Oh, Winnie." He kissed me on the lips then, fast, and I remember Ardeth laughing high-pitched. The fire crackled in the fireplace, and threw shadows of the three of us, jagged, gigantic, against the wall.

FIVE REASONS I MISS THE LAUNDROMAT

#1

Because once I was washing a load of clothes and a midget walked in with long, blond hair that was almost silver and I realized when I looked hard that it was a man, not a woman. He walked right over to one of the big drum dryers at floor level—he had a Walkman on—and got in. He didn't close the door but lay inside all curled up with his tiny feet ticking time against the metal. I was single then, and very young, and had only the one load to wash. I wore sunglasses to hide my eyes and leaned against my rumbling washer going at it like a belly dancer.

Before I knew it, it was time for me to dry. I pulled out the wound wet tentacles of cotton and denim and saw the only dryer open was the one above the midget. So that was it. I drove my big square basket over, unloaded into the second-story drum, and slid in dimes. The midget was still in the first-floor drum, snapping his fingers along to music nobody could hear but him. When I stepped away, he gave me a thumbs-up. Startled and confused, I did it back. He smiled then and folded his hands behind his head.

I stood by the bulletin board and read about a lost terrier named Alice, a super new megadiet that promised fifty pounds off in as many days, and three families in town who were selling it all at a yard sale dated three weeks ago. When my clothes were dry, I pulled them all out in a heap, the metal buttons nearly burning holes in my arms. It appeared the midget had fallen asleep. The television blared high up in the corner, and part of me wanted to stay, part of me wanted to go.

I drove back to my apartment, which was above a butcher shop. No killing on the premises, but lots of blood and fat and bone behind the counter. I bought my bacon there sliced fresh off a slab. I liked it that way. You could see where it came from.

In my apartment, I folded my clothes on the kitchen table, careful to avoid honey smears and milk dribbles. I lived alone, worked in telephone sales, and had been struggling through a pretty miserable patch of life. I had just broken up with the person I thought I'd marry, and was having trouble bouncing back. I thought about the midget, and wondered why he seemed so much happier than me, even though he was a midget and I was supposedly normal.

When I went back to find him, of course he was gone. He had been so tiny, so perfect, so comfortable with himself, I'd wanted to cuddle him in my arms.

#2

Because in Minneapolis I was in love with a man named Rudy who was a judge, although a young judge and certainly not a famous or well-known judge. He was married. I called him Judge for a joke and pulled on his ties with both hands. The Clean-o-Rama Coin-Op was in my neighborhood, a leftover hippie enclave that boasted old houses of the crumbling gingerbread variety. I lived in one of these with thirteen other people, all involved in theater except for me. I was fresh out of college and completely without a plan.

I had a thing for red hair, and Rudy had extremely red hair and tawny, almost invisible eyelashes and eyebrows and freckles everywhere including on his lips, eyelids, and penis. It was safe to meet at the Coin-Op because Rudy lived in New Brighton and knew no one in my part of the city. The best part of the affair, although *I* never thought of it as an affair, was that right next door to the Coin-Op was a bar with humongous plates of nachos—not the half-assed kind with cheese sauce on round chips but the real kind with hard triangle tortillas and jalapeno wheels and avocado chunks and tomato cubes and guacamole studded with onion and garlic. We met there every Wednesday at five, scarfed down two orders of nachos, chased them down with Rolling Rocks, then picked up my fluffy hot clothes in the dryer and proceeded to have oral sex in my station wagon. It always smelled like Tide and Bounce as we were doing it, and depending on the season, we could really manage to steam up the car windows like a couple of high schoolers. I always parked behind the dumpster so we couldn't be seen.

I can't remember how I met Rudy, but it must have been at one of the numerous plays I was always being dragged to by my roommates. Yes, it was at *Hamlet*! I was a smoker then, and anyone who smokes knows you meet people outside who are also doing the dirty deed. He needed a light, or maybe I did, but that's how we met. Something clicked in that proverbial love-at-first-sight way, although it wasn't really love. I do remember that later, when we were really at the height of our *affair*, he gave me rolls of quarters and dimes for the laundromat as tokens of his affection. What I really can't remember is how it ended, because although I distinctly remember continuing my laundry trips to the Coin-Op, eventually the pictures in my mind no longer include him. I stopped going to the bar for nachos, because I couldn't afford it. I definitely missed the rolls of quarters and dimes. Alone again, I sat reading deep and moody things like *Siddhartha* and Kerouac in the sunny plate-glass windows of the laundromat. The big windowsill where I sat was full of dying rubber plants and swirling linty dust and so much sunshine it hurt my eyes to see.

#3

Because when you're married and own a house and pay a mortgage and have a baby, you do so much laundry in your laundry room that you think you will collapse from exhaustion or boredom or both. And because your laundry room has a window and because it faces your neighbors' backyard, you overhear them, the Stringers, fighting and crying and saying, "You're out of control, Dick! You're really out of control!" (They will divorce later that fall.) Because you have whole loads now of nothing but dirty little stinky, stained baby clothes full of noodles and canned pears and Cream of Wheat and crusty boogers and poop. Because your laundry room is so dirty it shouldn't even be a place where you try and get things clean, but because you're so tired and spent (and not in any kind of sexual way *spent*) you can't summon the energy to care about such things anymore, so you drink cold beer every night on the couch and watch television.

You remember how lively it used to be in the laundromat downtown, despite the blush of shame at folding your black underwear in halves, then quarters, in front of rednecks and welfare moms and sixteen-year-olds just killing time at the video games. You remember the bright, cheery hum of possibility at all those clean clothes swirling together in tandem. You remember the soft, hot smell of Downy on other peoples' towels. You use scent-free now: everything has to be scent-free, because of your delicate nose, because of the baby's rash, because of your husband's belief system.

In the laundromat once—before you had a house and a husband and a baby and a washer and dryer—you ran into Bibs, a friend of yours who everyone thought was homeless because of the multiple tattered stocking caps he wore and his long, greasy beard and his muttering. But you loved him and listened to him and talked about art and writing and grandparents while your clothes spun. You stood on the stoop beside him in the ugly butt end of winter while you both smoked. The sun struggled to break through. People walked by, and he knew all of them, and you knew some of them, and everybody laughed or gave peace signs or offered Bibs whatever snack they were eating. Bibs had made a sculpture out of old laundry-soap bottles, he told you, and invited you to his apartment to show it off. You thought surely he really wanted to smoke pot or hit you up for money, but lo and behold, there sat the most *interesting* sculpture you had ever seen. It looked like Dr. Seuss with lots of royal blue plastic, with a drop of Picasso and a touch of Warhol for good measure.

You put your hand over your heart. *It's so wonderful! Bibs!* You almost kissed him, but he wasn't really that kissable, and you were engaged to be married to a plastic surgeon with perfect teeth whom you had met, of all places, at the dentist's office. Bibs made coffee. You sat staring at the piece, *the piece*, as you kept calling it—out of respect for his art. You had a nice conversation over coffee while the sun continued to make efforts at shine. Bibs played his radio softly. He kept it on top of the refrigerator.

Because now you have privacy in your own home, your own first-floor laundry room, so much privacy it makes you miss things you'd rather not. There's nobody like Bibs anymore. You think—you laugh out loud—you should have married Bibs.

#4

Because the Oregon coast was rainy and rocky and not the beach vacation I'd imagined, though my husband kept telling me it would be magical. Because clothes get dirty, even when you're on vacation, and our little boy, Winston, was of an age where he smeared avocado on his pants and smashed fresh blueberries against his T-shirts. Because clothes get especially dirty when there's wet sand around and nothing for a four-year-old to do but roll around in the wet sand. On the rainiest day of the vacation, we headed up to the Rockaway Beach Laundromat. We divided up our clothes into two loads: kid and adult. We were the only customers.

My husband had just bought a touristy little reed flute for Winston, who sat blowing sweet, empty notes like a Sufi on the floor, cross-legged. I bought miniature boxes of Biz and tossed them into the tumbling waterfalls drumming down against speckled metal. Winston was happy with the saltwater taffy we'd bought him, though I could almost hear the sugary slime rotting his teeth upon contact. He wore his swim trunks because they were the only thing clean. I wore my bikini as underwear for the same reason. Winston chewed and chewed and rolled the square laundry carts up and down the stained linoleum like a drag race.

It rained and rained, but it was Pacific Northwest rain I wasn't accustomed to: little fizz balls of tepid water with tails like minicomets. I sat on the counter meant for folding clothes and looked out the window: the soft rain, the little beach highway on the opposite coast of my continent. How do I explain . . . that I was happy? The flute music, the warmth, Winston's simple entertainment, our clothes being cleaned, just the three of us in this strange place. And the rain. It was part of the vacation process.

Then a couple walked in. I ruffled open a Dreamsicle taffy, chewed, said hello, and tried not to stare. It was obvious: we were vacationing and they were locals. How was it obvious? It just was. She was pregnant. He was wiry. Bad hair on them both. They looked very tired, and not the kind of tired you get on vacation from bland, shapeless days of reading and eating but tired from failing to manage any kind of career or prosperity or solidity. They didn't have any laundry, I noticed, and I shot my husband a raised eyebrow, which he deflected with a stoic shake of his head. The couple went back to the bulletin board and pinned up a couple things. Winston sidled up next to them and asked them their names. Mike and Crystal, they said, not unkindly. Then they left.

Of course I ran to look at what they'd put up. My husband shot me a look that I was being nosy, and I was. I *was*! Who wouldn't be? Mike's tatty little scrap paper said: "Need work, can do electrical, plumbing, lawn care, basic carpentry—I don't have tools—will need to use your's—355-2503." I frowned. No tools! The one from Crystal (clearly a woman's handwriting) said: "Need to sell, need the room! Therm-o-Rite hot tub, marble blue interior, never been installed. Bought for $3,000, asking $500. Sacrifice—Having a baby! 355-2503."

We should buy this, I told my husband, but he didn't even want to know what it was. Winston went back to drag racing the carts. The clothes were spinning.

My mind was spinning, and the rain came down outside, beading against the glass door, hanging on for all it was worth. My happiness had suddenly grown complicated, a luxury I was beginning to wonder if I could afford.

#5

Because as a kid, it was cozy. Going to do laundry meant being with Mom. Mom was strong and sturdy and no-nonsense, and even though we were poor, and even though I'm sure I didn't know the term "trailer trash" then, she got us by. The laundromat smelled like gasoline from the service station next door. It was big and roomy and yellow. It had a gum-ball machine by the door and another machine that dispensed swirly rubber balls and skeleton rings and miniature tattoos all captured in plastic bubble containers. Fifty cents each. But quarters were quarters and needed for the wash.

Mom was tall. Mom could heave-ho with heavy machinery, big armfuls of clothes, mean people. Mom could scoop me up and hold my butt cupped in her arm and at the same time spin the noisy dials on the machines and slide coins in. At the end, sometimes, if there was money left, we ate next door at the Tip-Top Lounge, a place that to me meant a grilled cheese sandwich and a chocolate malt but to Mom meant a Jack & Ginger and a cigarette. Later, I would learn she stripped there for cash. To feed me, to wash my clothes.

How could I know, even later, that I would be someone who'd appreciate the irony of the situation, really *love* the irony of it, and tell the story over and over to boyfriends who listened halfheartedly and thought me clever: the irony, I'd say, of washing *clothes*, clothes you take *off*, right next to the place where you *literally* take off those clothes, at a *strip* joint. I'd shake my head, remember Mom, miss her sturdy walking through the world. She was a heavy bleach user. She believed in the purity of bleach. Every time I open a bottle now, I am transported to visions of her big rusty eyes chunked with mascara on the lashes, her long jaw, her high freckled cheekbones, the slight sweat beaded across her forehead. She could stack and hoist all of our laundry in one fell swoop. She'd put the full baskets one atop the other, tell me to climb aboard, then—upsy-daisy—kick open the door with her foot and away we go.

FREEZE
======

That was the summer everything changed, and while I couldn't
know it at the time, it was to be a year of extremes. The
August temperatures lingered for weeks in the high nineties, literally
bleaching our new black roof shingles a charcoal gray. That winter,
after an agony of months during which we did not know if my father would live or die, the same roof shingles became coated with
so many layers of ice that, having nowhere else to go, the gradual
melt crept its way through the shingles, down into the attic beams,
through the floor, and finally through the ceiling of my bedroom
where I heard it splashing one January night, drop by drop, atop my
desk. The odd thing was that I immediately sprang out of bed and
called for my father to help, only to realize he wouldn't be able. That
was how it was at first: an accumulation of realizations that nothing
would ever be the same.

My mother had become a portrait of a girl after the accident. She let
her hair grow long with bangs, wore simple blue jeans with cardigans,
seemed smaller in stature than she really was; I had already surpassed
her in height by my twelfth birthday and stood, a year later, five full
inches above her. I remember flashes of her standing outside in the
cold, bitter wind that winter, hair flying into her face, navy peacoat

wrapped around her but unbuttoned while various vans, vehicles, and people pulled in and out of our driveway for my father. It was a year of strangers fronting as intimates walking around our house at all hours, reading books in corners while my father slept, sitting at the dinner table with us as if they were old friends.

My brother, Harry, I rarely saw. Three years my senior, he had no idea how to face what seemed the worst possible thing. He'd essentially retreated away from our family and into his girlfriend, Rebecca's, who lived across the canal bridge in a comfortable old house surrounded by pine trees. Although we were brothers, Harry and I had never been particularly close, and the accident only seemed to pull us farther apart and create a chasm I found defeating.

The thing that kept me going was my camera—a fully manual Pentax K-1000 given to me by my parents for my thirteenth birthday. For years I had been the family documentarian, the one who assumed responsibility for preserving memories of birthdays, anniversaries, ice storms, Christmases, and vacations. I'd used my parents' expensive little 35 mm automatic until it died one Halloween and was never replaced. A year later, I was finally given my own. It was an extravagant gift, certainly—I'd realized that as soon as I opened it—and I began to suspect something wasn't right between my parents. That same year, when Harry turned sixteen and got his driver's license, he was given, to his amazement, a used Honda hatchback. Both of us could sense something afoot.

After the accident, I photographed every person who came to help my father in some way. I simply asked their permission to do so as soon as they entered our house, and most of them, although confused, could not refuse me. My favorite shot was of Rhonda Fontel, a rehabilitation specialist from Rochester. She was sitting in the front entryway unzipping her winter boots when our cat, Nomad, ran by in a tabby flash. The look on Rhonda's face—both weary and astonished—reflected the general state of our household that year. That picture was hung, like all the others, in a simple black frame in my bedroom where no wall space remained save for a hard-to-reach corner or a finger of plaster between shots. Photographing people who came and went, who provided care and equipment, who did their jobs and left, allowed me to avoid looking directly at my father. Every time we made eye contact, it was as if my eyes—on their own accord—diverted downward to take in the effects of the accident, but then quickly, forcibly almost, ascended back to his face, only to see him looking out the window at the thick slurry of snow that seemed to constantly fall that year. I didn't photograph him when the accident was still new and fresh; that would come later and in its own odd time. But I did photograph the objects of his new life: the equipment, his new bedroom, his many medications from the pharmacy. We will want to remember this for what it is, I remembered thinking. We must make a record of it.

My mother refused to let me photograph her; in fact, the only shot of her is mostly a blurred swipe of the palm of her hand, her face turned away, her hair caught up in an exaggerated sweep. What I did instead was photograph her asleep. That year she often collapsed on the couch in front of the evening news or fell asleep, chin in hand, at the dining room table—forms and envelopes and piles of hospital bills all around her. My favorite photograph was of her asleep in the rocking chair. Her hands rested gently atop the rocker's arms, her head lay back, her legs crossed at the ankle. There was a peace in her slack jaw and lidded eyes I wouldn't see again in her waking hours.

Talking about it later, Harry and I decided we should have seen it coming—not the accident itself, but the slow disintegration of our parents' marriage. That June our father bought a fancy touring bicycle with whip-thin wheels and a small, hard tongue of a seat; the whole thing reminded me of a greyhound in its anorexic spareness. He had never been an avid cyclist before, but Harry and I, and our mother—from a distance—watched him cycle down the driveway in his tight Lycra wear, his hard, shiny helmet, and his special cleated shoes. On the weekends, he'd be gone sometimes whole days, and while Harry and I lazed around the pool, our mother smashed pots and pans around the kitchen, tossed the recycling out in the bins with a fury, rearranged the patio furniture in an awkward, chaotic way, then finally grilled us thick steaks for dinner with a look on her face that seemed to suggest she'd just as soon be turning our father on a spit. It was only later, much later, in that dim, sad dusk of summer when birds settle, bats begin to swoop, and children disband and run for baths, beds, and sleep, that we'd hear the light click of my father's bicycle chain coming up the drive. Our mother feigned nonchalance, although watching her carefully from the corner of my eye, I'd see her body physically tense up and could hear the ice cubes melt and shift in her gin and tonic as if mimicking the fall of her heart.

Later, I'd awaken from sleep to hear whispered screams, threats, tears, then low-murmured negotiations, and feeble-sounding, very temporary-seeming reconciliations.

When my mother—my mother, a birthday overdoer, a birthday sap to the extreme—spent her fortieth birthday alone, I knew I should take notice, possibly intervene, and yet, being thirteen, I hadn't the resources. On top of that, Harry and I were up to a lot of soccer playing that month, finishing out the season. To our credit, though, we did take our mother out to dinner at the newly opened Chinese restaurant in town, but watching her munch a soggy egg roll bathed in a horrible red sauce was finally more than we could bear. My gift was no better, although she'd smiled sadly and kissed me absently on the hair as she opened it. It was a small bowl glazed yellow and green bought at the college art department's annual sale. My mother never actually used it for eating, as I'd intended, but relegated it to special status as her coin and ring holder on the window sill above the kitchen sink. Harry gave her a box of stationery, his usual. My father, nothing.

For some reason, it was in me that my mother confided, and while I found the exchanges rather awkward ("Should I give your father an ultimatum? Do you think he would buy into that, or retract?"), I was forced to play both good son and close girlfriend; I was hardly prepared for the latter but tried to nod, question, rage, or enthuse when each seemed appropriate. I was jealous of Harry and how he seemed released from any responsibility in terms of our domestic situation. He'd always been the compulsive, scattered free spirit of the family; his sudden exits and manic mood swings were just enough to keep the focus effectively on him instead of the real sources of tension. "He's just like his father," my mother said to me one June evening as we watched Harry zip off on his rollerblades to Rebecca's. It got my attention that she'd said "his" father instead of "your" father, but she seemed for once so calm as we sat on the back patio, glasses of cool iced tea dripping in our hands, that I didn't want to rile her. Our father was still out on his bicycle and it was nine thirty, going on ten; the last strips of sunset fell pink and amber through the darkened tops of the trees. He'd certainly spent whole days away before but usually wheeled in closer to dinnertime than bedtime. Instead of being upset, my mother seemed resigned, at last, to something.

"It's finally cooling off," she said. She wiggled her bare toes in her sandals and folded her hands across her stomach. I was afraid anything I might say would ruin the mood, so I nodded and fell silent beside her. That's when we heard the phone ring, and lazy as we both were, I finally dragged myself inside, running to catch it before the machine picked up. I answered, breathless, on the fourth ring. "Hello?" My voice sounded young, even to me, and cracked on the second syllable; the person on the other end immediately asked for Mrs. Ginny Foster, my mother, whom I could see out the kitchen window. Something about the form of address alerted me to the fact that bad news somehow lay ahead. "Mom!" I yelled outside. "For you!"

I held the phone out to her when she came in, twirling a small black moonflower she'd picked from her flower garden. "Finally," she whispered, handing it to me, "it's blooming." Before taking the phone, she took out her earring, an old-fashioned gesture of hers I loved. "Yes?" she said.

As she listened, her whole body went limp but I grabbed onto her and steadied her. Somehow I felt my role as her sole support bear down on me with more peace and calm than dread and apprehension. It was a role I had been preparing for, though I didn't know it, all my life. I was a good listener, and whether by default or due to birth order or temperament, I had been groomed by my mother to be both sensible and strong, empathetic and unflappable; I was anyone's best bet for a confidante who would go the extra mile to get you to your destination. My reliability had always been the perfect antidote to Harry's jittery haplessness.

Later, I remembered the term "life altering" being used over and over again to describe what had happened.

At first our mother wouldn't let Harry or me come to the hospital to visit our father, although she spent almost every waking—and sleeping—hour there. It was just too awful and his situation so dire that we'd have to "wait and see," she'd said. In reality, I knew my mother was protecting us from a future of memories, seared forever, of our father: weakened, marred, maimed. It was as if we'd essentially been orphaned, and although it was fun in an illicit way to stay up late, ignore homework, watch music videos whenever we wanted, and eat out of cans and boxes, it quickly wore on me, and I soon felt abandoned by my parents in a way that made me feel six years old again. My sleep was fitful and interrupted; I'd awaken, only to feel exhausted. I had nightmares of horrible car crashes that woke me up in fits of sobbing.

In the mornings, I'd find my mother's tote bag flung on the dining room table where she'd left it the night before, health bars and insurance forms and Kleenex spilling out as if she'd thrown it there in haste. In reality, she'd make her way upstairs late for a few fitful hours of sleep and stay in bed until after Harry and I had left for school. I knew she was awake because I remembered looking up at her bedroom window as I got in the passenger side of Harry's Honda. I could see the curtains in her bedroom blowing in the breeze and would sometimes have to look away when I saw her peek out at us as we drove off. Her face was like a ghost's behind the pale lace curtains, and it nearly ruined me for the entire day to see her haunting us like that.

We knew the basics, certainly: our father had been hit by a car while riding his bicycle on Highway 21, which leads to Lake Ontario (what he was doing so far away from Bellport caused much speculation). Something had happened to both of his legs: they had been somehow broken or damaged in a way that I sensed was far more serious than we'd been told. Although he'd been wearing a helmet, he'd hit his head hard. What we also knew was that he had escaped spinal cord injury, and for that we all felt a tremendous relief. To me, though, it seemed like a false relief borne out of a desire to be happy about something, anything. Ah, I thought, so he won't be paralyzed! Thank God for good news!

As the days after the accident accumulated and then became a week, I think we all sensed the tragedy was larger than anyone knew, including our mother. When our father had at last stabilized and it seemed he would live and could breathe on his own, our mother capitulated and finally agreed that it was time for Harry and me to see him, for better or worse. We both took the day off from school, even though visiting hours didn't start until one, and even though our mother decided we should wait until three, which was "a better time for him." I sensed she was stalling.

The ride to the hospital felt long. Fall was coming on early, and the leaves, though still a hard green, blushed orange at the tips. Our mother, always a nervous driver, kept her hands in the ten-and-two position, her body erect, her face stoic. A light rain fell, more like a mist, and as we turned and followed the Erie Canal, an ominous cloud hung heavily over the water despite the dying sunlight to the west. Harry had wanted to drive, had made a brief nasty scene when my mother refused him, but had thankfully backed off at my urging.

"Boys," our mother said. I sat in back with my long legs spread out on either side. A compact car, it was barely able to contain the four of us on family outings, which had only rarely occurred anyway. She adjusted the rearview, then quickly placed her right hand back into position on the steering wheel. "There's something you need to prepare yourselves for." She eyed me in the mirror, and I nodded obediently, letting her know I was ready. "There's something you need to know," she said.

Harry was up front fiddling with the radio stations. I knew exactly which five had been programmed for each button: NPR, jazz, classical AM, 80s rock, and the college's alternative station. Our father prided himself on keeping up with current music and often went out and bought the newest albums before I'd even heard of them. To my surprise, Harry settled on the jazz station. "Highly overrated," he used to say, which would elicit a lecture from our father about innovation and experimentation and form and keeping an open mind.

"Now listen," our mother said. She turned onto the highway, only after craning her neck to look both ways several times. "I should've told you this—" she started, then shook her head.

"What?" Harry said, sounding fed up.

"It's just—it was all so uncertain," she said. I could hear the catch in her voice; she was scared. In the rearview mirror, I could see her eyebrows knit together. "Don't be mad," she said.

"Mad?" I said. "At who?" I was so far beyond anger her comment threw me.

She shrugged her shoulders and continued to drive in silence.

"Your father has lost both of his legs," she said finally. "They were injured so badly they had to be amputated."

We sped past little clusters of apple orchards, their spooky gnarled branches reminding me of old, evil witch hands. There didn't seem to be any appropriate response to her news. I had questions, certainly. Namely, why the hell couldn't the doctors do something to save his legs? Why hadn't she told us this before? Had it taken too much time getting him to the hospital? Why the hell had he been on his way up to the lake? Was he with anyone? But I asked nothing. She had scared me into silence.

Harry banged a knuckle back and forth against the window glass to the beat of a low bass drum. I thought he would stop upon hearing the news, but he did not. Thump, thump, thump. "When was this?" he asked.

"I don't know . . . two days ago?" she said. "I can't keep track anymore." She was trying to get over into the left-hand lane but kept slowing down and missing her chances.

"Shit," Harry said. He stopped the knuckle rapping finally as she slid the car over, barely missing a truck. The person laid on the horn and glared at us as he passed. My mother gripped the steering wheel harder. "I wanted to make sure everything turned out all right," she said. "You know? I didn't want to be giving any worse news than I had to." I puzzled over this for a minute, unsure what she meant.

"The thing is," Harry said, "we're his family. His *kids*, you know?" He turned to look at her, but she kept her eyes on the road. "I mean, I think we can take it. As much as you can, anyway." I didn't like him challenging her like that, so I changed the topic.

"How's he doing?" I asked. "Is he all right?" We were just approaching downtown where the highway split off and became freeway. The familiar cluster of buildings—the old Kodak headquarters, the new prison, the Frontier soccer stadium, the Xerox tower with the big red *X*—used to make me think I had really arrived somewhere, even though I knew we were not L. A. or New York City or even Boston but a third-tier, small-town city. I usually looked with special fondness at the old-fashioned limestone Hoover building that housed my father's law firm where he had always made enough money to keep us comfortable, to keep me and Harry in the latest jeans and tennis shoes, to keep us traveling to interesting places like the Grand Canyon and the Florida Keys, to keep two late-model cars in the garage so that anyone could tell at a glance we did not suffer. This afternoon the skyline seemed sooty and sad.

"He's all right," my mother said, but I could feel her editing things out again. "But he lost so much blood. You can imagine." She seemed unsure whether to continue or not. She put a finger to her lips, as if considering. "The couple who found him had given him up for dead. I mean, they had a cell phone and called 911, but they reported later they couldn't even get a pulse . . ." She wiped at her nose. "You don't know how lucky he is. Really."

I didn't. Or perhaps I couldn't possibly find a way to define what she was describing as luck. By this time we had exited the freeway and my mother was circling the hospital parking garage, looking for an empty space. I sat and tried to sort out the combination of things at work inside of me. After my father had gotten the bicycle, he'd become someone else, and although we all, I sensed, watched his transformation with some fascination, we could also see him leaving us further and further behind as he reached for some exhilarating notion of solitary flight.

The hospital was without details for me, save the elevator. A recorded voice narrated each floor we passed, announcing when the doors would open and close. I discovered, thanks to Harry, this was for the blind, or "the visually impaired," as our mother corrected. Harry was able to make great fun of this in his customary snide fashion and get away with it. I laughed hard when the Japanese-sounding voice said, "Fifth floor," but the mood didn't last. In fact, I felt the urge to vomit as we stood outside my father's room.

Before going inside, we were given surgical masks to wear because of our father's high susceptibility to infection, and this gave Harry even more comedic material with which to work, although my mother at last shushed him as if he were a young child instead of an adult towering over her with a wispy goatee and hunched shoulders. I'll admit it was very hard to keep a level head.

Our father was asleep and for this I was grateful; we were able to take in the basic situation without worrying about his reaction to our reaction. Harry and I both hung back by the window while our mother fussed with his bedding and bandages. She stood back, arms crossed, casting a brave grim smile over him, then nodded for us to come over.

"He's not in a coma, is he?" Harry asked. "I mean, or whatever."

"No," our mother whispered. "He's heavily sedated, for the pain. But he may be able to hear you."

The thing that kept running through my head was: Vietnam vet. My history teacher had just done a unit on the Vietnam War, and what stayed with me most clearly were the images of bandaged stumps of amputated limbs. Just like the vets, my father had gauze wound around his upper thighs (what was left of them), which looked oddly claylike where the flesh was visible.

I felt pressured to say something upbeat and hopeful, but Harry and I both stood there, mute. I touched my father's arm in one of the few places that was not compromised with needles and medical tape and monitors and stroked lightly. He was warm. Harry scratched his head and sighed. I could feel our mother watching us for some gauge as to how our future might play itself out; her stiff breathing told me that she needed us to be strong, capable boys. Just then a little yelp came out of my throat that was somewhere between a cry and a gasp. Harry flinched. My mother stared at the floor. My father's monitors continued to tick time on the black screen.

My father opened his eyes just a crack and looked reptilian when he did so. "Nick," he said in a voice that sounded drunk. "Harry. You—came." I wanted him to know that we'd actually wanted to come much sooner than this, and I gave my mother the eye, silently accusing her of not telling him she was the one who'd kept us away.

I could sense a new little war growing between us all, different territory at stake than before. But as all of this raced through my head, my father dropped off to sleep again. Soon a nurse came in to do vitals, in essence, ending the visit. We left, depositing the surgical masks in a large waste can in the lobby. Mine felt warm from all the breathing.

On the ride home, our silence was filled by NPR news and a long in-depth segment on the Israeli-Palestinian crisis. We let it drown out our concerns as city gave way to suburbia, and finally the Erie Canal led us home.

It wasn't until late November that my father was officially allowed to come home. There had been come-and-go infections in varying degrees of severity, and just when they'd thought he was "out of the woods" (according to his fly fisherman doctor, who always wore sand-colored clothing and a crisp blue bow tie), something else would present itself as a danger. Plus, his spirits were so down that the doctor had ordered us to work hard at cheering him up since his emotional health was jeopardizing his physical health. "And we can't have that, comrades," he said, I thought, somewhat glibly. But many was the day that Harry and I had sat by his bedside playing a round of hearts or backgammon, and many more were the days that my father sat there, unspeaking, enduring, it seemed, our constant campaign of enacting a "normal" family life.

"Try to focus on the *positive*," the doctor said on one of our last hospital visits. "Focus on what he *can* do instead of what he can't. You see?" He winked. There was a sparkle in his eyes that suggested he might actually *enjoy* this—the challenge our family presented to him as a medical and psychological problem.

The day my father returned home it snowed—in classic upstate

New York fashion—ten inches. All day big cottony flakes came down and settled themselves along the porch railing where you could see the accumulation, inch by inch. A mobile van service brought him home, and I remembered thinking: my father is now one of the people you see in those vehicles. From my bedroom window, I surreptitiously took a photograph of the van as it pulled up the driveway.

I watched as the aides rolled him up a newly built ramp. My father did not move his head or show any emotion. He sat with his hands folded in his lap, the snow swirling around him in a way that looked, from my perspective, artificial. I continued to peer down from my window like a spy. I knew Harry was in his room doing the same thing while our mother had to be the adult, provide the positive public face as the care workers got him into the house, which was anything but wheelchair accessible at that point. Extended family members had all offered to come and help, to cook us a big Thanksgiving dinner, but my mother had graciously held them off, saying that she thought our father might need some private transition time.

And there he was, sitting in the middle of the living room when I came down. "Dad," I said. "Happy Thanksgiving." I touched the back of his wheelchair.

"Yeah," he said, as if it were a joke and we were the only two people in on it. Whenever he spoke he sounded drunk, even though he had escaped serious head injury. "Thank God." But he laughed a little, the corners of his mouth twisting up in a familiar way. His green eyes looked huge and haunted, as if they had taken in a magnificent but horrible sight and would never quite be the same. He had the appearance of the religiously converted, minus the beatific glow.

My mother was like a nervous hostess at dinner, self-conscious about each and every dish, apologetic when the mashed potatoes turned cold, overly generous with the portions on my father's plate. I watched her drain wine glass after wine glass of chardonnay, her old standby; she preferred the tiny crystal glasses that necessitated small servings, even though she ended up drinking more of them than she probably should have. "So," she said, "just like old times, all of us here."

Harry kept getting up to check on the football game. My mother kept getting up to get butter, salt and pepper, serving utensils. My father sat holding his napkin, not eating. It seemed like there should have been some speech of sorts, some sage instructions for how to navigate the new terrain in front of us, but no one seemed capable of that, and I certainly wasn't going to be the one. Besides, what did I know? I could barely manage to look at my father as he sat pushed up to the table in his wheelchair. Everything in the house had been pushed back against the walls to make way for his chair. Luckily, at least one of his arms was still strong and he could push himself around, although he wasn't very good at it yet. He had told me about his physical therapy sessions, or "PT" as he called it, and how hard they worked him, how pissed off he'd get when he couldn't navigate the little obstacle course they'd set up as a test. "It's more complicated than driving a car," he said. "Doesn't seem like it would be, but it is."

Eventually, he excused himself from dinner and wheeled himself (at great effort) into the living room where he parked in front of the television set. I was reminded of a scene in *One Flew Over the Cuckoo's Nest* where the patients all sat in front of the television, drooling. I knew my father's mind was still, for the most part, capable, yet I couldn't shake the feeling that somehow he would always be viewed as incompetent. It seemed to go along with the chair. That's what he called it, too—"the chair."

I heard my mother crying that night for the first time since the accident. It was the middle of the night, and I'd had to get up to go to the bathroom. I stood frozen outside the door and listened. I could imagine her small shoulders shaking silently as she lay in their big king-sized bed all alone while my father slept downstairs in what used to be the family room. What I really wondered beyond the basic, how was my father going to survive this? was how their already rocky marriage would survive it. Later I would come to serve as observer, arbiter, coach, and snare. Harry, not surprisingly, dodged participation on any level.

By Christmas my father was able to maneuver the entire first floor of our house, even though the narrow old Victorian was not exactly easy on him. Ever since he'd come home, various contractors had been coming through the house with tape measures and blueprints for adapting our house to meet ADA requirements. My father, a civil rights lawyer, had had excellent disability insurance, and this offered the one single ray of hope in an otherwise bleak situation. Whereas many people in my father's situation would have been forced to downgrade and relocate to a more "ability-appropriate" living situation (i.e., one-floor, all-accessible apartment complexes), my father's insurance paid for almost all the renovations of our home, which thankfully allowed us to stay put.

It was painful to watch my mother sit down and sign her name to these contracts, however. After spending the early "lean" years of their marriage living in a small ranch house on the outskirts of town, my mother had finally achieved an address she could be proud of. The street we lived on was populated mostly with professors and high school teachers, retirees and Volvo-driving young couples who had fled Rochester when their children reached school age. Houses rarely went on the market on our coveted tree-canopied street, and I knew it caused my mother no end of agony to agree to let groups of men tear out the bull's eye molding around the doorframes, remove the original wainscoting in the bathrooms, take off the heavy wooden doors with glass knobs, and finally install a permanent two-tier wheelchair ramp onto the front porch, her pride and joy—graced with gingerbread detailing and ornate spindle work and painted in four rich but complimentary shades of green, a "painted lady" I had actually heard passersby envy and exclaim over.

On Christmas Day, the mood around the house was surprisingly cheerful. My mother had made a solid effort at normalcy by putting a turkey in to roast early in the morning, playing the old Bing Crosby and Elvis Christmas carols of our childhood, and gathering us all around the tree at an ungodly early hour to open gifts. Harry was not very amenable to this and sat there gruffly in his flannel pajamas, hair coned and twisted as if he'd been caught up in a storm, lips and eyes puffy from exhaustion. He'd been out the night before with Rebecca, which had caused my mother nothing short of agony. "On Christmas Eve?" she'd said plaintively, quietly, while our father took one of his customary late afternoon naps. "Don't you understand that we're all in this together?" She'd been rolling out cookie dough with me sitting obediently by her side. I had the Christmas tree, the Santa with his toy sack, and the star ready to go.

"Well don't you understand that I can hardly stand being in this house anymore it's so depressing?" Harry nabbed a pinch of dough between his fingers and popped it in his mouth. He'd pulled on his ski jacket and kissed my mother on the cheek before she had a chance to argue or scold. He grabbed his car keys off the counter, gave me the peace sign, and closed the door behind him, leaving a gust of cold air in his wake. My mother and I had both shivered.

As gifts were opened the next morning, it became obvious that Harry and I were being inundated with things to make up for the new sorrow of our household. We both received expensive new hockey sticks, matching (unfortunately) Irish wool sweaters, numerous new cassettes for our favorite computer games (which weren't cheap), and a television set for each of us to put in our bedrooms. The magnitude of these gifts worried me more than it pleased me. I knew my mother had orchestrated it all, since my father had not left the house since he'd returned home in November, save for a couple thwarted attempts to go downtown despite the treacherously snowy sidewalks. All the gift tags read "Love Mom & Dad," but they were all penned in my mother's expertly mastered Palmer's cursive that I knew I could identify out of thousands of writing samples if I had to.

My father received mostly clothes and music. Harry and I had gone in together on a Walkman that was supposed to attach around your waist for jogging but that we'd clandestinely discovered also worked perfectly around his wheelchair. It was unfortunately called a Jogman, scripted in flashy black letters across its bright yellow shell, but we figured it was the perfect gift for him regardless.

My mother gave my father an odd tool that looked like a giant silver duck bill but was actually called a Grab-It, used for reaching and grabbing things that were out of reach for someone in a wheelchair. Somehow my mother's giving him such a utilitarian, disability-focused tool tipped me off to how their relationship had shifted. I realized I hadn't seen them kiss or display any kind of affection since the accident. It had all become physical touch with a purpose: lifting my father with the help of the moving board (which Harry called a Ouija board because of its similar shape and composition); adjusting his clothing (they'd tried to alter his pants, but mostly they were just rolled up and pinned at the legs); bringing him medication and water; and generally helping him groom and tidy himself.

"Sorry I don't have anything for you," our father said as we were balling up the bright gift wrap and stuffing it into a garbage bag my mother held open. "But you can see how it is . . ." He gestured to his legs and shrugged. He looked down at the floor. I thought he was going to cry, and then I thought I might cry, until Harry broke in.

"Well, yeah," he said. "Hardly expected of you, Dad."

Our father nodded but didn't look up. I could feel my mother monitoring the situation, trying to gauge when or if we might need her mediation, but we were a fairly quiet, reserved group of males and not prone to deep or lengthy conversations. In fact, one of the things I'd always enjoyed about my father was the quiet understanding that seemed to carry us through the good and bad times. My mother had always been the talker, the busy, fluttering voice to help us all avoid the unspoken. Thankfully she didn't butt in but left us all with our private thoughts.

We ate at the small wooden table in the kitchen—feta, tomato, and onion omelets. I hated to admit it, but even the way my father ate seemed different now, like a handicapped person. I couldn't say what it was exactly, but something made me look away, out the window, where I directed everyone's attention to the chickadees snacking at the bird feeder in the patio. Beyond the garage, you could see the pool cover crusted over with snow like frosting on a cake; the sun reflected off the white stretch of yard in a fierce sparkle. It was hard for me to even remember anymore the evening my mother and I had sat out there so peacefully drinking iced tea, talking, cooling off, before the phone call that had changed everything.

Later that afternoon when the light was starting to fade, I heard a car pull up in the driveway. I figured it must've been another one of my father's aides who was here to help him bathe, go to the toilet, stimulate his limbs for blood flow. I glanced out the window and saw a vehicle I didn't recognize, though—a little foreign station wagon with a ski rack, sporty but sensible. Normally the aides drove older, rustier cars that had seen better days; in fact, one aide, Belinda, drove such a loud car that it often woke me up when she arrived early in the mornings. I got out my camera, readied myself in the front entryway, and after I let her in, asked if I could take her picture. "What?" she asked, uncoiling her scarf. She seemed flustered and surprised in a way the others hadn't; I sensed fear or entrapment. I noticed she was really quite beautiful, also unlike all the other aides who seemed to have a worn, underpaid look about them that suggested fatigue and early aging.

"I'm Nick," I said. "His youngest son." I held out my hand to her, and she shook it. "Let me take those for you."

Everything about her was bright and athletic, including her colorful jacket, hat, and gloves. "Rose Vancheri," she said. "Thank you." When she smiled and shook my hand, I instantly warmed to her. Her eyes, a squinty green, honestly sparkled. She was much taller than my mother, and something about her quick movements—running her fingers through her long hair, brushing snow off her pant legs, stomping her feet in a little two-step march—suggested youth and vigor, though I doubted she was really any younger than my mother.

"If you don't mind," I said, and pointed to the camera.

"I guess," she said, and stood holding the poinsettia she'd brought in her arms. She seemed more comfortable having something to hold onto. "You're quite the shutterbug."

"I take photos of everyone who comes to help my father," I said. She moved aside while I adjusted the light meter. "I mean, just so you don't feel self-conscious or anything."

"Well, I don't know how much help I can be," she said. She pulled a rubber band from around her wrist and twisted her hair into a loose ponytail, and that's when I got my shot. "But I'd sure like to see him and say hello." She stood on tiptoes for some reason and peeked into the living room; I took a shot of that, too. Harry and my father were watching a football game. The lighting was dim. It was already dark outside. I didn't know where my mother was or what she was doing.

"In here," I heard my father say. I realized he'd probably been listening the whole time. "The Jets are getting their asses kicked."

Clearly Rose was not an aide who had come to help my father. I could see it in the way she squeezed his hand and relaxed around him. "Peter," she said, "how are you?" She knelt by his wheelchair and presented him with the poinsettia.

"Okay," he said. This was his standard answer. I'd come to realize there was no way he would ever lie and say "good" after the accident; he was that kind of honest. "Just put it over there." He pointed to what I'd always thought of as my mother's plant table in front of the bay window. It was loaded with jade plants, African violets, wandering Jews, and one cursory spider plant that I'd given her for mother's day when I was a child and that was still amazingly alive.

It was funny what people brought to someone who had lost their legs in a terrible accident: backgammon, books, lasagna (we'd probably received upwards of ten lasagnas since the accident; what used to be a favorite of ours Harry and I could no longer stomach), long distance calling cards, notebooks and pens, bottles of wine, flowers, fruit baskets, crossword puzzles, *National Enquirers*, disposable cameras, even a two-gallon bucket of caramel corn, which Harry and I downed in a single afternoon. We actually kept a space in the pantry for visitor gifts and had an ongoing contest about which was the weirdest or most inappropriate—a set of juggling balls had most recently been holding first place.

Harry and I eyed each other as my father and Rose talked. They seemed to ignore us completely, and as I listened, pretending instead that I was engrossed in the game, I gleaned that they were coworkers or at least that she was affiliated with my father's law firm in some way. They referred to cases and subpoenas and appeals and hearings and laughed intermittently at things that didn't seem to me remotely funny. Rose sat in the rocking chair that I had always considered my mother's chair. Her foot bobbed up and down easily as she listened and talked. Instead of the many stiff, awkward visits I'd been witness to, this one seemed to draw my father out of his misery and into his old self again. This woman, clearly, was a friend, and a good one from the look of it.

I heard my mother thumping up the basement steps and felt a stab of guilt that I should've been helping her with the laundry. She brought the basket of whites into the living room, as she often did, to fold them in front of the television. "Might as well make it a little more fun," she'd say, then sit on her knees, folding our underwear and T-shirts, glancing up at Dan Rather between grabs into the basket.

Finally, she saw Rose. "Rose!" she said. "How are you? It's been a while."

They exchanged pleasantries, but I could see something was off.

My mother seemed wary, even though she appeared to know Rose, to have some vague familiarity with her. She pushed aside the laundry, too personal for public viewing, and rushed off to pour glasses of wine. When she came back, her cheeks were flushed and her eyes darted around the room as if she were looking for something.

"So how's the new job?" my mother asked. She sat beside me on the couch, elbows leaning forward on her knees, overenthusing her interest. Then, as if she'd just realized Harry and I were in the room, she turned to explain. "Rose used to work part-time at your father's office but quit for something more full-time." She hadn't said if Rose was a lawyer or a receptionist or a legal aide, and I couldn't guess. Something about her didn't seem lawyerly. She looked like a ski instructor or a tennis player. My mother swung back to Rose. "So how's it working out for you?"

My father watched their conversation like a tennis match, his eyes flipping back and forth. He held a hand up over his mouth, a ponderous lawyerly look.

The conversation took a turn then that failed to interest me. I let my gaze fall back to the television screen where players were tackling each other under a spitting snow. One coach paced back and forth nervously like an expectant father as his opponents inched toward the ten-yard line. In the stands, fans with green-painted faces shouted "Number One" at the camera in a way that suggested violence. Harry was rapt; occasionally he shouted admonitions or encouragement, depending on the play. He was barefoot and sat picking at his big toe absentmindedly. He acted as if he had no idea anyone else was even in the room.

After Rose finally left, I carefully watched how my parents reacted. My mother, who'd been so polite, hustled into the kitchen to fix dinner. "I can't believe she stayed so long," she said to no one in particular. "I mean, on *Christmas Day*?" My father sat fingering a single red leaf on the poinsettia. He wasn't used to drinking anymore and had been warned against it because of his pain medications. I could clearly see its effects on him. The next time I looked he was sitting in his wheelchair, head slumped down to his chest, passed out, and looking—I hated to even think it—like an old man. Even his hands looked ineffective as they lay in his lap, limp-wristed and useless.

We continued to have almost constant snowfall that holiday season. In fact, the winter had already been documented as the third snowiest winter on record since 1918, and it was only December. On New Year's Eve, when we were once again so socked with snow you couldn't really go anywhere, Harry announced to my mother, whose back was to him washing dishes, that he would not be home until the next morning. She spun around. "Excuse me?" she said, dishtowel flung over her shoulder like a toga. "And since when do you get to decide things like this, Mr. Harold Foster?"

He gestured impatiently at her mock formality. I was leaning against the kitchen counter picking at a pineapple upside-down cake someone had sent over. It was glazed with rum and encrusted with a brown-sugar glaze. I had to admit a sick part of me enjoyed watching Harry duke it out with my parents. He was braver than me when it came to such things, and part of me rooted for him, part of me rooted for my parents. I also had to admit he could be a total ass.

"I just thought I'd, you know, let you know." Harry joined me by the cake pan where we both gouged out chunks of the cake with our fingers and tucked them in our mouths. I knew this drove my mother crazy. "But you know, hey, whatever," Harry said. "I guess some people just don't appreciate courtesy."

My mother stopped washing a dish but didn't turn around. I wanted to say: Don't do this to her, Harry, not now. But it was almost as if he was trying to make her upset, knowing full well he was stirring up a fight.

"Well, where are you going, if I might ask?" My mother continued her dish washing. Although we had a dishwasher, she insisted that most of her things were too fragile for it. "Rebecca's?"

"Probably." Harry reached into the refrigerator for the milk. Just when I thought he was going to swig from the carton, he did the right thing and reached for a glass.

"*Probably*?" my mother asked. She stood wiping a cracked floral platter that had belonged to my grandmother. "What kind of an answer is that?"

Harry shrugged, drank down the glass of milk, then belched.

My mother handed me the platter to put away in the cabinet above the stove. For me it was an easy reach. "Well, why don't you ever bring her over here?" my mother said. They both seemed determined to beat the other at something; to me it was only a matter of endurance. "Harry?"

Again, Harry shrugged. This time she turned to face him, hands on her hips. I noticed, despite the cold outside, a thin film of sweat coated her face and her turtleneck was damp. "Is it because your father is in a wheelchair and you're ashamed for her to see that?" She stood there, all five feet of her, in front of Harry's towering frame, waiting.

"No! God!" Harry said. It seemed he had lost the showdown for he instantly retreated to the front entryway and pulled on his coat and boots. We heard the door slam—a sound muffled by all the snow outside. His Honda was buried, like both our parents' cars, and I assumed he would walk the half mile across town.

I'd thought my father had been down for a nap, but he wheeled in through the yet-to-be-adapted narrow doorway. "Can't you cut him some slack?" he said. The special black gloves he wore to wheel himself around had already frayed and pilled.

This was more direct parenting than my father had ever done, even before the accident. It seemed our whole lives were now divided in two: preaccident, a happy if not slightly dysfunctional time when none of us really knew how good we'd had it and were happy enough to operate in denial; and postaccident, an unreal and exhausting time that made me feel as if I were walking around like an actor in a play, unsure of my lines, unsure of my blocking, unsure of what might happen next. Postaccident, my father surprised me more and more often.

"I'm not sure you're one to be talking about slack," my mother said. It was a jab, certainly, but what stunned me was that this was the first time, postaccident, that she'd said anything to him other than words of support and encouragement. They were fighting just like the old times, and it was actually a relief to me. I longed to slink away into the living room or up to my bedroom, but my father was blocking the doorway. I had no choice but to stand there gorging myself on the upside-down cake.

"Here we go," my father said. "You've been waiting for this, haven't you?" He glared up at her from his sitting position, which felt unnaturally inferior. "You've been waiting for just the right time so you could say to me, 'Peter, this is all your fault.' If only I hadn't bought the bike. If only I'd paid more attention. If only I—"

"If only you hadn't slept with Rose Vancheri and acted like I was too stupid to know it," she said. "How about that?" She threw the wet dishtowel onto his lap. It landed right where his legs had been amputated. He'd taken to wearing sweatpants because the fabric could be more easily rolled up than jeans. He threw the dishtowel to the floor.

"That's not true," he said, but something in his voice caught.

"Isn't it?" She pushed his wheelchair out of the way, then rushed out of the room. Scared of any further confrontation, I followed behind her, but instead of going upstairs, I went and stood in the dining room and watched it snow. I pressed my forehead against the cold glass and let my hot breath fog it up so that I could see nothing but white inside and outside. Today marked the end of the twentieth century, I thought. Despite what had just happened between my parents, I thought we should make a note of it, do something special, commemorate what it was like to be alive in such an age. I could hear Harry's voice mocking me in my head ("Seriously," he'd say, "You are such a loser"); nonetheless, I went to get my camera and began to think up shots that would reflect the lifestyle of a twentieth-century person: the portable phone lying on the couch, my father's yellow Jogman tangled up in knots, the computer sitting on the dining room table as if it were a person. The latter seemed to me the most telling, but just as I was setting up the shot my father wheeled out of the kitchen facing me head on, and—I couldn't stop myself—I shot frame after frame of him advancing toward me, a grim look on his face, a dark smile buried in his eyes.

"Nick," he said, "come on. You understand." It was not a question but a statement—and an incorrect one at that.

My mother had taken a leave of absence from her job at the college day care center. She'd worked there even since its inception in 1985, when female faculty members began having children and needed a supportive, innovative curriculum that mirrored the Montessori schools, which all of them favored but couldn't afford. My mother was the executive director, and therefore no one gave her any grief when she announced she was leaving to help her husband and would return after the first of the year. She'd left the place (which smelled of canned peas, wet diapers, and bleach) in the hands of the assistant director, Lorraine Ford, a woman I heard my mother complain about absolutely every single day when she came home from work. Lorraine was old (in her sixties), set in her ways, had never had children of her own, and was simply, according to my mother, intolerant. Nonetheless, she was happy to be in charge and kept my mother abreast of the goings-on by calling her every Friday evening with a full report. My mother actually seemed to cherish these calls. She'd take the phone into the kitchen, pour herself a cup of hot tea, and sit at the kitchen table with her feet drawn up underneath her and exclaim, agree, nod, or question whenever it was appropriate. I could sense these calls gave her one last bit of contact with the outside world since it seemed ours had shrunk after my father's accident.

It's not that my father was helpless on his own. Most of the time my mother could leave him alone for stretches of time and it was fine, but once, and only once, my mother had run across the street to her friend Lucy's, ostensibly to borrow an egg for something she was going to bake, and didn't come home for at least a couple of hours. Harry was gone as usual, and I had been up in my room on the phone with a friend. When my mother came home, she'd reported to Harry and later to me that my father had been on the floor between the kitchen and the bathroom; he had fallen trying to get himself on the toilet and couldn't manage to hoist himself up. He'd cut his elbow and scraped up his face. "We must never, never leave him alone when there's not an aide in the house," my mother admonished us when he was napping later that same day. "Let's make that a family rule." It seemed she was talking more to herself than to us, though we both nodded sagely and agreed that the dangers were more than any of us had thought.

Our mother's going back to work coincided perfectly with Harry's and my return to school, leaving our father in need of an aide in the house from eight to three every day. He already had a steady crew with Belinda, Rhonda, Julie, and Hank, but they all worked for many different "clients," as they called them, and my mother feared my father might fall through the cracks if we didn't hire one of them permanently and exclusively. Again, my father's generous insurance plan had agreed to cover what for others would have been considered a luxury.

Even though it was freezing outside, we all sat around the dining room table the evening before our various returns to work and school eating bowls of maple nut ice cream. My father, who'd declined a bowl, presented a problem with this plan as we all ate: he insisted that he was ready to go back to work immediately and wouldn't be needing any aides at all. He vowed to plunge back into his old life with what seemed a falsely inspired enthusiasm. "I'm ready," he said. "Look at me!" He lifted his hands up in the air and made fists.

I'd heard him several times on the phone discussing cases he'd left in the hands of his two partners, but I was never able to gauge what their reactions were to his comments, which were sometimes off the wall and hard to understand. Sometimes his memory switch seemed to trip on and off at a moment's notice. One minute I'd think he was following what I was saying, then the next minute he'd ask me how school was even though he'd only just asked (and I'd answered) that very same question.

"Peter," my mother said, her speech padded by the ice cream

melting on her tongue. "You're going to have to give it some time, remember? We talked about this." I couldn't help thinking she'd started talking to him as if he were a child, but then that was the custom of someone who interacted with small children on a daily basis. "Try to be patient, huh?"

He glowered at her, then looked at Harry and me as if for support. "What do you guys think?" He placed his hands on his lap and waited. "I mean, wouldn't you guys like to see me out there being a *productive member of society* again instead of sitting around here all day?"

Being played as a pawn between my parents was more than I could stand; there was no way to win. I cocked a single eyebrow at Harry (he'd always been jealous of me for this skill he lacked) to help me out. He was older—let him step up to the plate for once, I thought. But I knew the only reason he was home with us at all was because Rebecca and her family were in Buffalo for her grandmother's seventy-fifth birthday party. He'd been moping around bored all day without her.

"Dad," he said. He licked his spoon clean on both sides and tried to hang it off his nose. It fell, clattering to the floor. "You don't need to prove anything to anyone," he said. He picked the spoon up and tried again. "Especially to us. I mean, come on."

My father turned instantly to my mother and laughed. "I see you've trained them well," he said. "They know just the right things to say. Gotta perk their old dad up, right? Gotta be supportive. Rah, rah, rah!" He pounded his fists on the wheelchair arms. Then, after turning his chair in a semicircle, he said, "I mean, wouldn't you guys like to see me out there being a *productive member of society* again instead of sitting around here all day?"

None of us said a word. For a second I wondered if he was having a laugh on us. But then he said, "I'm ready! Look at me!" He even raised his hands up in the air again as best he could and made fists. We listened as he rewound the whole conversation for us and seemed to have no idea he was doing so. "Can I have some ice cream?" he said. "What are you eating?"

My mother hung her head over her bowl like she was praying. Harry went to the freezer and dished him up a bowl. I sat quietly trying to make myself disappear.

Life settled into its own odd routine again after the New Year. We'd hired Julie as my father's caretaker not because she was necessarily the best but because she lived in town and could get to us even when the weather made the roads impassable. She also had a degree in psychology from the local college, was a trained aerobics instructor (and was strong, an important factor in lifting), and had once assisted a New York state congressman who'd lost both his legs in a car accident. She was twenty-eight years old, according to our mother, but looked my age. Every time she was in the same room as me I found myself dropping things, bumping into walls, excusing myself for some misstep or other. But Julie always smiled warmly at me. She'd place a caring hand on my shoulder or rub my back in quick, therapeutic circles and say, "How we doin' today?" What I loved was her thick blonde braid that hung down her back like a Viking's. In fact, everything about her seemed Nordic and indestructible: her large, wide frame, her cool blue eyes, her blunt and capable fingers that could lift, grip, tuck, and smooth.

"If you ever want to talk . . ." she said one day after I'd come home from school and stood watching the all-news cable channel in the living room. The millennium hadn't caused as much trouble as they'd thought, and now even that was a news story. I didn't realize she was talking to me until I turned around and saw it was just the two of us in the room.

"Oh yeah," I said, "right. Thanks." My backpack lay at my feet, and I quickly picked it up and ran upstairs. In my room, I lay on the bed looking at the picture I'd taken of Julie the first time she'd come to care for our father. The lighting was dark, which I liked, but the detail I really loved was that she held a piece of paper between her teeth. It was our address, scrawled down on a grocery receipt. You could tell from the photograph that she thought it was funny, getting her picture taken like that. You could tell she had a great sense of humor by the way her eyes gave off their own light.

That evening my mother had her monthly staff meeting, which was always followed by a round of drinks at Blue's Tavern; she had warned Harry and me that she'd be home late so we should help out with dinner. Since Julie was not just my father's aide but also a fabulous cook, she often went ahead and pitched in with dinner if it seemed like our mother was too tied up. I could smell a garlicky marina sauce that practically made me swoon as I went downstairs. The living room was dark, and I found the kitchen steamed up with water boiling for noodles. Julie stood holding a bouquet of noodles, waiting to drop them in. Harry was gone and my father was nowhere to be seen. I thought it was too late for his nap, though.

"Where is he?" I asked. I never knew if I should refer to him as "Dad" or "Peter" or "my father" with her, so mostly I just avoided it.

"Actually he's out," she said. She must have registered my surprise, because she said, "I know! Isn't it great? His first big outing." She threw the noodles into the water and stirred with a wooden spoon.

Even though the temperatures still hovered around zero, the snow had thankfully tapered off so that the snowplows had finally been able to clear the streets. Everyone had dug themselves out and most of the sidewalks were clear. Still, I couldn't imagine where my father had gone off to, and with whom, and I asked Julie these things.

She stood with one foot balanced against the other leg. It looked like a yoga move. "Well," she said, "friend of his from work, I guess. Rose?" She turned down the noodles just as they were ready to foam over the sides and make that horrible burnt smell I hated. "She said they were going to get some sushi, and—"

"In Rochester?" I asked. I was starving but couldn't focus on the thought of food.

"Well, you certainly can't get sushi in this sorry town," Julie said. "I mean, right?" Bellport was not exactly known for its restaurants. It had two Italian places, two Chinese places, pizza parlors galore, and one struggling Mexican restaurant that no one liked much because the food was authentically Mexican instead of the fast-food fare people had come to expect.

"So when will they be back?" I glanced nervously at the clock, gauging how long it would take my mother to return.

"Pretty soon," she said. "They left about an hour and a half ago."

I thought about this. I hadn't heard any vehicle pull up, but then I realized I'd been listening to music with the headphones on. I'd let my guard down, which I should've never done.

"How about Harry?" I asked. "Where's he?" Suddenly I had a panicked realization that it might just be the two of us for dinner.

"Take a wild guess," she said. She poured the noodles into a colander and spoke through a cloud of steam.

"Rebecca's?" I glanced in the dining room and noticed the table was set for two.

"Bingo." Julie ordered me to take my place at the table as she served. She pulled a basket of warm garlic bread from the oven and two fresh green salads she'd already prepared from the refrigerator. "Sit, sit," she said while I hovered uncertainly around my chair. "I'll join you in a second."

I sat. She came back with a bottle of red wine and poured herself a glass. "I shouldn't really be drinking on shift," she said, "but just a small glass. While your father's gone." She lifted the bottle towards me, then seemed to think better of it. "If you were old enough, Nick . . ." she said. "Sorry."

I laughed nervously and drank from the ice water she'd poured into my glass.

"Unless you can keep it a secret?" she said. She scrunched up her face uncertainly, and there was again that look I'd caught in the photograph of her: a sense of fun bordering on transgression.

"That's okay," I said. "Better not." I heard my voice crack on the word *not* and wanted to erase it.

"I'm sorry—do you pray before meals?" she asked, fork poised above her plate.

"Oh no," I said. I tried to modulate my voice so it wouldn't betray me. "That's something we never do."

"Well then," she said, "bon appétit." She raised her wine to my water.

I thought of my father eating raw fish in Rochester with a woman my mother had accused him of sleeping with. Up until this point, I'd been operating under the assumption that my mother's insecurities had simply given way to full-blown paranoia. Yes, my father was a good-looking man. Yes, he had a certain charm that was hard to resist—or he used to. But these days I didn't know what was true, and maybe, I thought, I didn't want to know.

One Friday night in late January, my mother and father were playing cribbage in the living room. Our cat, Nomad, kept batting playfully at the cribbage pegs as if she were a kitten and not the old timer she really was. There was nothing good on television, so I had it muted on a weight lifting program on ESPN while my father played jazz on the stereo. He kept telling me to really listen for the oboe, because that was what he wanted me to take up next year in band. I had never played an instrument and didn't intend to. I was all about my camera and harboring the secret fantasy that I would one day become a famous photographer known for my edgy portraits. I'd already decided I'd call my outfit simply "Foster" and sign all my photos that way, electing to keep my first name out of it in order to appear serious. I guessed that I'd likely have to move down to New York City to make an honest go of it.

That night it was snowing again in such a way that when I looked out the window, the flakes seemed to be flying horizontally across the sky. We'd all become so accustomed to it that winter, though, that people simply carried on as usual. Harry, in fact, had convinced our parents that it wasn't bad enough to keep him from going to the Black Cat in Rochester to see a new film noir with Rebecca. Her father was an English professor who specialized in film studies at the college, so she was always prodding Harry towards more intellectual movies than he was naturally inclined. Earlier, I'd heard him scraping his windshield in the driveway, then the muffled sound of his door slamming, then the little wind-up sound of reverse as he backed onto the street.

The phone rang and I was sure it had to be Harry, telling us he was stuck somewhere and couldn't make it home. I thought maybe he was even using it as a way to spend the night with Rebecca somewhere and applauded him his cleverness. I knew they had sex, because Harry, whether carelessly or purposely, left boxes of condoms in plain view on his dresser. Every time I went in there to ask him something or borrow something, they sat right there, exposed. I guessed my mother didn't even see them. She was too caught up in other things.

I was both right and wrong about the phone call—right in that it was Harry but wrong about the purpose of the call. When I picked up, I could tell he was on Rebecca's cell phone, because the connection was fractured and there were blank spaces punctuating his words. The only thing I could make out was that he'd totaled the car. "Totaled it—shit—" was what I caught. My mother eyed me hard and held her cribbage peg above the board. My father looked at me sheepishly, and the echo of my mother's words, "just like his father," rang in my ears.

"Where are you?" I said, then repeated it, louder. "Harry?"

My mother popped up. Even though it was only eight thirty, she had already changed into her pajamas and a light blue fleece robe I would later always associate with that horrible winter. "Is he okay?" She stood next to me, smelling like the peach-scented lotion she rubbed on her hands and arms every evening after dinner in long, smooth strokes that struck me as almost sexual. She grabbed the phone brusquely out of my hand. I figured she was responding in flashback mode to my father's accident and gave her a wide berth.

"Harry, what happened? Where are you?" Yet again I was left standing helplessly beside her while she received bad news. Assured that he was okay, she ordered him to call her back on a regular phone with all the details. After she hung up, we all sat looking at each other with big eyes. I thought it must've been illuminating for my father to experience what it had been like for us the night he'd had his accident. This way he could see how much pain one family member could cause another. But I was beginning to lose faith in our family's relationship with fate. What were the odds of two misfortunes so close together? I was beginning to think the best course of action was to simply stay housebound.

"He's okay," my mother said. "I mean, just scraped up." She put a hand on my father's shoulder, and kept it there. "He's at the police station. With Rebecca."

"And?" my father asked.

"DUI." My mother looked at me, rolled her eyes, shook her head. "Leave it to Harry." She seemed to imply that of course I would never act as recklessly as Harry.

"And?" my father asked. Perpetually cold all winter, he wore a black turtleneck sweater pilled at the neck and arms and a wool Hudson Bay blanket folded over his lap. I wondered sometimes if he ever felt what the doctors had described to us as "ghost limbs," but if he did, he didn't say so and I didn't ask.

After the second phone call came with more detailed information and directions as to their whereabouts, my mother tried to decide how best to proceed. Julie wasn't due to arrive for her shift until ten thirty to help my father get ready for bed. Although my mother tried calling to see if she could come early, she kept getting her machine. "Well, we have a few choices," my mother said. I liked her best when she shifted into this take-charge mode. It was so uncharacteristic of her yet so encouraging to see. "One, we all go. Harry and I lift you into the car, Peter, and we deal with it from there." She touched a finger to her nose. "Two, I go and Harry stays here with you until Julie arrives." I wasn't overly fond of that option, since I hadn't ever had to act as my father's caregiver before. The idea of helping him onto the toilet terrified me. I also knew my mother wanted me along for moral support. We could commiserate about the bad luck we'd been dealt and could gather forces about how best to deal with Harry.

"Three," my father said. "I have a three."

My mother and I looked at him to see if he was serious. "You have a three?" The condescension was thick in her voice. "Okay, Peter. Let's hear it."

She hustled into the front entryway to get her coat and boots and barely seemed to be listening. She threw my jacket to me, and I put it on. I wanted to run upstairs for my camera but could imagine the irritation I knew would be in my mother's voice if I even broached the subject of shooting Harry and Rebecca at the police station. "No boundaries for what's appropriate" was something she'd said to me before.

"Three is that Rose said anytime I needed any help to give her a call." I stopped on the landing. My father sat rolling himself in small back and forth movements in front of us. "So let's give her a call. Then you can both go."

The night of the sushi incident had come and gone without my mother ever knowing, as far as I knew. But her reaction to his suggestion filled me with doubt now. She held her purse stiffly against her side and walked right up to his wheelchair and just stood there, daring him to move. "Don't do this to me, Peter," she said in a voice so hushed I had to lean in to hear.

"Don't do this to me, Peter," he said back. Who knew anymore if he was mocking her or losing his grip.

"I'm still going to love you," she said, "because I'll always love you, *always*. But I want you to tell me the truth . . ." She glanced up at me on the stairs, watching like a spectator, then must've decided I wasn't going to stop her. "Did you?" she asked. She couldn't even say it. "Did you—with Rose?"

He shook his head, nodded, laughed. He threw his hands up over his face and hid.

Like an angel, Julie arrived and saved us from further scene. A blast of cold air slipped in with her as she shut the door. She'd gotten our messages, she said, and got here as quickly as she could. "How we doin', Peter?" she said. "Looking good." Then, looking up to see our blank faces, she said, "Is there something I should know?"

My mother gave her the quick story about Harry, then she and I left the house, squinting through the icy snow that stung our faces and coated the car. We let the engine warm up for a full ten minutes and sat there, silently, watching our breath cloud the air and then disappear.

"If you know anything . . ." my mother said. She adjusted the rearview and avoided my eyes.

"I don't," I said. "I swear." I had never lied to her before and realized, once I had, that it wasn't as bad as I'd thought. Instead of the tangle of the moral high ground, this path was smoother and easier to tread; I could breathe easier this way.

Rebecca's parents had beaten us to the station. Her father (Dr. Bob, as he liked to be called) was not full of the usual lively banter but stood stiffly in his fur-collared wool coat like a Russian soldier. His wife, Mary Annie (the name itself a giveaway she was from the South), greeted us by squeezing our hands and smiling grimly. It wasn't lost on me that tradition dictated that the boyfriend was responsible for the girlfriend, and therefore Harry, in addition to being in trouble with the law, was also now answerable to Rebecca's family. To make matters worse, she was an only child and certainly Bellport High School's most intelligent, well-read, well-rounded (tennis club, yearbook editor, study abroad in France) student.

After politely asking after my father, Mary Annie explained that the "kids" were with a couple officers having their paperwork processed. "Ya'll can rest easy. They're okay," she said. "Just a little shaken up." Her smooth, soft-looking face suggested ease, leisure, pampering. Next to her blunt blonde bob, my mother's long flyaway ponytail made her look like a ratty hippie housewife.

I always assumed that Harry drank no more or less than most students his age, but I also assumed he would never get behind the wheel of a car drunk, much less in a snowstorm. Apparently, according to Dr. Bob, Harry'd been turning off at the East Avenue exit ramp but had miscalculated the distance, then overcompensated, then rolled over after colliding into the guardrails. "Granted," he said, smoothing his beard, "the road conditions did not help the boy." Nor, I thought, had his heavy drinking. The Breathalyzer tests were off the charts, according to what my mother had managed to harangue out of Harry on the phone.

"I'm so sorry Rebecca had to be involved," my mother said.

Mary Annie shook her head politely. She wore all gold jewelry that shone warmly against her middle-of-winter tan. "Nonsense," she said. "There's no harm done, thank God. And we know it must be hard to manage everything at home now that—" She paused and touched a small gold hoop earring. "Well, now that you've got so much on your plate."

It was a polite way of saying "now that your husband has lost his legs in a terrible accident." I noticed nobody but us could ever face it head on. My mother, I could sense, was gearing up for some sort of rebuttal or speech. It was as if people assumed our family now leaked out an awful contagious poison, and she wanted to assure everyone that no, they would not become afflicted by mere association with us. Before she could defend her tribe, however, my brother walked out with his arm slung around Rebecca's shoulder. They both had Band-Aids on their faces, making them look like small wounded children.

"Hey," he said. Tears sprang to my eyes when I saw him—for what could have been a terrible loss. Harry had been working part-time at the coffee shop downtown and had saved up for a leather jacket—the black motorcycle kind with silver zippers and buckles and snaps. Instead of making him look tough and mature, it made him look young and innocent—his lips too red, his cheeks too soft. His eyes were bloodshot, and when he blinked they stayed closed just a fraction of a second too long. His movements were liquidlike and slow. At one point, he stumbled slightly on absolutely nothing. Rebecca clung to his arm like a damsel. Her skin was pale and her eyes unnaturally bright. They would have made a wonderful photograph, and the thought of my camera sitting at home caused me a small ache of regret.

Clearly no one wanted to yell at them or scold, but the silence felt excruciatingly loud to me. Thankfully a young cop came out and explained things to the parents. Harry was a minor, he said, and so he wouldn't be jailed tonight. Rebecca, apparently, was free and clear, but Harry would have to appear in court for sentencing within the next two weeks. Everyone murmured their thanks and apologies and the cop left, handing my mother a thick envelope of papers and carbons. "Keep an eye on him," he said, which seemed to suggest it was somehow her negligence that had caused him to drive drunk in a blizzard and crash. I wanted to shout at the cop: "Look, we've got a pretty fucked-up family situation on our hands here and I would appreciate your cutting my mother some slack." But I didn't, of course. I put an arm around her shoulder and led her outside while Harry and Rebecca separated with an intensity that made me think of Romeo and Juliet, which I'd just read in Advanced English. They groped and cried and Harry ran his hands over her rumpled hair until finally her parents said it was time to go.

At that moment I had an overwhelming urge to be Harry. There was an intensity inside him that glowed brighter than any of us. It compelled you to look, to listen. I didn't know what it was. Walking out to the car with him, I figured it out. The pain, the danger, the drama were his own. He'd created the terms. He was not spectating. He was not living in reaction to my father's accident like my mother and I were. He had his own agenda now. Maybe he always had.

By Valentine's Day our house had been widened and expanded and opened up in such a way that it felt more like a small, bright gymnasium instead of an old Victorian. When Harry and I were little we used to hide in the small front-hallway closet tucked under the staircase. I could almost smell the rich spike of cedar and could almost feel the rough brush of wool against my cheeks just thinking about it. Sometimes Harry would lock me in the closet and not let me out for just a second or two too long, and I'd whine and squeal like a trapped animal until my mother came running around the corner with a wooden spoon, threatening to use it on Harry's backside but never following through. Now the closet was gone, and in its place were a wider doorway and a perfectly smooth transition from the hardwood floors of the hallway to the Berber carpet of the living room. All the doors—at least those that remained—had gold-plated handles that could be grabbed easily and practically pushed open. The bathroom off the kitchen used to be so small you could hardly turn around in it; in fact, you used to be able to touch the small pedestal sink while sitting on the toilet. Now, the bathroom had been bumped out and expanded so that our kitchen was half the size it used to be. Our kitchen sink was now so low I kept accidentally reaching into the air for it, and all the appliance knobs jutted out against my legs when I brushed by. Quite frankly, the renovation had left our house stripped of character in a cheerless, antiseptic way. "We might as well have moved," I muttered to Harry, who sat at the computer in the pantry (also expanded) making a clip-art last-minute valentine for Rebecca. "I mean, it's like a new house now anyway."

"Yeah." Harry clicked at the keyboard, ignoring me in favor of his project. He and Rebecca seemed to have bonded even closer after the DUI fiasco, as if the trauma had served to rekindle some spark that had faded. Our mother had grounded Harry for one month, and although she'd been firm that that meant no visitors and no going out, gradually Rebecca started to come over after school and in the evenings, and my mother seemed too weary to fight it. The fact was I knew she liked Rebecca, and more than that, I knew she liked the idea of her son dating a professor's daughter. Our mother had always wanted to get a graduate degree but had stalled out at the bachelor's after Harry and I were born.

Rebecca's family had a certain cachet in town due to their unconventional lifestyle (Dr. Bob drove a tiny old VW Bug that you could hear puttering down the street from blocks away) and behaviors (during a brutal heat wave one summer, they showed old black-and-white home movies in their front yard and invited the public to attend). But they never went too far over the top so as to offend or alienate. Most people, myself included, had always found them strange but knew that strangeness was bred out of an intelligence and irreverence not often evident in a small town. I could very much understand the attraction Harry must've felt towards them.

Harry pushed his chair back and stood up. "So is this cool? What do you think?"

I walked over to see what he'd done. On the computer screen was a stock black-and-white photograph of two dogs lying on top of each other, their ears and tails overlapping. Over the photograph Harry had superimposed the words *Be mine* in a bright red lashing font. Along the bottom, some song lyrics from his current favorite band spoke about "love like a tidal wave / Tsunami I'm breaking the bank for you." Frankly, I didn't get it, but it seemed harmless and sweet enough. A big black heart hung over the dogs.

"I mean, since you're the big photographer and everything," Harry said before I could respond. He shrugged his shoulders, as if the whole thing were a big joke and didn't mean anything to him. "I mean, whatever."

"Very cool," I said. "She'll like that."

"Really?" Harry went to the refrigerator, grabbed a diet soda, and cracked it open. "You don't think it's too gay?" He drank lustily from the can, and I could hear the carbonation fizzing in his mouth.

"Gay?" My heart beat double time for a second. Did he think I was gay? Was he trying to tell me he was gay? But then I realized it was just Harry picking up on the latest slang. Last month it had been "wicked"; the month before that it had been "strapped"; before that, "sweet"; before that, "dag" as in, "Dag, that is one serious snowstorm out there." Frankly, I found it rather affected, but then I was not nearly as cool as Harry.

Harry grew impatient with me. "I just wanted to get your opinion," he said. "I mean, no biggie."

"I think it's great," I said without hesitating. "Really. That photo is perfect."

He gave me a leery eye and reached into the bag of chips I'd been eating. "I wish Mom would cook once in a while," he said. "I was busting her chops about it the other day and she practically whaled on me."

"I know." I felt a strong urge to defend her but restrained myself. I missed just sitting around like this in the kitchen talking about things. Ever since the accident it seemed all we did was argue over who got the shower first or who'd drunk the last of the milk, never daring to have real conversations, since we didn't know when our father might come wheeling in to interrupt us. The floors were so smooth there was never any warning. The thresholds had been removed, and it was all one big continuous plane like a skating rink. He could stealth us, and so it seemed safer to stay quiet than to risk him overhearing us.

"It sucks, doesn't it?" Harry said. He sat back down at the computer, his back to me. I froze, not wanting him to stop.

"Big time." I hopped up onto the kitchen counter, which was so low now my feet dragged against the floor.

"I just wish none of this had ever happened," Harry said. "I mean, it's never going to be any good now. You know? I mean, whatever." The printer slowly chugged out a copy of his valentine, heavy and wet with ink. "His life is basically fucked. Which means our lives are basically fucked. I mean, right?"

"Well," I started to say, but our father wheeled into the room and I quickly backpedaled. We should've really known better.

If he'd heard us, though, he didn't act like it. He was bright eyed and quite possibly jazzed up on painkillers. Why he still took them

I didn't know and didn't ask, although my mother had informed me that even though he seemed all right, he was sometimes in a lot of pain. Mentally or physically? I'd wanted to ask, but knew it was best not to push her.

"Guys," he said. He'd lost muscle weight from being in the chair, and his clothes hung off him now and showed his newly angular frame. Before, I would have described my father as athletic to the point of brawny or even buff. He used to lift weights while he watched television at night. Our garage was full of in-line skates, cross-country skis, a treadmill, a volleyball and net, and a wet suit he'd bought one summer, vowing to take scuba lessons at the college. Now his arms had that soft freckled look of someone who didn't get out much. Granted, it was the middle of a most hellacious winter, but still. You could tell the summer months wouldn't help him much either. "I've got news," he said. His speech, oddly, did not sound like him anymore. A slight echo rang through his words, and a hesitancy skipped between every syllable.

"What's that?" Harry said gamely. His valentine was ready to go, and I could see he was eager to move on to other things. Our talk was over, and I was disappointed that it was. There were so many things I'd been filing away in my head for just this occasion, and now it was too late.

"I'm going to walk again!" our father said. He looked up at us both, I felt, challengingly. He rolled back and forth in the chair, which was, I was learning, his version of pacing back and forth with excitement. "I'm going to get legs!"

At first I thought he was delusional, but then it dawned on me that he was right: he could get artificial legs, prostheses. Why not?

"Right on," Harry said, but I could see he was checking out. He inched toward the doorway, nodding. "That's very cool, Dad, but

I gotta fly." Ever since he'd totaled the Honda, Rebecca had taken to coming over to our house in her mom's white Subaru wagon. It would sit in front of our house camouflaged by winter. Apparently, she was here now, because the front doorbell rang as if on cue, and Harry ran for it.

"So, what do you think?" While my father waited for my response, I saw my mother pull up in the driveway and knew it was grocery day.

"Just a sec," I said. "I've got to help Mom with the groceries." I slipped on Harry's boots, which always sat by the back door unlaced and at the ready, but when I got out there my mother met me on the walkway carrying only a small white bag and a bouquet of roses.

"Takeout chicken from that new place your father likes," she said, and asked me to carry it. The warmth seeped through the bag and onto my fingertips. I wanted to prepare her for my father's news, but a drab winter's light hanging over our backyard made me think better of it. The light was the perfect color of loneliness, and I wanted to photograph it before it faded but knew I wouldn't likely get the chance.

Inside, my father waited for us in the kitchen. I wondered what it must've been like to be him—trapped in a body that was now half of what it once was, unable to walk or run or spontaneously do anything. The guilt factor must have been high, too. No one had ever said anything, but I predicted that one day he and my mother would have it out.

"Happy Valentine's Day, sweetheart," my mother said. She laid the roses in my father's lap. Their musty hothouse scent filled the kitchen when he drew back the paper wrap. She kissed the top of his head, I noted, not his lips.

"Thanks." He smiled and handed them back to her to put in a vase. "I didn't get you anything," he said. "You know . . ."

My mother shrugged and laughed. "Don't be silly," she said, opening up the cardboard containers full of chicken. It was all I could do not to pounce on the food and stuff everything into my mouth. "The fact that you're with us at all is enough for me." But she was all business and didn't even look up. "Nick, could you set the table?"

I rushed plates and silverware onto the dining room table, even though I thought the beauty of takeout was supposed to be that you didn't have to do dishes. But this was a special romantic day, I reminded myself, even though I didn't have a girlfriend; seeing Harry and Rebecca constantly together never failed to remind me of that. Earlier I'd heard them laughing in the living room, then chasing each other up the stairs to Harry's room. Ostensibly they went up there to play a new video game on his television, but I had to wonder. What amazed me even more was that my mother let them get away with it.

Finally we sat down to eat, and I loaded my plate with an extra plump chicken breast, a dollop of mashed potatoes and gravy, and a small soupy puddle of coleslaw just to be polite. I started eating before they'd even served themselves.

"So did Harry and Nick tell you about the legs?" my father asked. He helped himself to a drumstick and wing, then handed my mother the box.

"The legs?" Her eyes looked glassy and tired. The day care center had been having a lot of turnover lately, and she'd been putting in long days and sometimes nights.

"I'm going to walk again," he said. He hadn't touched his food yet—another new trait since the accident was his seeming lack of appetite. I rarely saw him eat. "I'm going to get legs."

"You are?" My mother was peeling all the good crunchy breading off her chicken breast. She was one of those people who read labels on food religiously, refraining if the fat content, especially the saturated fat, was too high. Her chicken, without its coating, reminded me too clearly of an actual bird now, and I looked away. "So where did this idea come from all of the sudden?" She ate politely with a fork and knife. "I mean, do you think you're ready for something like that?"

My father put down his food. "Do I think I'm ready?" He gestured to himself in the chair. "How much more ready could I be?" I thought he winked at me then, but I couldn't be sure. At any rate, he hadn't seemed to have lost his enthusiasm, even though my mother, for some reason, was doing much to dampen it.

"I just mean," she said, chewing. She patted a napkin to her lips and cocked her head to the side, considering. "Didn't the doctors say that might not work for everyone? I mean, that you'd have to wait and see?"

My father pushed himself back from the table and crossed his arms. If he couldn't stalk away at least he could do that. "So what are you really saying, Ginny? Would you prefer I stay in this wheelchair for the rest of my life? Is that what you want?"

"I just don't want you to get your hopes up," she said. She fluffed her potatoes with her fork like a little kid trying to pretend she'd eaten them.

"Why not?" my father said. The way he draped one arm around the back of his wheelchair provided a glimmer, for just a second, of his old confidence, his almost cocky self-assurance. It was part of what had made him such a good lawyer. Why couldn't he still practice law? I thought. Even from his wheelchair? "What's wrong with someone getting their hopes up?"

She looked at him, her chin pointed down. "You know why."

My father turned away, staring out the window. I wished there had been a way for me to leave gracefully, but I was stuck in the middle of them with my mouth full. "In your world," my father said finally, "nothing works out, does it? Nobody wins. You've always been an incredible pessimist."

My mother's eyes widened. "And what's *that* supposed to mean?"

I got up and cleared away the discarded boxes stained with grease spots and littered with bones. Let them clear the air, I thought. Let them finally do it. Neither one of them stopped or acknowledged me as I ducked out of the room and took the stairs by twos only to hear Harry and Rebecca laughing in his bedroom. The contrast with what was going on downstairs was acute—and welcome. The door was open a crack, and I knocked with a knuckle. "Guys?" I said. "Can I come in?"

"Sure," Harry said. They both lay sprawled on bean bag chairs in front of the television. His room had been newly painted navy blue, but my mother had insisted he at least keep the trim white. It looked nautical and sporty instead of the brooding den he'd likely imagined. He'd bought a couple of Indian bedspreads from the head shop in town and had one hanging on a wall and the other billowing from the four corners of the ceiling. They gave off a scent of smoky incense and dark, earthy hemp. "What's up?" Harry sat up, revealing matted messy hair. He'd inherited my mother's kinky curls, which he wore, in my opinion, a little too long to look good.

"Not much," I said. We all looked at the door when we heard loud voices erupt downstairs.

"They going at it?" Harry said.

"I guess," I said.

Rebecca leaned back against the bed and crossed her arms over her knees. She wore two long ponytails like a child. "I didn't think they ever fought," she said. "They just seem so . . . I don't know. Under control." She pulled at the fraying white hem of her jeans. "Unlike my parents, who are, like, totally whacked."

"Dad wants legs," Harry said. "He thinks he can walk with fake legs."

"Well, couldn't he?" Rebecca asked. She balled up a bunch of threads from her jeans and pitched them in the garbage can across the room.

"In theory," Harry said. "I mean, I guess, right?"

I shrugged. I'd never really let myself consider the possibility after the accident. "Maybe with crutches or arm braces or something." I sat on the edge of the bed and couldn't help feeling I was interrupting something. I stood up. "So I thought I'd take a picture of you guys," I said. "You know, for Valentine's Day and everything."

"That's sweet," Rebecca said. She took off her little wire rimmed glasses and folded them up in her hands. Her eyes were perfectly round, like giant bright blue marbles. Something about her reminded me of a frog.

"You want to do that?" Harry asked. "Picture of us?"

"Sure, why not?" I went to get the camera in my bedroom, which sometimes felt like a shrine to all my father's caregivers, with their pictures on the walls like some sort of museum. I looked again at the one of Julie with the grocery receipt in her mouth and felt a pull in my chest. She still worked for my father, but it was often the late shift and I wouldn't see her unless I had to run downstairs for something. Even then, we hardly spoke.

Back in Harry's room, I walked in on them kissing. They'd clearly heard me but must not have cared. "So, okay," I said.

"Like this," Harry said, muffled. They kept their arms around each other. They turned their faces towards me, but kept kissing. "It's the perfect Valentine's shot. Come on."

I fiddled with the light meter, then, just when I was about to take it, Harry placed a hand on Rebecca's breast. All of us froze, but I took the picture anyway. Neither of them laughed, although I wished they would've. "Harry's so uncouth," Rebecca finally said, and slid his hand back into his lap. "You'll have to forgive him."

Harry shrugged it off. Ever since the DUI it seemed he cared less and less about what people thought; in fact, getting the DUI seemed to give him even more license to shock and disrupt. Shortly after the incident my mother had timidly suggested he get therapy, which was not a big hit with Harry. "I'm not the one who's fucked up around here," he'd said. "God!" I remembered that Saturday morning; I'd been sitting at the piano playing Bach. Harry kept spinning the basketball on his finger, then letting it drop to the floor where it bounced, upsetting everything in the house. At one point it crashed into the glass hutch where my mother kept all her mother's valuable dishes. When my mother told him to knock it off, he left for the entire day and didn't return until midnight.

I went back to my room after Harry had so deliberately embarrassed me and lay on my bed. My room was dark, save for the glow-in-the-dark stars on the ceiling I'd put there on my eleventh birthday. Amazingly, they still kept their glow. I closed my eyes and gave myself permission to masturbate for just a little while. I liked to think of Julie the most, but images of what Rebecca must've looked like naked crept in as well: her pale, veiny skin, her small round breasts under tight T-shirts, her collarbone jutting up out of her clothes. The climax never really felt like a cleansing, though, but more like the way a hard, sweaty climb left you breathless and exhausted.

Afterwards, I thought about my parents. They didn't even sleep in the same room now, even though the downstairs den had been renovated and enlarged to accommodate their big king-sized bed whose tall mahogany spires had always read medieval to me. My mother stayed upstairs in their old bedroom; sometimes I caught her watching television and folding laundry up there, even though she'd said she was so tired she could absolutely not stay awake another minute. I guessed I couldn't blame her.

The thaw that year was incredible. Although the meteorologists had forecast a very wet spring, given the record-breaking volume of snow we received that winter, no one had predicted how torrential the month of April would be. I'd taken to carrying my umbrella with me no matter what. The ground felt spongy underfoot, and the old slate sidewalks—uneven and pocked with age—became red-tinged lakes that stained my shoes and socks a pale orange. Our basement had flooded, and then flooded again; the old sump pump could be heard underneath the floorboards desperately trying to keep up, but nothing could stanch the continuous flow of water that came from both above and below. Religious pundits began appearing on television to declare the floods biblical in proportion and prophetic in scope. Perhaps, they claimed, the new millennium had indeed served as a warning to us after all. I was unsure what, exactly, they were suggesting, but I knew I had never prayed, had never believed in God, and could think of nothing particularly sinful about my behavior save for my private masturbatory sessions that had increased in frequency as the months wore on.

One cold, rainy Friday evening found us all at home with no plans, no good television to watch, and nothing good to eat. I knew this meant our usual pizza order to Mamma Mia's: two thin-crust sausage-and-mushrooms with extra cheese and a liter of cola. By now this had become our standard backup meal after the constant flow of casseroles, soups, and baked pastas had tapered off. We'd had a good laugh when we realized the sympathy period after a misfortune ran almost exactly six months, especially if the misfortune was particularly debilitating and "life altering" as my father's had been. I actually found it a relief not to sit through another foil pan of baked ziti, the noodles so melded together by cheese they looked like brain matter, the sauce so sweet it could not be cut with any amount of parmesan cheese or hot sauce.

Having long abandoned formal meals at the dining room table, we all sat around the living room watching The Weather Channel, even though we all knew the forecast by then: rain, rain, rain. My father's wheelchair sat in its usual position, which was adjacent to the couch and perpendicular to the leather club chair that he used to occupy almost exclusively. Harry lounged in it now with his feet dangling over the edge. My mother had bought it for my father for their tenth wedding anniversary, and it was his pride and joy, with its supple oxblood leather, its matching ottoman, its traditional nailhead trim. Recently he'd begun testing himself in terms of lifting and moving himself onto furniture, but most often he seemed to prefer his wheelchair, which was starting to take on a slouchy, lived-in quality. He now had a swing-armed tray attached to the side that he could use for eating, writing, or holding his shortwave radio; when he didn't need it, it folded down out of sight. There was also a little tote bag snapped to one side, with pockets full of papers, pens, magazines, and the portable telephone.

"I have something to tell you," he said apropos of nothing. Nothing was ever just a simple conversation with my father anymore but a series of bulletins, updates, and challenges. We'd all been watching yet not watching the television, eating merely to sustain ourselves, what my mother called "maintenance eating," a term she used, I thought, to assuage her guilt over not preparing home-cooked meals. For a while she'd tried, but then she was simply too tired by week's end to put in the effort. Julie, my father's aide, still helped out in that regard, but she only came in the late evenings to help bathe him and get him ready for bed. Sometimes she left us containers of chocolate chip cookies she'd made while we were all asleep, which helped explain what I could've sworn were my vanilla-scented dreams.

"Yes?" my mother said, not unkindly. It seemed she'd become immune to his pronouncements by that point and could no longer be shocked.

"I'm thinking of moving out," he said. A huge triangle of pizza was draped over his paper plate. He hadn't touched it. "Try things on my own for a while."

Harry changed position in the leather chair, causing it to squeak loudly like an animal. He shot me a look of disdain, as if it were me who was abandoning ship.

My mother, who had been supporting my father—however un-enthusiastically—through his initial inquiries and examinations for prostheses, did something then that I knew I would never forget: she screamed. It wasn't a quiet or ladylike scream, or even a tired, anguished little scream, but a full-on, from-the-throat scream. Then she cried, "No! No! No!" And again, "No!" before running out of the room with her hands on top of her head. In my mind I remembered thinking: such is the beginning of a nervous breakdown. For a second I contemplated calling an ambulance, but Harry ran after her and I thought it best to wait a while, let the dust settle, see how serious both of them really were. This left me alone to deal with my father.

"The legs . . ." he said, but didn't finish. "It would take too much out of her."

I got up and turned off the television. Later in my life when I would remember these moments, I didn't want them cheapened by a flashing television in my memory. "What do you mean?" I sat down in the club chair and put my feet up on the ottoman, something I rarely felt entitled to.

"It's an uphill battle," he said, then laughed a little. I didn't know if he was acknowledging the understatement, or referring to their marriage. "But then it always has been with your mother and me."

The rain lashed against the windows with little ticking sounds as shadows of headlights moved across the walls, growing and then lurching as they got closer. I grabbed Nomad and rubbed behind her ears until she purred appreciatively and slumped down in my lap for more. Until last year, I'd thought they'd had a pretty happy marriage. I remembered one particular vacation we'd taken quite vividly, even though I'd only been about eight years old. We'd driven all the way to New Orleans, stopping only once at a chain motel just outside Nashville, then driving the next day straight through until we reached the French Quarter. My parents were both younger and thinner then, more apt to try new things and experiences without analysis or debate. They'd brought along a small fruit crate of their favorite tapes, and each got to take a turn at selecting as they drove. "Except driver trumps all," I remembered my father saying with a sly smile since he was most often the one behind the wheel. Harry and I sat straight up in the back seat of the old BMW station wagon, eying the men dressed like women with fear and intrigue. Clowns juggled, artists painted caricatures, and everywhere musicians played the Dixieland jazz my father so loved and admired.

Our European-style hotel (read: small, quirky) spilled right out onto Bourbon Street, and the very first time we ventured outside a woman lifted her shirt and showed us her tattooed bare breasts and laughed in a way I remembered sounding like a mean cackle. Harry and I walked in front of our parents, who held hands and kept making sure we wouldn't get snatched. They both seemed so happy during that trip, popping into any shop as they walked, buying freely, holding sequined masks up to each other's faces and laughing. Harry and I were each so festooned with Mardi Gras beads around our necks that I could still remember the hot weight of them in that tropical August humidity. We ate muffulettas, big, round, flat sandwiches stuffed with greasy meats and cheeses and cut into triangles like pizza. We threw coins into the cups of street performers, one of whom terrified me to the point of tears. A man, spray-painted in silver, stood on a podium and pretended to robotically disassemble all his limbs. My mother later claimed she'd had to shield me from him every time we went by his corner.

At night, Harry and I slept in a bed just inches from our parents'. When I opened my eyes, I found them seemingly locked together face to face, lying on their sides as if they were stuck that way. The city lights that leaked through the curtains allowed me to see their faces—pale, waxen, quietly charged. In the distance was the music, so lively and gay, reminding me we were far away from home.

My father now moved his wheelchair closer to me, and I felt myself pulling back instinctively. "You would understand, right?" he asked. "If I had to leave for a while? We'd still see each other, of course."

Somehow everyone assumed I was older than my age and could take just about anything they dished out. "Is this about Rose?" I countered. A few times she'd come over to visit, but always when my mother was at work. "Or is that all over with?"

"Harry," he said. Even before the accident he'd sometimes confused me and Harry, as if we were interchangeable. "Things get complicated. I mean, it doesn't affect how I feel about you. You know that, right?"

"I'm not lying for you anymore," I said. It was the closest I'd come to refuting or crossing him, ever. I looked down. I could hardly stand to look at the sad flap of his pants rolled up to his groin. His body was so . . . brief, so ineffectual, so damaged. The few times we'd all gone out as a family, to the mall or to a restaurant, people had stared with pitying shock, a brave few gracing us with lean, hard smiles that looked more like grimaces. I got a sense it made them feel fortunate by the way they seemed to take deep breaths as they passed us, husbands throwing arms around their wives' shoulders, children drawing up close to their parents' pant legs, grateful not to be us, especially not to be him.

"It's going to be okay," my father said. "I think it's part of the process." Then, as if he realized he was still my father and should somehow soften the blow, he put a finger under my chin and lifted my face up to his. I had so rarely ever seen him at such close range. I saw his ingrown whiskers at the chin, the red puffy rim around his eyelids, how yellowed the whites of his eyes had become. His lips were chapped and flaking. "You have no idea," he said, "how sorry I am." He kept his finger under my chin, and my eyes roamed around, desperate for some distraction to interrupt us. "For all of this. Everything." He let me go, and I slouched back in the chair as if it had all been my fault. But my father wasn't done. "I hate myself for what I've done to your mother. That's why I think I should leave for a while. Let her see what she wants to do. Let things settle themselves out."

He shrugged his shoulders, waited for me to say something, then wheeled away.

And so it was that my father moved out. It was raining when he left in an unknown van. My mother made sure we were all out of the house with various errands and appointments, but I'd tricked her by skipping my dental exam. Instead, I'd stayed up in my room, camera in hand, and taken an entire roll of black-and-white through the window as my father was wheeled out and helped into the van by two large men I had never seen before. At one point, I thought my father looked up at the house, but the rain was coming down in wet misty sheets, and I doubted that he saw me. Nonetheless, I drew the curtains and rewound the film, holding the little canister in my hand like an amulet. The only thing I knew for certain was how tired I felt; I longed for the clarity of a clean print in my hands: black and white, positive and negative, light and dark. These were things I understood.

After my father moved out, my mother seemed to flourish, though it was in a slightly overboard, nervous way that to me suggested denial. Nonetheless, her new competence and independence was a surprise that everyone—coworkers, friends, neighbors, and mere acquaintances—instantly picked up on. Of course not everyone knew she was buoyed up by a small but potent pharmaceutical supply that involved antidepressants, Valium, and some kind of pain reliever I didn't quite understand the need for. She was truly a poster child for the benefits of antidepressants, though; they instantly cheered her, made her a more bubbling, vivacious person, made her eager to talk and less likely to mope. Frankly, it startled me. There was something about the way her eyes flared every so often that read manic to me.

One Saturday morning in May I found her standing on the kitchen counter cleaning the tops of the cupboards with a blue feather duster that had always seemed like a comedic prop from a play set to me. I'd recently become interested in theater at the behest of my English teacher, Cal Corrigan, who said I had a flair for the dramatic after reading my required one-act play about an old couple arguing over who should be the one to die first; neither of them wanted to be the one left behind, but in their argument they'd forgotten about how sad they would be to lose the one person they truly loved. I'd received an A+ on it and was now being railroaded into trying out for the fall play, "The Fantastiks." I had still not decided if I would.

"Nick, I hope you're okay," she said. She wore her old khakis that were stained dark green from when they'd painted the house a few years ago and a navy blue T-shirt I was pretty sure belonged to my father. "Because it's all going to work out," she said. "Somehow it is. Your father just needs a little adjustment period. It's part of the grieving process for what he's lost."

I shrugged, popped an English muffin in the toaster, waited for it to crisp up.

"A person in my position could mope around and be bitter," she said, "or they could rise to the occasion and use the time for, you know, personal growth." She was whipping the dust up into a frenzy, and I could see it dancing inside the bars of sunshine. Finally, the rain had retreated, and we'd had a string of beautiful days that seemed to nudge us closer to an early summer. All the appliances and dishes shone in the sunlight.

I spread strawberry cream cheese on my English muffin and stood eating it while she cleaned. It was my day to go over to my father's new place, which was just across town in a newly constructed development of one-story townhouses; a couple of them had been made handicap accessible by state mandate, and my father had luckily been the first in line. Neither Harry nor my mother had been there yet, and I was beginning to feel like a secret liaison every time I ventured from place to place. I had become the unofficial messenger between both parties.

"Tell your father his social security papers are here," she said.

"Should I just bring them over?" I asked.

"No," she said. I knew that would have been too easy; despite her veneer of acceptance and her positive attitude, I could sense she still wanted to make things hard on him, as if they weren't hard enough already. "I need to explain some things to him. It's complicated." She grabbed onto my shoulder and jumped down to the floor. "Have you ever seen Rose over there with him? Does she visit?" She clapped her hands free of dirt and wiped them on her pant legs.

"A couple times she's come over to help." My new policy of not covering for my father had its downfalls—namely, that I had to cause my mother further agony and watch her face settle with things she didn't really want to hear.

"Well," she said a little too brightly, "that's good he's got someone to help. She's probably got a really flexible schedule." She moved over and began putting away the toaster and wiping up my crumbs, things I would've done if she'd just given me a minute.

I wanted to tell her that Rose was someone she didn't need to worry about, but frankly, I didn't know if it was true. "So, I'm off," I said. "I'll tell him you said hi?" I reached for a ball cap Harry had handed down to me: navy blue Yankees with a frayed bill. I never wore it backwards like Harry did, though.

"Tell him I send my love," she said. "And I'm here if he needs anything." She crossed her arms and rubbed her hands up and down her skin. "Tell him he's always welcome to come back, whenever he's ready." I thought I saw her bottom lip jut out just a little bit, but she didn't let herself miss a beat. She waved me off enthusiastically and moved on to her next project: cleaning out the refrigerator. I left her on her knees with half-empty bottles of salad dressing and ancient cartons of yogurt spread out all around her.

I had to cross the Erie Canal to get to the new townhouses, and just as I was heading towards the bridge, the bells starting ringing and the draw gate went down to stop traffic while a boat passed. The old green bridge creaked and groaned on rusty sprockets you could hear turning with all their might underneath the crossing. Every year the canal was drained in late October and filled again in April. The whole town came out to watch each occasion, and even our family walked down for what had come to feel like a sort of seasonal rite of passage. Now the murky water looked overfull, and I watched as a big white leisure boat was careful to obey the no-wake zone the bridge master was notorious for enforcing militaristically. The boaters always waved to the local townsfolk as they did to me now. I waved back and even saluted the captain until finally the bridge went back down. Local traffic tended to get antsy, but being on foot, I was more patient than most; I did not exactly look forward to reaching my destination.

My walk took me past Rebecca's house, and while no one was outside, I saw through the screen door what looked to be Harry and Rebecca pulling up chairs at the dining room table. Ever since Harry's punishment for the DUI, he'd taken to staying overnight at

Rebecca's a couple times a week. I believe my mother thought it easier to let it happen than to try and raise interference.

I crossed the one busy highway that led out of Bellport and rushed through a green light since there were cars impatiently advancing to take their right turns. Bellport was infamous for its utter disregard for pedestrians. There were always petitions and movements afoot to make the village a more walkable place, but so far nothing had stuck.

The townhouse development, Gray's Landing, was tucked behind the Gas 'n' Go, shielded by a stand of fluttery new poplars whose shiny leaves glowed silver from a distance. Each unit boasted a two-car garage, making it look more automobile oriented than residential. The buildings were all various gradations of muted browns: taupe, cappuccino, caramel, cocoa. My favorite touch was the little faux lighthouse that sat next to the timber-wood entrance gate. What it had to do with a suburban housing tract in the middle of nowhere I had no idea.

The weather was so nice my father was actually sitting outside on a small concrete patio in front of his unit surrounded by a border of pale yellow crocuses. I slowed my pace for a minute and watched him. He was having a cup of coffee and read the newspaper folded in quarters. He wore shorts and had some special white vascular stockings over his stumps so you couldn't see the actual flesh. Still, it was the first time I'd really seen his legs, or lack of legs, without pants since the accident.

"Dad," I said. He turned around as much as he could in his chair and smiled.

"Oh, hey, Harry," he said warmly.

"Nick," I said. "It's Nick."

"That's what I meant," he said. "Nick. You look good."

I sat in a brightly colored lawn chair I'd never seen before. "So how's it going?"

"Going," he said. He now had a cup holder attached to his chair, and placed his coffee in it. "And you? Is your mom doing all right?" He wore a baseball hat, I realized with some embarrassment, just like mine, only his was on backwards.

I heard dishes clattering inside, and for a second my heart pounded, thinking it might be his aide, Julie, whom I hadn't seen for weeks. "Mom's cleaning the fridge today," I said. Then, thinking that might've suggested too much unhappiness, I revised. "I mean, she's doing really well. She's, you know, getting things in order."

"Yeah?" He itched his elbow. Lately he'd picked up a rash, which my mother told me was from inactivity and problems with his circulatory system. "I worry about her."

"She's really good," I said. "She's been busy." I looked around and could see no one else out enjoying the near eighty-degree temperatures. There was a slight breeze, and the sun had that sharp, hard angle that suggested summer was imminent. You could smell freshly cut grass again and hear lawnmowers in the distance. Oddly, though, the place felt deserted. Despite its many units, it seemed more private than our house in the village.

"Well, I think she's putting on a front," he said, and pointed out a robin that had landed on a tree branch.

"For who?"

"I don't know," my father said. "Me? You and Harry? All of us?" He shook his head, as if chasing out a conflicting idea. "On the phone the other night," he said, "she was crying." He closed his eyes as if trying to stay focused. "I can't remember what about," he said. "Something . . ."

"Doesn't matter right now," I said. "She's doing fine. Let's go inside."

What I actually liked about his new place was its lack of furniture and clutter. Although I knew our big Victorian was a place to be envied, over the years my mother had accumulated so many things it felt claustrophobic and a little too precious to me. At a barn sale last year, my mother had found an old glass window with peeling red paint on its mullions and hung it, like some sort of ghostly portal, at the top of the stairs. Everywhere you turned there was some eclectic, primitive, or exotic item looking back at you. When the old elementary school integrated with the junior high, my mother had eagerly gone to the auction and come home with an old, musty pull-down map of the United States that now covered one whole dining room wall.

My father's new place, on the other hand, was sparse and cool and airy. The walls were all white and the furniture, what little there was of it, seemed Asian in its spare lines and monochromatic colors. I didn't know where he'd gotten it, but I liked it; it was easy to ignore my jumbled, bifurcated life when I sat on the cool blue couch with extremely low arms and tiny legs like thin little branches.

Rose came out of the bathroom, surprising me, and gave me a quick kiss on the cheek in greeting. There was something about her, against my better judgment, that pulled me in. Just standing in the living room talking quietly, she gave off a charismatic glow that made me want to do her favors, ask her questions, be near her, and be liked by her.

"Still taking photographs?" she said. I found it sexy the way she sat with her bare legs curled underneath her, and I clutched a couch pillow in front of me for cover.

"When I get the chance," I said. "Not as much as I'd like to." I realized I sounded like a middle-aged man talking about his golf game. "I've been busy with school. You know, lots of things."

"Sure," she said. "Life conspires against us." She laughed lightly and sipped at a tall glass of iced tea.

I thought it was an odd comment and waited for my father to participate in the conversation or at least to steer us towards something more meaningful. As pleasant as Rose was, I found it difficult to know how to behave around her. It was role conflict at its most extreme: was she like my father's aide now? a friend? an aunt? a buddy?

"Nick's going to be famous someday!" my father said. He wheeled over towards me and tapped my leg with the rolled up newspaper. "His pictures'll be on the cover of *Time* or something. Big famous Nick Foster won't even know us anymore, will you, Nick?"

I shrugged my shoulders and laughed. "Right," I said. "You can all say you knew me back when."

"Seriously," my father said. His eyes were getting that bright wet look about them that alerted me to the fact that he was tiring. "Big famous Mr. Nick Foster won't even know us anymore, will you, Nick?" He yawned and slumped back in his chair. "Nick. Nick. Nick."

"Why don't we all go for a walk?" Rose said. She pulled out her running shoes stuffed with socks from under the coffee table and put them on. I stood up and waited for her while looking at the photos magneted to the refrigerator. One showed me and Harry our last Christmas, preaccident, when we'd both received ski hats that looked like jester's caps with long pointed ends in bright colors. Another picture showed a girl roughly my age riding a jet ski in her swimsuit on Lake Ontario. When I looked closer, I thought it looked like a girl from school who'd been killed a couple years earlier by a hit-and-run while walking along a busy street in broad daylight; I couldn't remember her name. I'd never considered that Rose might be this girl's mother, but now it hit me that she must have been. She'd been one year younger than me in school, and what I could remember of her (Wendy! Wendy was her name) had been her wavy red hair, which she always wore in one long braid. The story got a lot of attention because they never found the person who'd hit her, and the newscasts kept running her school picture for weeks. I wasn't sure what her picture was doing up on my father's refrigerator, though, and I didn't ask. Some things were better left unknown.

I'd never really walked around town with my father since the accident and realized, as Rose and I helped him outside and onto the main sidewalk, that I was battling some shame about it, which was quickly compounded by guilt. No matter how polite people tried to be, a wheelchair drew stares. People went out of their way to give us space on the sidewalk, and cars actually slowed down at the crosswalks to let us pass. My father, I noticed, made eye contact with no one.

There was a small grocery store at the edge of town, Jack & Jill Foods, that I'd always found sad for its hard-luck clientele, and it was there that we headed now under the auspices of buying ice cream for dessert later. The store was housed in a mini strip mall also inhabited by a cheap haircut franchise, a dollar store, a VFW bar painted battleship gray, and a credit union that I had never once seen open. As we crossed the freshly tarred parking lot towards the automatic doors, my mother came out the exit with a single brown paper bag in her arms. We were far enough away so that she might not have seen us, but we were close enough that she could, and did. We all stopped: me pushing my father in his chair, Rose standing by his side, my mother in front of us like a stranger, using the grocery bag, it seemed, like a shield.

Naturally we exchanged pleasantries, but after that there was quickly a deficit of things to talk about. The fact that I felt like a traitor ignited in me the urge to draw my mother into our triad in a way that I knew was inappropriate. "Just getting a little something for dessert," I said. "You can join us for dinner later if you want." I obviously hadn't cleared this with my father but he seemed nonplussed by it all. I didn't know if Rose was planning to stay or not.

"Harry won his soccer match," my mother said, and adjusted her grocery bag. Harry had kept up with the game even after I'd abandoned it the season prior.

"That's great," Rose said. "He's such a gifted athlete, isn't he?"

My mother nodded but seemed suspicious that Rose knew much of anything about her sons. She was putting on her best face, though, and I couldn't help but feel proud of her. People kept walking around us and cars kept avoiding us by backing out awkwardly, and I knew eventually we had to get out of the way and go inside, but no one seemed to want to pull away first.

"So I was just getting some more cleaning supplies," my mother said, and nodded down at her bag. "I should probably get back . . ." She squinted into the sunshine, and I saw sweat break out across her face.

"You sure you don't want to join us?" I asked. When I said this, my father looked up at me as if checking my sanity level. I watched my mother register this, vacillate, then decide.

"Well, I suppose I could stop by," she said. "If it's all right with you, Peter." She raised a hand over her eyes to shield them from the sun. "It'd be nice to see the place."

My father nodded but didn't say anything.

"Good," Rose said. "Then it's settled." She was the take-charge type, and for that I was grateful. Apparently my father had been struck mute.

"Ride with me, Nick?" my mother said. "You can show me exactly where it is." I could tell this was a command, even though she knew precisely where my father lived, right down to the number of his unit.

"We'll see you there," my mother said to them. "I have to pick something up at the drug store, so we'll be a few minutes."

My father waved us off. Rather, he held up a hand and kept it there until we were out of sight. Rose, in her Lycra shorts and running shoes, looked even taller than she really was, towering over the back of my father's wheelchair.

My mother started the car and acted as if everything were perfectly normal. "So does she cook for him?" she asked me as she nosed her way out into traffic. "Is that how it works?"

"Are you sure you want to do this?" I said.

Her entire body sank down in exasperated frustration at my lack of understanding. "This is good for him," she said. She accelerated abruptly and made a hard left into the Walgreen's parking lot across the street. "He needs to see that he can have an independent life again," she said. "Once he feels he's a capable, functioning person again, he'll probably be more comfortable at home."

"Let's not go over there," I said. I rolled down my window and stuck my elbow out. "Let's just go home and say we had things to do."

My mother left the car running in the lot. "I'll be right back," she said. "I have to get your father's prescriptions." She gave me a small wave and headed inside, dodging the hot sun.

So this is it, I thought as I watched people go in and out of the drug store. Instead of choosing to fight, my mother was going to wait him out, prove she was still the primary caretaker, the wife, the one who knew the important details and was still watching out for him even though he was no longer under the same roof as her. I knew she was scared about Rose's role in his new life, but perhaps it was more complicated than that. As I watched her push open the door and walk towards me, I had a glimpse of what she must've looked like as a little girl. The slight wind split her bangs apart in the middle and flipped her hair up at the ends. Her walk was determined and straightforward, not a hint of elegance or ease about her. She was so short some clerks in the mall actually directed her to the girls' section for better fitting clothes. But there was that smile that spoke volumes; it was a smile pushing against all the odds. It was a smile that swallowed sadness and strained for hope. It was a smile that always broke my resolve to defy her.

"We're going over there, Nick," she said. "I bought some Mint Milanos as a gesture," she said. "You know, your father's favorites." I held the bag of cookies and knew I couldn't argue with her. She had to lay claim to him somehow; she had lost so much already. Fortunately, the bell started ringing and the draw gate went down across the bridge, giving us a couple minutes to think and prepare. We both sat silently in the car as we watched the bridge lift to let a boat through. Finally, a small white boat glided past with buoys dangling over the sides like garland. "Darling Jane," it said across it, and I wondered if the old woman sitting on the deck reading was Jane. The man who I imagined was her husband waved to the bridge master and then to us; good sports that we were, my mother and I both waved back enthusiastically, never for a moment letting up, letting go, letting on.

At my father's townhouse, my mother and I ate salmon grilled on a cedar plank; that was the kind of cook Rose was, and I watched my mother take it all in as if recording it to tell someone later. There were fresh, feathery sprigs of dill, a light lemon caper sauce, and crusty French bread. Steamed asparagus, my mother's favorite, was laid out in a milky white dish, which accentuated the vivid green. For dessert, Rose served small bowls of fresh blueberries with vanilla yogurt drizzled on top. She'd politely arranged my mother's store-bought cookies on a small glass plate shaped like a fish.

Midway through dessert, when the three of them were discussing Harry's soccer game yet again, I began to silently curse my brother for having so expertly extricated himself from our family and having left me to pick up all the pieces. It simply wasn't fair that while I sat enduring this awkward meal he loitered around Rebecca's house watching movies and shooting baskets in the driveway. What was worse, I somehow knew in my heart that Harry, the one who tried the least, cared the least, disappeared the most, would be the one to really make it someday. Yes, my grades were first-rate, whereas his were mediocre; yes, my photographs had garnered some attention in the art department at the high school, whereas he was happy to simply fly under the radar; yes, I was the son both parents looked to to perform and contribute beyond expectations, but still. Harry had what I could never seem to achieve: freedom. As I looked around at my mother, my father, and Rose sipping decaffeinated coffee—my mother regularly glancing at me to see that I was still "with" her—I knew I could never fully escape her no matter how far I fled. This fact settled down on me like the hot, humid storm clouds that had begun rolling in from the southwest and rumbling overhead.

"Nick? Are you okay?" my mother asked. She got up to clear plates, even though Rose told her to just leave them.

"Yeah, fine," I said. "But we should probably get going." I stretched loudly like an old man and sighed.

"Well," my father said, "if you have to." He wheeled himself away from the table and backed himself closer to Rose.

"You're sure you're going to be all right here?" My mother stood up and held the chair in front of her.

My father didn't answer but looked around with wild eyes as if he were lost.

"Peter," Rose said. For once, she was flustered and stumbling. The muscles in her tanned legs flexed and flinched. "Peter?"

"It's all right," my mother said. "Anyway, we should go." She went to retrieve her purse in the living room and bent down to embrace my father lightly.

Rose nodded and began clearing the dishes while my father sat silently, his eyes beginning to close.

Outside, it was already growing dark, and the tiny flash of fireflies lit up the squat bushes lining the parking lot. The thunderstorm was still lighting up the sky, but it was far off now and seemed like it might miss us. My mother drove by Rebecca's house, always lit up like there was a party going on, then over the canal bridge, then past the old movie theater toward home. Our house was completely dark. The wheelchair ramp looked like part of a broken maze. I saw Nomad in the living room window and thought about my camera but didn't feel any real drive to pick it up anymore.

My mother cut the engine and got out, leaving me behind. Everything at that moment seemed impermanent. In fact, I had every reason to believe my father would be back after he'd had a little time to process the events of his life. I had every reason to believe this was all a phase, a sharp corner we'd all turned that would one day find us back on track. I got out of the car and looked at the house. My mother was inside and already on the telephone. Nomad hopped off the windowsill and followed her to the kitchen, where

I saw my mother shake some cat food into her bowl as she spoke and laughed into the phone. She took off her earring, set it on the kitchen counter, and ran her hand through her hair.

"What a day!" I heard her say as I walked in the back door. Whoever it was she was talking to, she was definitely putting on the bravado.

Upstairs, I peeked into her bedroom: a tangle of patchwork quilt, slippers upended on the floor, a bra hanging on the doorknob, the blinds at half-mast. All the signs of a living, breathing person there. Nothing of my father remained, save their wedding photo nailed above the bed. In it, my mother's slightly crooked teeth smiled in an overbite that was heartbreakingly familiar to me; my father loomed large in his tuxedo with his big arms wrapped around her from behind. Smiling at the camera, they both squinted into the hard sunshine at a future they could never have seen coming.

I turned away, went to my bedroom, and stood on the bed. I took down some of the pictures I'd taken that year, then put them up again after seeing the big gaps they left on the walls. There were so many possibilities, I thought, so many ways things could have gone. Downstairs, I heard my mother laughing like a teenage girl into the telephone, and then she hung up. Then there was the sound of nothing but the rain, soft and then suddenly hard.

ACKNOWLEDGMENTS

Special thanks to the following literary journals in which some of these stories, in various versions, first appeared, or will appear:

The Beloit Fiction Journal: "Super America"
The Florida Review: "Five Reasons I Miss the Laundromat"
Terminus: "Pinned"
The Kenyon Review: "All-U-Can-Eat" (forthcoming)
Five Points: "Tidal Wave Wedding" (forthcoming)

Thanks also to the Millay Colony for the Arts for that wonderful month in the woods during which some of these stories got their start.

Thanks to all the good teachers I've had over the years, so generous with their time and encouragement: Jonis Agee, the late John Mitchell, Robbie Shapard, Steve Heller, Jeff Carroll, Richard Messer, the late Larry Brown, and Christopher Moore, who started it all.

Thanks to Barb LeSavoy, Dena Levy, Ruth Childs, and Andréa Parada for the "Solution Circle" and years of friendship, laughter, and lunches.

Thanks to Rachel Hall and our writing "group" of two, for reading every single one of these stories and helping them along, and for saying, "Let's write novellas!"

Thanks to Steve Fellner for his constant encouragement, valued friendship, and always dead-on feedback. What did I ever do without him and his "assignments" that kept us both going even when the writing well seemed dry?

Thanks to Christine Green for her unconditional friendship, love, and support.

Thanks to my family in Minnesota, who—though far away—are never far from my thoughts.

Thanks to the old Augsburg College gang for their complete irreverence, their scathing wit, and their warmth, creativity, and love that still manages to lift and sustain after all these years. And to John Mitchell, of course, for throwing the champagne glass against the wall.

Lastly, thanks to my husband, Mark, who has always supported my writing life, even when it meant giving up time of his own. His good eye and ear for fiction have helped shape many of these stories.

Finally, thanks to my son, Hudson, and daughter, Lily, who have given me more than they will ever know. xoxo.

THE FLANNERY O'CONNOR AWARD
FOR SHORT FICTION